The Arrangement

Bancroft University Chronicles, Book One
By S.D. Lettie

The Arrangement
By S.D. Lettie
Copyright 2025

This is a work of fiction. Names, characters, businesses, places, events, and incidents are either the products of the author's imagination or used in a fictitious manner. Any resemblance to actual persons, living or dead, or actual events is purely coincidental.

The Arrangement

Chapter 1

Emilia

The ballroom is unbearably warm.

It always is.

The kind of heat that clings—not the physical kind, but the weight of eyes, of old money, of legacy lacquered in gold leaf and protocol. Chandeliers sparkle like they're judging you. Every woman here smells like power wrapped in jasmine and Chanel. Every man looks like he's trying to win something: attention, funding, forgiveness. Who knows.

And somewhere in this overpriced museum of ambition, I'm supposed to smile.

My mother's hand lands softly at the small of my back as we reach the top of the staircase. "Chin up," she says, voice low, clipped, trained for event spaces and unflattering acoustics. "Posture."

"I am standing up straight."

"You're slouching in the eyes."

I don't respond. We both know this is the best it's going to get.

1

The Arrangement

The cameras flash below us—soft, timed bursts. The press is cordoned off behind a velvet rope like trained zoo animals, lenses focused on whoever walks down these stairs next. Not me. Not really. I'm just part of the background tonight. A Langford daughter: well-dressed, well-bred, and the best part, silent … for now.

But even from up here, I see them catch my face.

That flicker of recognition. That tiny beat of, *Oh, right—her*.

I straighten my spine, tilt my chin a half-inch higher. Not for them. Not for the photographs. For me.

My mother adjusts the neckline of my gown with quick work of her fingers. "Remember what we discussed about the Cortland delegation—"

"I'm not speaking to Senator Cortland's son again," I murmur.

"He asked about you. That's enough."

"He also told three people I look like a 'marketable virgin'."

Her hand stills. Her eyes don't flinch. "Then use it."

I turn my head just enough to meet her gaze. Her expression is void of any emotion. It's eerie, unyielding in a way that makes her seem less like a mother and more like a conditioned robot.

"You do realize that's not normal, right?"

She sighs, like she's tired of my antics. Like years of emotionally beating this into me should have worked, but it didn't. "Normal is for people with fewer responsibilities."

I bite back the sigh. She's already stepped forward, gliding down the staircase like royalty. Her hair is lacquered into submission by gallons of hairspray no doubt. Her gown is dove gray and stunning. And behind her, just to the left, are two secret service agents who follow every step we take like a shadow with credentials.

My detail waits beside the champagne tower, Agent Keller and Agent Ruiz. I spot them immediately. They're trying not to look like they're watching me. They're failing.

I descend slowly, heels silent against the marble. Every few steps, I feel the buzz of whispers. Every few seconds, someone says my last name like it's currency.

It is.

"Holy crap" a voice says just behind my left shoulder. "This place smells like inherited stock options."

I don't have to turn. I know the voice. Thalia Reyes—first daughter of a Supreme Court justice and sworn enemy of subtlety.

"You're late," I say without looking.

"They held me at the checkpoint. Apparently, my dress sets off metal detectors."

"You're wearing chainmail."

"It's couture."

She falls into step beside me—bare-shouldered, smirking, her dark hair twisted into a knot. Thalia has never once apologized for taking up space. It's one of the things I love most about her. That, and the fact she once told a diplomat's wife to choke on her own lineage.

We've been best friends since boarding school. Paired for a debate tournament. Argued so viciously in the first five minutes, the judges thought we were enemies. We won.

She eyes my dress—champagne silk, off-shoulder, spine-straightening. The kind of thing my mother calls "timeless".

"You look like you're here to announce a Supreme Court ruling and then stab someone with a shrimp fork."

"I'll take that as a compliment."

She plucks a glass of champagne from a tray as we pass.

The ballroom is lit like a stage. All soft gold and illusion. You'd think the walls themselves were watching, recording, waiting for someone to crack under the weight of their own performance. The light clings to bare shoulders and champagne flutes, refracts through crystal and ambition, and turns the air heavy with perfume and strategic alliances.

I know most of the faces here. Not by choice.

Thalia and I stand just left of the orchestra, near an arrangement of white roses so aggressively expensive they could probably pay off a senator's gambling debt. She's sipping champagne like it's her last with an expression that could curdle cream. We've been here less than fifteen minutes, and she's already whispered three threats, all of them with elegance.

"Tell me again why we came?" she mutters under her breath, adjusting the cuff of her velvet shawl like she might strangle someone with it.

"Because my father said I had to," I reply, eyes skimming the room. "And you said you wouldn't let me be alone with these people unless I promised to sabotage the wine list."

She considers this. "Ah. Right. Civic duty."

From across the room, I catch a flash of familiar blonde.

Brandi Walters. Perfect posture. Perfect teeth. Wearing a shade of pink that resembles Pepto Bismol.

Her Chi Omega pin glints on the curve of her collarbone—a small, sharp reminder that we share letters, a house, a sisterhood. She's a legacy. Her mother was Vice President of the chapter in the early '90s, and every time Brandi walks into our dining room, she carries herself like she's auditioning for a future national board seat. She's exactly what nationals wants in a poster girl: smiling, well-connected, impressively pliable.

She wasn't always like that. I remember how, freshman year, she used to cry in the shower after PR committee meetings, say things like *"I'm trying to be what they want"* through tears she'd never admit to now. But tonight? Tonight, she's wearing the dress of someone who's won. Or thinks she has.

Because Preston Carlisle, my ex, is standing next to her.

4

Thalia notices him the same moment I do. She groans like she's just seen a snake in a dinner jacket. "Tell me he's just here for the dessert table."

"He's here for the press."

"Still gross."

Preston's hair is a little longer than it used to be. He's doing that thing where he leans in just a little too close, pretending to be interested in what Brandi's saying when, really, he's checking to see who's watching.

I don't flinch. I don't freeze. I simply catalogue.

The way her hand curls around his arm—tight, possessive, practiced. The way he doesn't pull away. The matching posture. The carefully chosen proximity. Someone planned this.

"Do we like her tonight?" Thalia asks, voice low and syrupy.

"I'm undecided."

"We hate her then."

"We're civil."

"Civil is for treaties. I want blood."

"She's our sister."

Thalia lifts her brow. "And Judas was a brother."

And then, of course, Brandi spots us. Her smile breaks across her face like a champagne cork popping—loud, unexpected, a little forced.

"Emilia!" she calls, weaving between tables with practiced grace. "I didn't see you come in!"

Of course she did. Brandi doesn't miss entrances; she just likes pretending she does.

I plaster on a soft smile, the kind that could pass for warmth from across the room but dissolves into ice up close. "Brandi. You look very ... pink."

She beams. "Preston said it's my color. Said it reminded him of the first time we met."

5

Thalia exhales through her nose, unimpressed. "Was he concussed?"

Brandi's smile wavers for a fraction of a second. "I didn't realize you were coming, Em. Thought you were skipping this one."

"Vice President's daughter. You know how it is, can't hide forever."

Her eyes flick toward my Secret Service detail, stationed subtly along the ballroom's edge, dressed like guests but tracking every movement like hawks. One of them meets my gaze and gives a discreet nod. I return it without thinking.

"Well, you look amazing," Brandi says brightly. "Very diplomatic. Very 'future senator's wife'."

"That's funny," I say sweetly. "You always struck me as the one gunning for that title."

Her smile freezes. Not visibly. Just around the edges. Like a fault line waiting to slip. "We should catch up," she says quickly. "Maybe coffee next week?"

I nod once. "Of course. After chapter?"

"Perfect." We both know it'll never happen.

She turns before I can say more, walking away with her chin a little higher than it was a moment ago, her back stiff like she knows exactly how many eyes are on her. Preston doesn't glance back. He never does.

Thalia sips her champagne again. "You are terrifying in heels."

"I didn't do anything."

"You didn't have to."

We turn toward the crowd, letting the conversation fall behind us like shed skin—another performance shed, another glass of forgettable champagne in hand. I'm halfway through pretending to care about some donor's thoughts on yacht taxes when I see him.

It's the stillness that draws me first, a sudden halt in the churn of motion and ego. He's standing just beyond the perimeter of the crowd, in that liminal space where the light softens and the music dulls, one hand in his pocket, the other curled loosely around a glass he hasn't touched. The suit is black, sleek, tailored in a way that whispers money without flaunting it. His collar is open, no tie in sight, his hair slightly tousled like he walked in late and didn't care. Because he probably did. There's something about the ease of his stance that sets him apart from the pack of overeager heirs and polished political climbers milling like sharks in Loro Piana.

It takes a second to place him. Not because he's forgettable—*how could anyone forget those steel-colored eyes*—but because the memory doesn't sit neatly in the front of my mind. It's buried, tucked somewhere deep under years of galas, press dinners, polite lies, and summers I don't talk about. But the second I see him—really see him—it clicks.

St. Petersburg. The letters.

I was sixteen, wandering around a palace I had no business being alone in, trying to avoid another night of speeches and small talk and whatever polished version of diplomacy my parents had dressed me up for. I remember gold ceilings and velvet curtains. I remember the cold, how it crept in through the windows even from the inside. And I remember *him*. By the window. Alone. Calm in that strange, watchful way, like he was listening for something no one else could hear.

He told me his name was Nikolai. No last name. No country. Just a look that said he knew exactly who I was, and that it didn't matter. We talked for hours. Or at least it seemed that way. But there was something about him, even then. The quiet. The way he spoke like he meant every word, even when he wasn't saying much at all.

Later that night, I asked my mom if she knew a boy named Nikolai, someone who might've been there with one of the Russian delegates. She barely looked up from her phone. Just said it was probably a house boy or an aide's kid.

"Don't let your imagination wander," she told me. "He's no one."

And now—watching him from across the room, older, sharper, like he walked through fire and didn't flinch—I know exactly what I'm seeing. He's not no one. I've met him before. Wrote letters to him.

He's different now. Rougher. Sharper around the edges. Like whatever softness was there once has been stripped away, and what's left is something harder. Something dangerous. And yeah, holy moly, he's still gorgeous. Even more so than I remember. Not in the Instagram-perfect way the guys at Bancroft all aim for. Not the pretty-boy type who's constantly fixing their hair or waiting for someone to look. No, this is different. It's quieter. Like he doesn't need the attention, because he knows it'll find him eventually. The sharp jaw, the lazy blink, the way he watches the room like he already knows how it ends; it's all just … unfair. That slow-burn kind of attractive that sneaks up on you, gets under your skin, and makes you feel like it means something. Even when it probably doesn't.

I don't expect him to look up. I'm just watching, quietly, like I've done with a hundred other people in a hundred other rooms.

But then his eyes find mine.

And everything inside me pulls taut.

They're not the soft kind of gray people romanticize. They're storm-gray: cool, unflinching, and precise. They don't widen with surprise or narrow in suspicion. They just lock on and hold. Still. Measured. Like they already know too much.

I don't expect him to recognize me. I was younger then. My dark hair was shorter. My confidence, quieter. I hadn't yet learned how to cut with my words or use my smile for gain. The girl he met in St. Petersburg wasn't allowed to wander without a minder and still asked permission before speaking. This version of me doesn't ask. She calculates.

But then, his mouth moves. Just barely. The corner lifts, subtle, like something remembered and kept quiet.

And that's when I know. He remembers.

And for one beat longer than I want to admit, something in me stirs. Not panic. Just ... sharp awareness. My heel catches, just slightly, and my fingers tighten around the stem of my glass. The moment passes.

No one notices.

Except him.

Of course he does.

His gaze doesn't move. Doesn't falter. And it burns—not in that sweet, dizzy kind of way, but in the way that makes your spine stiffen. Like being watched by someone who sees through the facade. Someone who's already imagined all the ways it could fall apart.

My cheeks flush before I can stop them. I haven't moved. Haven't spoken. Haven't done anything except exist in his line of sight, and somehow, that's enough. I feel ... exposed. Not dramatically, not in a way anyone else would notice. But underneath it all, there's this quiet unraveling. Like he's pulled a thread I didn't know was loose.

I look away, slow and deliberate, as if choosing not to react is its own kind of armor. My pulse drums steadily at the base of my throat, reminding me of every rule I've ever been taught. I've stood in rooms filled with power since I was twelve. I've smiled through deals worth more than my trust fund. I've charmed, negotiated, deflected. I don't get rattled.

But this version of Nikolai—older, unreadable, dangerous in that too-quiet kind of way—he gets under my skin without even trying. And the worst part? He knows it.

My fingers twitch at my side. It's automatic, barely a thought. Before I can stop myself, I lift my hand. A wave. Small. Controlled. Just enough to be noticeable.

And the second I do it, I want to take it back. Because it's not me. I don't wave at men across rooms like we're old friends in a coffee shop. I don't hand people like him anything that could be misinterpreted.

But it's too late.

His expression doesn't change. Not really. Maybe the smallest tilt of his head. A faint shift in the way his mouth moves. Not a smile. Not even close. Just that same quiet awareness that says: *I see you.*

I let my hand fall slowly, pretending it was nothing. Pretending *I'm* still nothing to him. But deep down, I know better. Because if I'm feeling this off-kilter, this thrown, this *exposed*... Then he's already won the first move.

-

Emilia - Five Years Ago

The cold in St. Petersburg settles differently than it does back home. It doesn't just bite, it burrows, threading itself through wool and silk and spine until it becomes something you carry, even indoors. I remember the way the doors closed behind me that night, heavy and quiet, muffling the hum of the summit behind them like the world itself had lowered its voice. I wasn't supposed to be out wandering on my own, not in a place like that. Sixteen-year-old daughters of U.S. diplomats are expected to smile, nod, sit quietly during opening remarks and compliment the host nation's table settings. But no one stopped me when I slipped away. No one asked where I was going. Not because they didn't care, but because they assumed, as always, that I was going somewhere important.

The Arrangement

The palace was endless with corridors stretching like silk ribbons under frescoed ceilings, each hallway spilling into another room lined in gold and velvet. I didn't know what I was looking for, only that I didn't want to be where I was. Eventually, my steps carried me into a quieter part of the building, a long room that felt older than the rest that was less polished, more private. The ceilings were still high, the details still ornate, but there was dust in the corners of the floor, and the room reeked of mildew and stale air. But then I saw him.

He was standing by the window, half-silhouetted by the whitewash of snow outside, hands tucked into the pockets of a long, dark wool coat he hadn't taken off. His posture wasn't tense, but it wasn't relaxed either—he stood the way someone does when they're used to being watched and have learned exactly how to be still. His dark hair was slightly mussed, like he'd just come in from the biting wind, and the faint flush on his cheeks made him look a little less untouchable, a little more real. At first, I thought he might be older—early twenties, maybe—but when he turned slightly and caught me watching him, I saw it. Not quite a boy, not quite a man. Late teens, if I had to guess. But his eyes were older. Not jaded, not cruel, just quiet. Like someone who'd grown up much faster than they should.

He didn't smile. Didn't even flinch. Just said, "You're not supposed to be in this wing."

There was something both curious and unsurprising in the way he said it. Not scolding. Just ... stating. His accent was there—possibly Russian, definitely not American, softened by British consonants, the kind that screams old money and danger in the same breath.

I didn't move. "Neither are you," I stated, and that made him turn fully toward me.

The Arrangement

His eyes flicked down to my heels, then back up to my face. "You're American," he murmured. It wasn't a question.

I nodded.

"Delegate's kid?"

I nodded again, slower this time. He caught on fast. Which meant he knew my father was here on behalf of the U.S. government. Which meant this wasn't his first summit. "And you are?" I asked, straightening my spine slightly, more curious than nervous.

He paused, hesitating just long enough to feel intentional. Like he didn't want me to know who he was. "Nikolai." No last name. Noted.

I moved closer to the window, still leaving a few feet between us, enough to keep the moment balanced. The snow was falling in slow spirals outside, soft and quiet, blanketing the courtyard in that way only Russian winters know how. "Why are you hiding?" I asked, still watching the glass. Mesmerized by the scene.

"I'm not hiding," he said. "I'm avoiding."

I looked over at him. "Is there a difference?"

"No," he shrugged, and there was no sarcasm in it. Just a quiet kind of certainty, like someone who'd spent enough time being told to show up that he'd started choosing his moments instead.

I studied him, careful not to be obvious about it. His coat was expensive. His shoes plain but perfect. Not a scuff in sight. He didn't look like the other sons and nephews and future ministers that filled the summit rooms. He looked like someone who could vanish and still take the attention with him.

"My mother's still talking to some EU rep about wheat subsidies," I muttered softly, like a confession. "So I figured I had twenty minutes."

His mouth curled slightly, barely more than a breath of a smile. "Irina's probably somewhere in that room telling an ambassador to stop pretending sanctions mean anything." He said it like it wasn't a complaint, more like someone describing the weather.

"Irina?" I asked.

He gave a half-nod. "My aunt. She brought me."

There was something final about it, like the subject of his family didn't go any further than that. And I knew— instinctively, quietly—not to ask about the rest.

"Do you live here?" I asked.

"No," he said. "England. But I come back."

I nodded, then asked, "Do you like it?"

He was quiet for a moment. "The city, yes. The people, no."

I laughed a little. "That honest?"

He looked at me again, directly this time. "You don't seem like the type who likes these events either."

"I don't."

"Then why come?"

"Didn't get a choice."

He nodded, and that felt like something. Like agreement. Or understanding. There was an awkward silence after that.

Finally, he asked, "Is this your first summit?" I nodded. "They don't get better," he said, and this time I laughed for real, my breath fogging just slightly in the cold room.

A voice called out in the distance—my name, maybe. My family's security detail. I turned to it, slowly.

He didn't move.

"See you around," I said.

And just before I stepped out of sight, he said quietly, "You will."

-

It's been twenty minutes.

Twenty minutes since Nikolai and I locked eyes. Twenty minutes of nodding while a lobbyist's wife—Caroline, I think—talks about tariffs and trade routes like I haven't heard the same speech at three other galas this year. Ten minutes of keeping my expression polite and just interested enough to seem engaged. Like this isn't complete bull. Like I care.

A few feet to my right, Thalia's deep in conversation with Cole Mercer, a Kappa Sig whose dad runs some cybersecurity firm out of Manhattan and thinks that makes him someone worth talking to. She's laughing, but I can tell she's already cataloging his entire personality as 'predictably boring'.

But I'm not really listening. Not to Caroline. Not to Cole trying to slink his way into Thalia's orbit … or her bed. Not to the champagne-soaked undercurrent of power-hungry ambition threading through the room like secondhand smoke.

Because he's still here.

Nikolai.

And I'm trying to figure out if what I'm feeling is just curiosity laced with history or something heavier. Something worse. Like maybe I'm not just remembering a boy I met once in the wrong room of a Russian palace but watching the man he became walk straight into the world I thought I understood.

And then I watch my father, Trent Langford, Vice President of the United States, and a few of his closest confidants stroll over to Nikolai like he's just another networking opportunity instead of whatever the heck he actually is.

So I do something entirely stupid. Entirely out of character.

I walk over there.

Not slowly. Not dramatically. Just ... directly. Like I have a reason, like I was always meant to be standing in this particular pocket of power with my dress zipped and my mask on. Except my heart's doing this quiet, traitorous thing in my chest, like it knows something I haven't admitted yet.

Nikolai sees me first. Of course he does. But he doesn't flinch, doesn't smirk, just gives a polite nod—cool, smooth—while his eyes stay locked on mine. And they're doing that thing again where they make you feel like he's waiting for you to say something important, even if you don't know what.

I step up next to him, and that's when my father finally notices me.

"Emilia," he says, that clipped, pleasant tone reserved for televised interviews and tightly controlled family photo ops. "Didn't expect to see you mingling over here."

I shrug. "Change of scenery."

Translation: I'm tired of pretending to care about committee appointments and champagne with weak carbonation.

Then I turn to Nikolai, and my voice softens just a touch. "Nice to see you again, Nikolai."

His mouth lifts, just barely, and he raises his glass like it's some shared secret between us. "The infamous Emilia Langford." His tone is casual, but the edge is there. "You're no longer sixteen." So he does remember.

And oh man, his voice. Still that strange mix of quiet confidence and accent I can't place—European of some sorts. The kind that should be illegal in all fifty states.

I raise an eyebrow. "Yeah, well, growing up will do that to you."

He lets out a low laugh, and sweet mercy, it's even better than I remember—quiet, genuine, like it's a rarity to do.

Then my father—never one to miss a chance to redirect the spotlight—cuts in. "You two know each other?"

Nikolai doesn't even hesitate. "St. Petersburg. A diplomatic summit. Emilia wandered off the beaten path."

I feel my lips twitch. He's not wrong.

"She does that," my father says, chuckling like it's some charming quirk instead of something that's been meticulously corrected since I was ten.

"She wandered into the wrong room," Nikolai adds, glancing at me. "Or maybe it was the right one. Depends on how you look at it."

I meet his gaze. He's toying with the memory, sure, but he's not wrong. That's what makes it dangerous.

"Still undecided," I say, tilting my glass just slightly. Cool, composed, but my skin's humming.

My father doesn't clock any of it. He's too busy jumping into his favorite sport: talking about me like I'm a LinkedIn profile. "Emilia's a senior now. Public Policy major. Chi Omega president. She's fielding internship offers all over Capitol Hill. Senator Briggs' office reached out personally over the summer."

Oh good. We're doing this.

"She manages a full academic load, a leadership position, and still finds time to keep the Langford name looking sharp in social circles."

And there it is. The brand pitch. Wrapped in paternal pride but aimed like a résumé.

I don't react. I don't need to. I've heard this enough times to tune it out like background noise. But then I glance at Nikolai, and he's just watching me. Waiting to see if I'll jump in. I don't.

"Sounds like you haven't changed much," he says quietly. Just for me. Like he knows me. Like he's been following my achievements over the past few years. Like he didn't read all my letters.

I smile, but it's thin. "Neither have you." Then I flick my eyes down to his suit. "Except the wardrobe. That's new."

He shrugs. "Had to blend in."

"And you're doing a bang-up job," I say. My voice is light, but my thoughts are a mess. Because I'm trying to decide if I want him to keep talking or if I should walk away before I fall into something I can't climb out of.

Someone calls my father's name—something about messaging strategy for an upcoming press cycle. He excuses himself without missing a beat, already back in performance mode.

Nikolai turns back to me, stepping close, leaning down so only I can hear. "You've grown up well."

It's simple. It shouldn't make me feel any way. But it does.

And before I can come up with a clever way to dodge it, he puts his hand on my shoulder and murmurs, "Enjoy your evening, Emilia." Then he's gone.

I stand there a moment too long, finishing the last sip of champagne even though it's gone warm. Like how I'm feeling.

Thalia finds me in five seconds flat. She's already mid-sip, one heel angled against the marble column like she's starring in a perfume ad, her expression equal parts wicked and bored. "There you are," she says, pushing a flute into my hand like she's offering a weapon. "Was starting to think you'd fled to Monaco."

I take the glass, but I don't drink. I need to slow down on my alcohol intake. The crystal is cool between my fingers, and I grip it like I need something to anchor me. "I was mingling." I air quote mingling.

"From the stench of lies and someone's Walmart version of Tom Ford?" She eyes the room. "Understood."

I glance toward the east wing again. I don't see him. He must have left, or he's mingling in another hall.

"Where'd you go?" she murmurs, barely tilting her head.

I don't hesitate. "Talking to my father." It's true. Technically.

She hums, skeptical but not pushing. "You always come back from those chats looking like you aged five years."

I exhale through my nose, the closest thing I can manage to a laugh. "Must be the lighting."

She snorts. "Right. And the tension in your jaw is just from smiling too much."

I don't answer. Just sip the flat champagne and let my eyes flick across the room, carefully not searching.

Thalia bumps her shoulder lightly against mine. "Tell me when you're ready."

I give her a sidelong look. "To do what?"

"To lie better," she says, deadpan. "You're slipping."

But there's no bite in it. Just that familiar, easy Thalia concern wrapped in sarcasm.

I let the corner of my mouth twitch. "Give me five minutes. Then we leave."

She hums, satisfied enough, and links her arm through mine like we've just sealed a deal.

We move slowly through the room, smiling, nodding, accepting compliments from people who couldn't pick us out of a lineup last week. A congressman's wife stops us to comment on Thalia's earrings. A Bancroft alum makes a lazy joke about Chi Omega brunches being more cutthroat than Senate hearings. We laugh. It's fake. We let them see exactly what they expect to see. Composure.

But under it ... beneath the practiced posture, the easy charm ... I can still feel the weight of his gaze from earlier. Still wondering if he's watching. Still pretending I don't want to look back.

And when Thalia leans in, brushing a strand of hair off her shoulder, she says softly, "Time to get out of here."

I nod.

We start walking toward the exit, slow and deliberate, shoes sharp against the marble, hips aligned, shoulders poised. Every head that turns catches only the version of me I've chosen to show. Graceful. Controlled. Untouchable.

"Emilia," a woman purrs, stepping into our path with practiced grace and a smile so tight it should come with a surgeon's watermark. "Radiant as always. Will we be seeing you at the campaign kickoff next month?"

Burgundy lace. Flawless blowout. I already know her type: legacy donors with legacy egos.

"I'd love to," I say sweetly, "but I'll have to check my class schedule. It's senior year." I leave it at that.

She laughs too loudly. "Oh, of course! But truly, we need more young women like you in this space."

I nod. "Let's hope they need more minds than faces."

Her smile freezes for just a breath, then reanimates as we drift past.

Thalia leans in just enough to whisper, "Dang, you're good."

"I'm trained."

We barely get five more steps before the next interruption comes with a voice like bourbon and bravado. "Emilia Langford! You look more like your mother every year."

I turn slowly, already preparing the diplomatic mask. Senator Carlisle, Preston's father. Red-faced, puffed up, and carrying the entitled weight of too many closed-door handshakes.

"Senator," I say evenly. "Good evening."

"You're stunning, truly," he says, giving me a once-over like he's awarding points. "Tell me—when are you and Preston going to quit playing games and find your way back to each other? That boy still talks about you."

From my right, Thalia makes a noise so close to a laugh it earns a look.

I don't blink. "Does he mention which sorority house he snuck into the night after our last anniversary?"

Carlisle's smile falters. "Boys will be boys."

"Right," I say, calm as ever. "And girls grow up." Before he can recover, I nod once. "Give him my best."

We move past. Thalia's practically vibrating.

"That was rude," I murmur.

"That was immaculate."

But we're not done.

Meredith DeCorte stands like a jeweled barricade in head-to-toe Valentino, mid-monologue about her "formative" summer in the Hamptons. Her voice lilts with the kind of self-importance that can only come from generations of money and perfectly choreographed family scandals. She's recounting lobster boils and private regattas like they're sacred rites, punctuating each memory with sweeping gestures that belong more to a Bravo confessional than a real conversation. This is Meredith in her natural habitat: center stage, spotlight firmly fixed.

We manage to sidestep her just as Thalia—ever precise—brushes a hand against her arm. The contact is featherlight, deliberately casual, but the intent is surgical. A practiced strike.

"Oh," Thalia says, her voice syrupy with sympathy, "Nationals heard about the yacht video. You might want to start drafting your statement before recruitment starts."

Meredith freezes mid-sentence, spine rigid, lips parted in a silent gasp. The effect is instantaneous, like someone poured a bucket of ice water down her couture.

I glance at Thalia as we pass the catering station. "What was that?"

"I said good luck with her fall calendar."

"You're terrifying."

"And you're welcome."

The exit doors come into view. The air outside is finally close enough to taste. I keep my expression smooth, spine straight, chin up. And as we walk through the grand arched foyer for our carefully-timed exit, I feel the exact number of eyes track our departure.

Just the way I like it.

-

The black SUV pulls to the curb outside the Chi Omega house just before eleven. The headlights cut across the lawn like spotlights, catching the columns and manicured hedges in brief, clinical sweeps. One of the agents, Keller, steps out first, eyes scanning the street before opening my door with quiet efficiency. The porch lights are still on, though most of the windows are dark, save for the usual sliver of lamplight behind closed blinds where girls claim they can't sleep unless they know who's coming and going.

Thalia slides out beside me, her heels already dangling from one hand, her hair pinned half-crooked from a rushed trip to the powder room. "Frick," she mutters, shifting her clutch to her other arm. "Remind me to burn these shoes in the morning. Or tonight."

"You said that last week."

"Last week I meant it less."

The front door sticks, like it always does—old wood and bad humidity management—but the agent behind us doesn't intervene. My detail rarely crosses the threshold unless there's a threat, and Clara has already made it clear that the house is not to be treated like an operations post.

"We're not a security perimeter," she said once during a chapter meeting, smiling so brightly you'd almost forget it was a complaint.

The entryway greets us with its usual blend of lavender linen spray, expensive eucalyptus candles, and the lingering haze of a dozen dry shampoos competing in the air like some unofficial sisterhood cologne. The floorboards hush beneath our feet as we cross the threshold, passing beneath the familiar mosaic that stretches across the far wall—our annual composite, a curated archive of symmetrical smiles and blowouts perfected through trial, error, and institutional memory. Curls, glossed lips, the occasional pearl stud for tradition's sake. I spot my own photo in the center row, crooked. I don't bother fixing it. I know Clara will be annoyed.

"Why didn't anyone tell me I look like my mother here?" Thalia says, her voice climbing an octave as she narrows her eyes at her headshot, which glows faintly under the soft burn of the entry sconce.

"You are her daughter," I reply without looking back. I can feel her glare hit the back of my head like heat from a stove.

"You look like you're running for office."

"Gotta live up to the family name." The words are easy, automatic, but they taste like something else. Like theater. Like a lie I've been repeating so long I've almost forgotten where it started.

I'm already halfway up the stairs before she finishes the sentence. It's been a long night, and the only thing I want now is to crash—hard, face-first, and preferably into silence.

Thalia follows, skipping the third step out of muscle memory—it creaks loud enough to wake someone in the back hallway bathroom, and no one wants to be the girl who disturbs a Chi O executive's sleep unless it's for a real emergency or a lip gloss crisis.

Our room is at the end of the hall—larger than the others, not because we earned it, but because Clara insisted on a single. I could've said sucks to be VP, claimed seniority, but I didn't want to throw Thalia to the wolves. So I took the double and moved in with my ride or die. I haven't regretted it once.

Thalia collapses face-first onto her bed, limbs splayed, heels still on, dress still clinging to her like a second skin. "Okay," she groans into the pillow, muffled but clear, "let's recap. Brandi looked like she was moonlighting for a Pepto Bismol campaign, Preston's new hair isn't fooling anyone, and his father just casually suggested you both play house again."

I let my clutch fall onto the desk and begin working the zipper down the back of my dress. "You missed the part where Cole tried to take you home."

She flips onto her side in one smooth motion, mascara smudging into the pillowcase. "That man is equal parts disgusting, equal parts ... fine." She stretches the word out like taffy, biting the last syllable. "Honestly? Criminal that someone that annoying can look that good."

I sigh, letting the gown slide down my frame, stepping out of it with care before folding it neatly over the back of my chair. "You have standards."

"I can lower them."

I say nothing because Thalia is like a dog. A loyal dog. If you keep giving her scraps, she'll come back for more, no matter the cost.

Thalia hums, amused at herself and already fading into sleep.

The corner of my mouth lifts as I reach for my phone on the nightstand. The screen glows to life, lighting up with the one group chat I never asked to be in: **Chi Omega Exec + House Leadership**. Not a real conversation. Just Clara playing commander-in-chief again, wrapping directives in fake niceties.

Clara Schulz: *Hi ladies! Just a quick note before brunch this Saturday! noticed the composite frames are* *still a little off from photos—would be amazing if someone could straighten them. Also, heard Ava is planning to wear navy for the alumni mixer next week! Just flagging so we don't all look too matchy.*

It's Clara in her final form: cheerful, controlling, and disarmingly polite. She doesn't ask. She flags. Names the girl. Names the offense. Then lets the weight of the room do the rest.

From across the room, I feel Thalia watching me with one eye open. I don't have to look.

"Exec group chat," I say. "Composite's crooked. And Ava's navy dress is apparently a national security risk."

Thalia exhales sharply. "Let me guess—Ava's wearing what she wants, and Clara's spiraling."

I flash her a dry smile. "You know the drill."

"She's such a fake troll. Not sure how you put up with her."

"Years of practice." I scroll past the message without reacting, but my screen lights up again, this time, private.

Ava Hawthorne: *Hey. Soooo did I apparently ignite some kind of navy dress crisis without realizing it? Didn't know we were pre-clearing colors with Chi O leadership now. Clara could've just texted me if she had a problem instead of turning it into some group thread spectacle - Poppy told me. I'm not changing. Dress is bought, I look good, and I'm not about to start color-coordinating out of guilt.*

My fingers hover, then move.

Me: *You're fine. She can't claim an entire color.*

A few seconds later, a thumbs up. No emoji. No exclamation. Just simple acknowledgment. Ava's not oblivious. She's just not stupid. She knows Clara plays for dominance, not harmony. And she knows enough to avoid sparring with someone who can cut her from brunch tables and speaker rosters without ever raising her voice. But with me? She doesn't pretend. Not because she's intimidated, but because she knows who actually holds the cards here. And she's smart enough not to bluff.

I set the phone down, face-down on the duvet, and recline slowly against the pillows. My lashes are still on, makeup fractured across my cheekbones like a cracked mask. The corset boning in my gown presses into my ribs, leaving faint lines I won't notice until morning.

The house settles around us in quiet waves—pipes creaking behind the walls, footsteps fading on the stairs, a laugh spilling briefly from someone's room before the door clicks shut. There's a rhythm to nights like this. A performance that extends even into rest.

Thalia's breathing has slowed. She's either asleep or pretending to be, but the effect is the same. I don't move. The overhead light is still on, casting clean shadows across our bookshelf, the closet, the stack of laundry I meant to finish folding. I lie perfectly still, but my mind continues its quiet dissection: the donor's wife with the thinly veiled threats disguised as compliments. Preston's father, all sleaze and calculated nostalgia. Clara's emoji warfare. And Nikolai—sweet mercy, Nikolai—with the suit, the smirk, the storm-colored eyes.

How in the world am I supposed to get through the first week of classes with him on my mind? Wait … is he staying in D.C. for the foreseeable future? I need to find a way to ask my father.

A cabinet closes downstairs. A door latches at the far end of the hall. Somewhere below, the bones of this house exhale with me. Not loud. Not dramatic. Just enough to mark the end of the night.

I close my eyes. Not to sleep. Just to stop analyzing. For now.

Chapter 2

Emilia

The day starts before I'm ready for it—before I've had a chance to brace, before my body catches up to the choices I made last night. My alarm buzzes at 7:00, early enough to keep control, late enough to pretend I slept. I silence it with one hand and use the other to block the morning light spilling through the blinds. My mouth tastes like flat champagne and passed hors d'oeuvres, the kind you eat out of politeness, not hunger.

For a moment, I just lay there. Still. Quiet. Waiting for the rest of me to catch up. Then I sit up slowly, peeling the covers away, before standing up and padding across the room towards the bathroom. In the mirror, I look like a mess someone tried to clean up—mascara smudged, hair pulled loose from the messy bun I threw it in last night, mouth still painted like I had something to say and didn't say it. It's a look.

I get dressed in stages. First the pajamas, then the version of myself that played the dutiful daughter and smiled through three hours of small talk. I wash my face, layer caffeine serum under my eyes, swipe on tinted moisturizer and pretend I'm ready for the day. By 7:40, I'm in a pair of black running shorts and a soft white crewneck sweatshirt with the sorority letters stitched across the front: clean, collegiate, comfortable enough to move in but still pulled together. My hair's up in a ponytail, slicked back tight at the crown. I look casual. Controlled. Awake. That's the illusion, and that's all that matters.

At 7:52, there's a knock at the door.

"Exec board in the kitchen," Clara calls, chipper in that forced, performative way that always makes me want to laugh. "Pins on. Eight sharp."

I glance back at the mirror, tucking a loose strand of hair behind my ear, then adjust the hem of my sweatshirt like it needs fixing. Does she not realize I'm the President? I scheduled the meeting. Sent the calendar invite.

Across the room, Thalia groans into her pillow. "Tell her to bite me."

"You're not on exec," I call to her from the bathroom. "You don't even have to be awake."

"She's still annoying," she mutters, rolling over. "Tell her I said that."

I glance back at the mirror. My skin looks better than it should. No eye bags. No redness. Nothing that betrays the fact I spent half the night in a silk dress listening to senators lie and watching my sorority sister hang off my ex-boyfriend like she just discovered power in cologne form. I pin the Chi O badge to the center of my sweatshirt—gold and pearl, perfectly aligned—and smooth my ponytail back into place.

"I hate that you look this put together," Thalia says from the bed, one eye open. "Tell Clara you're running five minutes late just to mess with her."

I smile. "Tempting."

"You'll behave."

"I always do."

By the time I head down, the kitchen is already full: espresso steaming, laptops open, the table surrounded by seven women in some combination of cashmere, crest sweatshirts, and high-functioning ambition. No one's speaking yet. Just the quiet clinking of mugs, keys tapping, Poppy adjusting the lighting with the dimmer app on her phone like it's a scene she's producing.

I grab a bottle of water from the fridge, twist the cap without looking, and take my seat without announcing myself. I don't have to. My chair is always at the head of the table.

I scan the room to see who's all here.

Clara Schulz, Vice President. Political science. Her dad runs a hedge fund, her mom owns a chain of plastic surgery clinics, and she hasn't had a boyfriend since freshman year—not for lack of trying. She color-codes her planner and builds agendas like she's prepping for a deposition.

Sloane Carrington, Recruitment Chair. Economics. Old Westchester family. Generational Bancroft donor. Single and visibly unbothered. She treats rush like a military operation and knows more about our pledges than they do.

Marist Vanderbilt, Social Chair. Communications major. Technically related to the *Vanderbilts*. Has a boyfriend at Georgetown and makes sure we all know it, usually by casually referencing his last name. She's quiet in meetings but controls most of our social calendar by proxy.

Tinsley DeWitt, Philanthropy Chair. Criminal justice major. Charleston born, southern bred, planning to join the FBI after graduation. Single. Sharp-eyed, steady-handed. Never raises her voice, never misses a deadline.

Poppy Sinclair-Kingsley, PR Chair. Media studies. Grew up between Malibu and Notting Hill. Single, technically, but not particularly lonely. She's already posted three Instagram stories today, each one captioned with enough emojis to make you roll your eyes.

Kennedy Ames, Treasurer. Finance. Her parents are divorce lawyers in New York City who specialize in high-net, high-stakes settlements. She tracks every receipt like it's evidence in a trial.

And me? Emilia Langford. President. Public Policy major. Daughter of the Vice President of the United States and a mother who can make or break careers over lunch.

I didn't join Chi Omega because I wanted to braid hair or sing Greek songs in a stairwell. I joined because I understood what the letters meant: Protection. Position. Proximity to the right people at the right time. But just because I know how to play the game doesn't mean I like the board. I want to burn the board and the players on it.

"Alright," I say, tapping my pen against the margin of my notes. "Let's get started. Alumni Brunch is five days out, so we're opening with that. Tinsley, run us through final prep?"

Tinsley lifts her chin with practiced cheer. "Tables confirmed, linens arriving Wednesday. We're doing individual pastry boxes instead of passed plates ... keeps things cleaner. Favors are done, Tiffany blue bows are on-brand, and every alumna over fifty is getting a personalized place card because they apparently still care about that."

A few polite laughs. I nod. "Are we good on volunteers?"

"Thirty-eight signed up. I shifted a few from Friday night cleanup to Saturday morning."

"Perfect. Marist, what's the schedule for the day?"

Marist checks her agenda. "Doors at 10:30, program at 11:15. Em, you're speaking right after Clara. Kennedy and I will tag-team transitions. It's women-only, but I confirmed with alum relations, two guests from Nationals will be attending. Low-key, but eyes-on."

"Got it," I say. "No last-minute changes. Every table needs to be set by 9:45, no exceptions. If you're not on shift, you're still expected to show up on time."

I glance next to me. Clara is sitting straight-backed, lips glossed, pen uncapped like she's about to launch a campaign.

"I'll have talking points to you by tomorrow morning," she says quickly, almost cutting in. "We want to be really aligned for the brunch, especially with Nationals there."

I nod. "Send them by ten."

She blinks once, like she expected more pushback. I don't offer it.

"Poppy, PR," I continue.

Poppy flips open her tablet. "Teaser photos for the brunch go up tonight. I've scheduled a 'thank you' graphic for Sunday morning with tagged sponsors and alumnae chapters. We're also running a flashback story series for Halloween starting Thursday, counting down old costume highlights to build hype."

"Clean the captions," I say. "Keep them tight. No hashtags. We're not a brand."

"Copy."

"Speaking of Halloween," I pivot, "Marist, update on co-hosting with Sigma Alpha Epsilon?"

"They're locked in. We've got the venue—the Atrium house—which gives us weather options if it turns cold. Their risk chair already cleared it. They're handling bartenders and security. We've got decor, wristbands, and check-in. Theme not yet decided."

I shift to Kennedy. "Treasury?"

Kennedy adjusts her glasses. "Alumni Brunch is fully paid. We'll have actual numbers by next week, but we're still projected to land under budget for the semester, barring Halloween."

"Allocate $250 to discretionary. Keep the receipts."

Then, as I turn to wrap, Clara clears her throat.

"I just want to flag something," she says lightly. "Brandi texted me this morning. She brought up the gala. Said there were ... questions about Chi O visibility. Just wondered if we had a messaging plan."

I look at her, puzzled. "I wasn't at the gala on behalf of Chi Omega."

"Of course," she says quickly. "It's just—your dad speaking, the press coverage, the social posts—it might've helped if leadership had been looped in. Proactively."

"It wasn't a sorority event," I say. "It wasn't about the chapter."

"Right, but some people might not separate the two—"

"Then they should," I reply, calm as ever. "Brandi included."

A beat of silence.

Sloane glances down. Marist caps her pen. Poppy leans back in her chair with a hum that almost sounds like approval.

Clara gives a small, toothless smile. "Just something to keep in mind."

"Noted."

The meeting continues: committee reminders, merch designs, a housing maintenance request that I flag for later. We wrap at 8:17, clean and quiet.

Everyone stands. Chairs scrape softly against the tile. Clara lingers behind, still typing something into her planner, her eyes fixed on the page.

I gather my notes, tuck the pen into the spine, and stand without a word. I step out into the morning with cold water in my hand and less patience than I started with.

My phone buzzes in my pocket.

Thalia's already texted.

Thalia: *Breakfast. Same table.*

I don't reply. She already knows I'm coming.

It's the kind of morning that can't decide what season it wants to be. Warm in the sun, cool in the shade. That in-between September feeling where the air thinks it's autumn, but the sweat behind your knees says otherwise. I've got my sunglasses on, my headphones in, and a light sweatshirt thrown on.

The quad is alive, students moving like ants from one obligation to the next. There's a buzz to Bancroft this time of year with events ramping up, Greek life in full swing, professors pretending to care. I've done this walk so many times, I don't even have to look up. My steps know the route.

Behind me, I know I'm being followed. Two agents. Same every week. Rotating detail, federally trained, emotionally stunted. One's Keller—wound tighter than a spring, always scanning like he's expecting a sniper in the student union. The other, Ruiz, is less obvious. Quiet. Watches everything, says nothing. Both pretending they're just part of the campus crowd but moving in formation like I'm the briefcase from a heist movie.

I ignore them. That's the deal. They follow, I pretend they're not there, and we all get through the day without another overreaction. Or so I thought.

Because just as I shift lanes to pass a couple stopped on the path, one hand halfway in my bag for my phone to change the song, I slam directly into someone solid.

Hard.

My shoulder clips his chest, my sunglasses nearly go flying, and I let out a startled, "Crap— Sorry—" I instinctively reach out to steady myself.

But I don't have to.

Because he's already caught me.

His hands find my arms, firm and careful, and I look up, ready to snap something sharp and rehearsed, only to lose the words entirely.

He's tall. Not tall in that gangly, unsure kind of way. Tall in that calm, grounded, built-for-sin kind of way. Tousled brown hair, lightened from the sun, like it's permanently stuck in golden hour. Eyes so blue they almost knock the breath from my lungs. A mouth that curves into a smile, slow, easy, a little crooked. And dimples. The kind you don't recover from in a day.

"You okay?" he asks, voice smooth and deep with the kind of warmth that could wreck lives if you let it.

I blink once. Twice. Nod.

"I wasn't watching," I say, my voice softer than I mean it to be. "Sorry."

"I noticed," he says, smile deepening just enough to make it worse.

And then—all chaos breaks loose.

"Ma'am—step back," Keller barks behind me, and suddenly there's a wall of black and earpieces and entirely too much testosterone between me and the perfectly innocent man who just got caught in my orbit.

Keller's already got a hand half-raised like he's debating pulling a weapon over a shoulder bump, and Ruiz is speaking low into a comm I didn't even see him touch.

The guy raises his hands a little, a mixture of confusion and calm in his expression. "Uh ... is this a bad time?"

"She's under protection," Keller snaps like the words mean something to a guy wearing Vans and an easy grin.

"I can see that," he says, glancing at me now like I'm the one with a SWAT team on standby. "I wasn't trying to kidnap her. She hit me."

"She didn't hit you," I hiss, stepping around Keller and shooting him a look that could cauterize. "I ran into you. Not on purpose. Calm down."

Ruiz, thankfully, says nothing. Just stands there like a statue with better judgment.

The guy's smile returns, lighter now. Like this whole thing is mildly hilarious. "Honestly, I've had worse run-ins. Literally."

"You good?" I ask, finally facing him directly again.

He grins, dimples and all. "Better now."

And then, just like that, he steps around the scene, gives me one last look amused, curious, maybe a little impressed—and disappears into the crowd.

Keller exhales like he just defused a bomb.

"Are you serious right now?" I mutter under my breath, adjusting my bag and brushing my sweater smooth.

"He came out of nowhere," Keller replies, still bristling.

"I came out of nowhere. I walked into him."

"Still a proximity breach," Ruiz adds, quieter, more diplomatic.

"Jeez," I say, popping my earbud back in. "I can't wait for you to explain to your boss how you almost tackled a student because of my doing."

I keep walking. They follow. And somewhere, two dimples and a pair of blue eyes are still messing with my equilibrium.

Mondays are a trip.

Thalia is already at the café when I get there, stretched out in her usual spot by the planter wall, one leg tucked under her like a cat in the sun. She's halfway through her drink, condensation slipping down the side of the plastic cup, her oversized sunglasses perched on top of her head like a crown. Her hair's twisted up in that lazy, I-didn't-try way that somehow still looks editorial, and she's wearing a faded Bancroft sweatshirt like it's designer. She doesn't look up when I approach, but she doesn't need to. She senses me the way she always does, like the air shifts and gives me away.

"You're late," she says, her eyes still fixed on her phone, voice flat and unconcerned.

"You texted me before I left the house."

"Still late," she replies, thumbs moving with practiced ease, slow and unbothered, like she has nowhere else to be.

I drop into the chair across from her, heat still clinging to the backs of my knees and the tops of my shoulders, my skin flushed with more than just the weather. My heart hasn't fully settled since I passed him, since that look, that faint twitch of his mouth that sent a jolt straight down my spine and left a thrum in my veins that hasn't let up. I exhale, low and steady, and peel off my sunglasses like that might help reset my entire nervous system.

The barista catches my eye through the window and nods. Same order as always. I don't even need to move.

Thalia finally sets her phone face-down on the table and leans back, stretching out like she's waiting for me to spill. She doesn't ask anything at first, just studies me with the same quiet precision she uses to take people apart during chapter meetings. It makes my skin itch.

"What the heck happened to you?"

"I walked into someone this morning," I say, calm, casual. Like it's a footnote, not something that's been replaying in my head since it happened.

Thalia glances over her cup, one brow arched. "And by 'walked into,' you mean…"

"Full-body collision. Wasn't looking and slammed straight into him."

Her mouth twitches. "You okay?"

"Physically? Fine. Emotionally? A little bruised."

She leans forward, interested now. "Do I know him?"

"I have no idea who he was," I admit. "Tall. Athletic. Hoodie, joggers, Vans. Just … existing. And I barreled into him like a freshman late to Econ."

Thalia snorts but keeps it mostly contained. "Was he cute?"

I hesitate. "Yes. Unfortunately."

"That does make it worse."

"I had a water bottle in one hand, phone in the other. My detail started to move like he was a threat, and I had to step in before they tackled someone who was just standing there."

"Oh no."

"And then," I sigh, "because my brain completely short-circuited, I said, *'You good?'* Like *he* had done something wrong."

Thalia blinks. "You didn't."

"I did."

A slow grin spreads across her face. "That's … deeply awkward."

"Thank you."

"I'm just impressed. I think that might be the first time I've ever heard you sound rattled."

"I wasn't rattled," I say quickly, then pause. "Okay, I was rattled. But he just … walked away. Like the moment didn't touch him at all."

Thalia hums, a quiet sound of amusement. "Your thighs clenched, didn't they?"

I glare at her but don't deny it. "I think I almost blacked out from embarrassment."

"You've got a type," she says, stretching. "The hot, potentially dangerous kind who look like they could carry you with one arm but also calculate tax fraud in their head."

"You're disgusting," I mutter.

"You're flustered. It's charming."

I want to respond, to lean into the banter, but something—or rather someone—catches my eye.

Across the quad, leaning against the stone railing outside the administration building like the campus was built to frame him, stands Nikolai. And he's not alone. Next to him is a guy I've never seen before. Trust me, I would know. Tall. Blonde hair. Looks like he works out for fun. He's laughing, which is a rarity in these parts.

Thalia tracks my gaze with a sigh sharp enough to cut through the hum of the quad and mutters, "Ugh. This guy again," in that particular tone she reserves for people who speak too confidently in class and never bother to cite their sources.

I glance sideways, following the direction of her stare, and ask, "Which one?"

She doesn't miss a beat. "Blonde guy. He was here earlier. Huge ego, even bigger opinions."

As if summoned by sheer force of her disdain, the blonde turns and immediately spots her, his expression sliding into something cocky and theatrical before he offers a slow, deliberate wink that practically leaves a trail of cologne in its wake. Thalia, unbothered and unimpressed, flips him off without looking away, and I catch myself blinking, not because of him, but because I've never seen her waste the effort. It takes a particular kind of ego to earn Thalia's visible irritation, and apparently, this guy's the reigning champion.

He grins, clearly enjoying himself, and leans toward Nikolai to whisper something, a motion that draws my attention away from Thalia's quiet fury and directly into the stillness of the man beside him.

Nikolai isn't scrolling or feigning disinterest like the rest of us might, just standing there, patient and composed, as if this entire setting—the campus, the noise of students, his friend's antics—has nothing on him. When he finally looks up, his eyes settle on me without hesitation, and there's a brief moment where the air between us shifts, not dramatically, not loudly, but enough that I feel the weight of recognition pass through it.

He doesn't smirk or nod or make a scene out of knowing me, but he does offer a subtle tilt of his head, the kind you give someone whose presence you expected, maybe not here, maybe not now, but eventually. There's no heat to it, no false warmth, but there's an awareness. A grounded sort of ease that makes it impossible to accuse him of being cold.

I raise my hand in a brief, instinctive wave, the motion too casual to feel intentional but too deliberate to be ignored, and to my surprise, he lifts his hand in response, a simple echo of mine, restrained and understated, but somehow more pointed because of it.

Then, without ceremony, he turns back to his friend, says something quiet, and swings his backpack off the ground with the efficiency of someone who has other places to be. They start walking in the opposite direction, the blonde glancing back once with a look that screams confusion, and I feel an involuntary flicker of agreement.

Thalia doesn't comment on the interaction—too focused on the foam patterns swirling in her cup to clock the sudden tension pulling at my posture—so when she finally asks, "You good?" her voice is casual, distracted.

I answer with a nonchalant "Fine," because I am, and there's nothing remarkable about seeing Nikolai here except that I didn't expect it. Not today, not on this stretch of campus.

Last I knew, he was in London, so seeing him here, on this campus, in broad daylight, standing outside the psych building like he belongs, makes no sense at all. I don't know why he's in D.C., let alone why he'd be anywhere near this place. And the fact that he doesn't look the slightest bit out of place only makes it worse.

Maybe he's here for a guest lecture. Maybe for a meeting. Maybe for his family. Whatever the reason, I tell myself it doesn't matter. Because we aren't anything. We never were.

-

Thirty minutes later, I'm one group chat away from launching my phone out the nearest window. There are moments I regret saying yes to being chapter president, this is one of them. I didn't realize "referee" came with the title, but apparently, it's in the fine print between leadership and damage control. And with girls, it's never just surface level. It's subtle. It's sharp. It's exhausting.

I set my phone down and bite the inside of my cheek to keep from groaning out loud. Thalia doesn't notice. Her thumbs are flying across her screen, a storm of motion and zero eye contact. Then she sighs, a deep, dramatic exhale that makes her sound like she's personally responsible for carrying the emotional weight of the entire university.

She takes a long sip of her coffee, winces, and sets it down like it betrayed her. "Ugh. What is in this?"

"Oat milk," I mutter.

She glares at the cup. "Figures. I haven't even had my first class yet and I'm already over the semester."

"You've been awake for less than an hour."

"And somehow it's already too much."

I smile into my drink. "Psych major problems?"

She shrugs, slow and deliberate, one gold hoop glinting in the sun as if even her jewelry agrees with her irritation. "Not yet, but give it a week. I've already met three people who think their childhood drama makes them qualified to diagnose strangers on TikTok."

I don't say anything. She doesn't need me to. Everyone assumes Thalia picked psychology because she's quick—quick with people, with words, with the kind of observations that leave you feeling both seen and slightly exposed. And they're not wrong. But what they miss, what they never even think to question, is that she was raised in a house where arguing wasn't just expected, it was a competitive sport. Her father sits on the Supreme Court, her mother turned federal prosecution into a launchpad for political consulting, and her brothers went into law without hesitation, like gravity. Thalia could've followed effortlessly, but she didn't. She chose psychology instead. Not to win, but to understand. That's what sets her apart.

She crushes the napkin she'd been absentmindedly doodling on, not quite annoyed, just bored with the conversation already forming in her head. "Anyway, I can

40

already tell I'm going to end up doing all the work in every group project. Some girl with a crystal collection is going to submit a Pinterest board and call it research."

"You haven't even been to class yet," I point out.

She lifts her chin with mock seriousness. "I've seen enough."

I roll my eyes, but she's already watching me differently now—subtle shift in her posture, the slight narrowing of her gaze. She's not talking just to talk anymore. She's circling.

"You're still flushed," she says casually, sipping again.

"It's warm."

"It's September."

"And sunny."

She hums, unconvinced. "Is this about the guy?"

"What guy?"

She gives me a look. "The one you walked into like you were trying to merge with him."

I groan. "Thalia—"

"Tall, athletic, suspiciously hot, vaguely mysterious? That guy?"

"I don't even know who he is."

"You sure *noticed* him."

"I collided with him."

"And then supposedly stared after him like you forgot how your legs work."

I glance down at my drink, swirling what's left of the ice. "I was distracted."

"Mm-hmm," she says, leaning back, stretching like a cat in the sun. "It's been three months since Preston."

"I know how time works."

"It's senior year. You've spent the whole summer being good. Clean. Controlled. Nothing even remotely messy."

"That's not a bad thing."

"No," she says, "it's just ... when's the last time you hooked up with someone? Like, no expectations. No strings attached. Just because you wanted to."

I don't answer, not immediately, and that's all she needs.

Her smile fades into something quieter, less teasing, more knowing. "That's what I thought."

She doesn't push. Doesn't say I'm repressed or uptight or carrying too much on my back. She just stands, brushing the crumbs from her skirt, and lifts her tote with a single, smooth motion.

"You should let yourself be curious," she says lightly, slinging the bag over her shoulder. "About him."

"If I see him again, I'm walking the other way."

"You won't," she calls over her shoulder as she starts across the quad. Her hair slips from its clip, long waves falling in soft, dark strands. She doesn't fix it. Doesn't glance back. Just lifts one hand in a lazy, parting wave.

"Why not?" I call after her.

She tosses the answer back without stopping. "Because now you *want* to see him."

And I hate that she's right. Because I do. Not in a way that makes sense. Not in a way I'd admit to anyone else. But he's still in my head—his voice, that brief flash of his jawline, the weight of his shoulder against mine like it left an impression deeper than it should've.

But so is Niko, and that's what makes it worse.

I stand slowly, tossing my empty cup into the bin and adjusting the strap of my bag. I don't have class for another fifteen minutes, but I take the long way around the quad anyway—not because I need the extra steps, but because the idea of walking into a room, sitting still, and pretending I'm not still thinking about that stranger feels unbearable.

Because I am still thinking about them both.

And I really hate that I am.

The Arrangement

-

The lecture hall is grand, like all things at Bancroft are. Polished wood paneling, wide-tiered seating, recessed lighting that makes the space feel more like a courtroom than a classroom. The kind of room built to impress visiting faculty, donors, and the occasional dignitary who decides to "drop in" mid-semester. Everything is just slightly too curated with symmetrical rows, gleaming brass fixtures, a podium that looks like it belongs on a debate stage. Even the silence has a weight to it, thick with the pressure of expectation. Students trickle in with practiced ease, pulling out laptops, arranging notebooks, speaking in the kind of low, hushed voices that make even small talk sound strategic. I find a seat near the center and settle in without issue, fingers already reaching for my laptop, the start of the semester tightening around me like a familiar collar.

I've barely opened my laptop when the chair beside me scrapes backward and someone drops into it with the kind of smooth, unhesitating motion that suggests familiarity where there isn't any. I don't have to look. I already know.

Wells Ballard.

Of course.

He sits like the seat was reserved for him—like the room is. Navy Bancroft quarter-zip, pressed khakis, hair cut to precision but tousled just enough to feign effortlessness. The smile he offers is confident, practiced, the kind of thing that probably worked on freshman girls and family friends at political dinners. It lands between us like a business card I didn't ask for.

"I didn't know you were taking this class," he says, tone casual but edged with curiosity, as if he's been keeping track of me and just missed this one detail.

"It's required for my major," I reply, eyes still on my screen.

43

He lets out a quiet chuckle, measured, smooth, just performative enough to be useful in fundraising rooms. I'm sure he thinks it's disarming. It's not.

Wells Ballard is the kind of man who's been treated like the answer his whole life. His father's a federal judge with a last name that's appeared in three circuit courts and one amicus brief with national headlines. His mother chairs a foundation that turns donor galas into policy previews. Wells was raised on access, groomed for relevance. He knows how to ask questions that sound like compliments, how to flirt without sounding like it, how to insert himself into a conversation and make it seem like he was invited. What he doesn't know—still, somehow—is how to handle people who don't immediately bend to his charm.

Before he can launch into whatever follow-up line he's rehearsed, the room shifts around us—conversations fading, bodies straightening—as Professor Kerr walks in.

He looks exactly the way I expected him to—shirt slightly rumpled, blazer with one thread near the cuff coming undone, and a leather satchel that's been through more airport terminals than some of the students in this room. He walks with purpose but not urgency, and when he drops the bag on the desk and turns to face us, it's with the tired authority of someone who doesn't care if you like him as long as you remember what he said.

"Welcome to Comparative Political Systems," he begins, voice steady but unimpressed. "If you're here to learn how to run for office, transfer departments. This class won't teach you how to win elections or craft palatable soundbites. We're here to study structure. Power. Failure. Which institutions fall apart, and which ones pretend not to."

A few people chuckle. I don't.

He flips to the first slide—*POWER ≠ CONTROL*—and launches into the day's material like he's on a timer. The history of European regulatory systems, policy adoption models, regional variance in implementation. It's dense, but I'm used to that. I take notes quickly, silently, fingers moving faster than my thoughts, catching the rhythm before it slips away.

And then the door opens.

Late.

It's not loud, but the room turns anyway. Curiosity is contagious, and first-day lateness always draws attention.

I'm barely paying attention to the latecomer, but the unmistakable murmur around me has been glancing up only to bang my knee against the table.

"Crap," I whisper so quietly I think I imagined it. It's the guy from the run-in.

T-shirt, joggers, a backpack slung low across one shoulder. He looks like a normal college student, like someone who's never been a part of the Bancroft crowd. He looks around, scans the space like he's assessing something—not just availability, but possibility—and then his eyes land on me.

There's recognition in them. A slow, knowing grin crosses his face, and I can feel the heat rising up the back of my neck.

I straighten slightly as he chooses a seat in the row in front of me. He sits with his legs stretched slightly in front of him, body angled like this is just another day.

I try to focus. I try so hard. Professor Kerr presents a scenario involving enforcement delays in EU privacy law. A few students answer, offering the usual surface-level insights. Then there's a pause, and the voice that follows cuts through everything.

"Because they're buying time. Fines are manageable, domestic backlash isn't."

I didn't notice it before—maybe I was too busy playing interference with my security detail—but his accent is

English. And yes, I'm pretty sure the girl behind me whimpered.

Professor Kerr flicks his gaze to the guy. "Name?"

The guy shrugs once, lazy but not dismissive. "Max." So that's his name.

Kerr doesn't push. "Correct. Strategy isn't always about winning. Sometimes it's about delaying until no one's paying attention anymore."

The class continues, but I'm no longer fully present. I'm tracking Max. The calm in his posture. The confidence in the way he spoke. The way his shirt hugs him. The cut of his hair—tight on the sides, messy on top in a I-just-ran-my-fingers-through-it way. Dark. Tattoos running down the length of his right forearm.

I'm not sure why I'm noticing him so much. He's just a guy. I've talked to plenty of guys before. Trust fund guys who think the number in their bank account attracts women like me. It doesn't. I've seen enough crap in this lifetime to know the DC arena is not where I want to find my person.

When the lecture ends, people start packing up fast. I take my time, lingering as if a certain someone will engage with me. I'm halfway through zipping my bag when I feel him next to me.

Max close, but not in a way that crowds, just enough that I notice. Enough that I smell the unmistakable scent of Armani. Subtle, expensive, and clouding my judgement way too much for a Monday morning. For the first day of senior year.

"We meet again," he says, tone easy, the words rolling off his tongue.

I glance up at him slowly, keeping my expression in check. "And I didn't run into you this time."

His mouth pulls into an easy grin, but he doesn't say anything else. Doesn't explain himself. Just meets my gaze with the same quiet precision I remember from earlier, and adds, almost as an afterthought, "Try not to run into anyone else today."

Then he's gone.

And I hate how long it takes me to look away.

-

The air outside is cooler than expected, that particular kind of late-summer chill that slips beneath sleeves and brushes against your skin just enough to make you think about layering without actually needing to. I've got on a light sweatshirt—half comfort, half uniform at this point—and the wind threading through campus feels more like a warning than a shift. Behind me, one of my security guys follows at a distance that walks the line between casual and strategic. It's easy to pretend he's not there until I see people noticing him instead of me. I check my phone as I head into my next class: International Law. Still nothing. No new texts from the Exec Group. Small mercies.

North Hall looms ahead—square, severe, and utterly humorless. The kind of building that was probably designed to discourage joy. Its windows are strips of frosted glass, glowing faintly like they're concealing something radioactive inside. Apparently, this is where the "serious" classes happen. Law and policy. Theory and teeth.

Inside, Room 206 hums with fluorescent tension. The classroom is maybe a third full, but people already move like they've claimed territory. A few have laptops open, some pretending to read. I slip into a seat near the center. Not eager, not distant. I know how this looks. I've been taught.

I open my notebook even though I won't need it, not yet. It's the motion that matters, the optics.

Behind me, voices hiss in hushed urgency.

"They say she failed half the class last year."

"For real?"

"First paper. One guy had to drop. Couldn't hack it."

I keep my face forward, but my stomach tightens.

I've read the same stories online. Professor Layton: unflinching, unsparing, untouchable. The kind of professor who can end a semester with a single raised eyebrow.

The door clicks open again and a guy saunters in like he owns the syllabus. Tall, disheveled in a curated way. He grins. "Sorry, Professor. Interview ran long."

Layton doesn't even look up. "Save the excuse for someone who cares. Take a seat."

He flops into one without waiting for permission. The girl next to him doesn't hide her recoil.

Layton finally looks up, sweeping the room with the kind of gaze that makes you sit straighter without realizing it. She picks up a pen.

"I don't know any of you. That changes now." She gestures to the front row. "Name. Full name. Something I'll remember you by. Go."

The first girl rattles off her name and passion for human rights law. Another says she worked a summer at a prosecutor's office in Philadelphia. A few try to be clever. Layton remains impassive, scribbling down only what matters to her.

It gets to our row. My pulse picks up. The girl beside me introduces herself—some vague interest in international trade and NGOs. Then Layton's eyes land on me. Not hard. Just curious. Uninvested.

I lift my chin a fraction. "Emilia Langford."

A flicker. Just the tiniest change in Layton's expression. Recognition. Not of me, exactly, but of my last name.

"Langford," she repeats. "As in…"

"Yes," I say, before she finishes. "But I'm here as a student."

Layton stares at me for a beat longer than anyone else, then writes something down without looking up. "Understood." She moves on.

Dylan—the late one—goes for charm in his intro, talking about moot court and "being allergic to boredom." Layton doesn't even blink.

Once introductions are over, she sets her pen down and says, "No slides today. We're doing this the old-fashioned way. You'll need your notes, your brain, and the ability to think under pressure, which, judging by most of your intros, is still up for debate."

A few people laugh. I don't.

She glances over us like she's flipping through dossiers. "Who can explain the core conflict between judicial independence and collective enforcement in transnational law?"

Silence.

Then Dylan raises his hand, of course. "It's about sovereignty, right? Like … courts don't want to follow someone else's rules?"

Layton stares. "That's not an answer. That's a vague shrug in sentence form. Try again or move on."

He leans back. "Pass."

"Brilliant. Anyone else?"

More silence. Then the girl from the front row offers a clean, textbook-perfect response. Layton gives one crisp nod.

"Enforcement without authority isn't enforcement. It's theater. Remember that."

The next forty minutes slide past in a slow drip of nerves and thinly veiled panic. People stumble. Someone tries to challenge Layton and gets intellectually gut-checked. I don't speak. I listen. I take notes.

When class ends, Layton shuts her folder like she's closing a case file. "Bring actual opinions next week," she says. "Not just outlines."

Dylan glances my way. There's something calculating behind his lazy smile, like he's deciding whether I'm the kind of person worth charming.

He opens his mouth, but I beat him to it. "Don't."

He blinks, pauses, then closes it again.

Good boy.

-

Dinner is already a mess when I walk in. The Chi Omega dining room looks perfect, as usual—dim overhead lighting, table centerpieces unnecessarily curated for a Monday night, pasta in ceramic warming dishes that probably cost more than most people's first car. But the energy? The energy is trash. You can smell the tension before you even sit down.

Clara's in the middle of the room, exactly where she wants to be, with her elbows poised just right on the table like she's leading a board meeting. She's mid-rant about color palettes—again—still seething about Ava's navy dress like it's a personal betrayal and not just a basic outfit choice.

"I'm not saying she can't wear navy," Clara says, her voice high and tight, "I'm saying if more than one person wears the same tone, it looks like we didn't plan. And that's ... embarrassing."

Across from her, Ava's twirling pasta around her fork like she's bored to death. "Clara, it's a color, not a trademark."

"It's my signature color for the brunch," Clara snaps. "You literally said you were wearing navy after I already announced it."

"I literally said I had the dress picked for two weeks before you even booked the brunch."

"Okay, but that's not the point—"

50

Thalia cuts in from two seats down, voice deadpan. "The point is, Clara thinks your navy is sabotaging her navy. And honestly, this is the most stressed I've ever seen someone be over chiffon."

"Thank you," Ava says sweetly, without looking away from her plate. "Exactly."

I slide into the seat beside Thalia, grab the serving spoon, and pile vegetables onto my plate without comment. Clara's already shooting daggers in every direction, probably waiting for me to chime in and save her honor or whatever the heck she thinks this is.

She looks directly at me. "Emilia, don't you think it sends mixed messages if two members are dressed the same at an alumni event?"

I sip from my water first. Slowly. "I think the only message being sent is that navy is universally flattering. And you're blowing it out of proportion."

A few girls muffle their laughs. Clara doesn't.

"Image matters, Emilia," she says stiffly.

"I know. Which is why this meltdown looks worse than the matching dresses ever would."

Clara clutches her glass like she's deciding between sipping it or throwing it.

Brandi, who's been quiet up until now, suddenly perks up like she's just realized we're not paying attention to her. "Wait, is this about the navy dress again? I thought we were past that. I literally wore the same top as Tinsley last semester, and the house didn't burn down."

Typical Brandi. She's the kind of girl who borrows your lip gloss and your boyfriend in the same breath, then acts surprised when anyone notices. I don't respond. Some things aren't worth adding to the record. They're just meant to be remembered.

Clara snaps, "You wore it after her."

"Holy crap," Thalia mutters, "are we doing a chain of dress custody now?"

Willa, one of the new girls, whispers to the girl beside her, "Is this, like … normal?"

I cut a glance at her. "Welcome to Chi Omega. Smile, nod, and never wear the same dress as Clara unless you want to get verbally sacrificed."

The tension breaks into a wave of laughter. Not all genuine, but enough to release some of the pressure. Clara looks like she wants to scream into a throw pillow.

Dessert hits the table—crème brûlée, cleanly torched, with a sprig of mint that feels more decorative than functional. I crack the shell with the back of my spoon, take a single bite, and set it down. Thalia's already finished hers and is sipping her espresso with amusement.

Across the table, Brandi's deep in her latest monologue, this time about a teeth-whitening brand deal that's "projected to triple her engagement rate by Sunday." She says it like it's something to be proud of. It's not.

Thalia doesn't look up. "God bless. Nothing builds credibility like bleaching your gums."

I choke back a laugh, the kind that curls in my throat instead of coming out. Under the table, I feel her foot nudge mine once.

Brandi keeps going, oblivious. I don't look at Thalia, but the corner of my mouth shifts anyway.

Five minutes later, she's still going on about her brand deal when Clara shifts in her seat like she's physically restraining herself from interrupting. I count to three in my head. She doesn't make it to two.

"Can we go over Round One logistics before everyone leaves?"

And just like that, the air tightens.

Thalia doesn't look up, just mutters, "Jeez," into her water glass.

Ava lets her fork clatter to her plate in protest. Brandi sighs and adjusts her sweater like someone just asked her to show up for jury duty.

Clara, undeterred, launches into it. "We're still missing three bios, and if we want to stay competitive this year—"

That's when I tune her out. I already know her pitch. Clara's been performing this same song since we were fourteen back at St. Bart's, where group projects were war zones and school elections ended in silent feuds. She wasn't my friend then. Still isn't. We were rivals, technically. She just wasn't fast enough to keep up, and I wasn't petty enough to tell her that to her face.

Now we're stuck playing grown-up in a house built on manicured sisterhood and matching tote bags, pretending we don't remember the way she once told me I was "better at looking confident than *being* confident." I was fifteen. And she was already keeping score.

Willa's eyes flick around the table like she's trying to figure out the rules of a game she never signed up for.

"So ... do we have, like, actual scripts?" she asks, voice small.

Clara pounces. "No *scripts* but talking points. We're emphasizing community, leadership, balance—"

"Jeez," Ava says. "It's recruitment, not a Senate confirmation."

Brandi twirls her spoon. "I thought our brand was like, warm but ambitious?"

"You said that," I remind her.

"And I stand by it."

Thalia finally looks up. "We're not a brand. We're a vibe with a zip code."

Clara bristles. I watch her carefully. Her hands are too still. That means she's pissed.

"This matters," she says. "We're not just competing with Kappa and Delta. This is Bancroft. Everyone is trying to win."

There it is. Trying to win. That's the truth no one says out loud—not to potential new members, not in recruitment videos, not in welcome letters signed "With love and sisterhood". At Bancroft, Rush isn't about finding your people. It's about building a résumé in heels. You don't join for the house. You join for the doors it opens. For the way it looks on paper. For the quiet, ruthless ladder that starts with a curated Instagram feed and ends in a corporate boardroom or a country club brunch.

Willa's still blinking. "So ... what do we say?"

Sloane, who's been silent until now, finally looks up from her phone. Her voice is calm. Deadly. "Say what makes you sound likable. Then shut up before you say too much."

The table goes quiet. Sloane is Recruitment Chair. Her job is to manage the chaos, make it look effortless, and never break a sweat. She's terrifying in the way only someone who's *never needed to raise her voice* can be.

Willa swallows. Brandi pulls out her lip gloss like we're done.

Clara, of course, pushes forward anyway. "We should at least be aligned on language," she says. "Otherwise, it's disorganized."

"It *is* disorganized," Thalia says. "We just say it with better hair now."

I feel the tension building in my jaw before I realize I'm grinding my molars. I don't want to step in. I don't want to have to be the adult in a room full of grown women who still measure power in tone and seating arrangements.

But I'm president. So I do.

"Clara," I say, finally. "Let Sloane run the conversation. That's her job. Yours is support. Let's not overcomplicate it."

There's a pause. Clara's mouth pulls into a tight smile, the kind that looks like it hurts to hold. "Of course," she says, but her eyes scream *you humiliated me in front of them.*

Which is rich, considering she's been trying to do the same to me since sophomore year chem class.

Thalia catches my eye. I raise an eyebrow, and she raises hers higher. It's a dumb game we've been playing since we were twelve.

She texts me under the table.

Clara's gonna write a whole essay about that in her burn book.

I type back:

Let her. I'll fix her formatting.

Ava's checking her nails like this whole conversation is beneath her. It probably is. She joined because her aunt is an alumna and stayed because she figured out how to weaponize charm while living off iced coffees.

Brandi is taking a selfie.

Willa is scribbling notes in her phone like this is a lecture.

Sloane is already back on her screen. Probably coordinating a spreadsheet, a rideshare, and someone's emotional breakdown all at once.

And me? I'm sitting in the eye of the storm, pretending like I'm not thinking about my freshman year rush, when every girl already knew my name, my mom's voting record, and the fact that I wore the wrong shoes on Day One. I got the bid. Of course I did. But I bled for it quietly. Smiled through the taste of metal in my mouth.

Now I run the house. And sometimes, I think I hate it, but I'd rather burn it down than hand it over to someone like Clara.

Thalia nudges my foot. I don't look up.

"I'll see you upstairs," she says, already rising.

"You're leaving me with Brandi?"

"Consider it penance for making me Rush in the first place."

I grin, but it fades fast. She's right. I did drag her into this. And we both stayed longer than we meant to.

By the time I get back to my room, I'm spent. The house has finally settled down with only the sound of doors closing.

I close the door behind me and let it rest against my back for just a second. The first day was unusual. I can't really pinpoint why. In fact, the past few days have sent me into a tailspin with Niko, Max, and now Rush week looming upon us. I look up and see Thalia in her bed, cross-legged on her comforter, laptop in front of her as she taps her pen idly against it. She looks up and sends me a *What a fiasco* look.

I laugh, walking to my side of the room, pulling off my sweatshirt and tossing it on the chair by the window. I loosen my scrunchie, allowing my hair to flow past my shoulders. My phone buzzes in my shorts pocket. I ignore it, thinking it's a text, but then it buzzes again. I look down and see my father's name lighting up the screen. Groaning, I answer.

"Emilia." His voice is calm, clipped. Not cold, just clean, like everything else he controls. He says my name like punctuation.

"Yes, sir."

"Your mother asked me to check on the brunch."

She didn't want to ask herself. She never does. She strategically delegates through him, like always.

"It's done," I say. "Final headcount is confirmed. Catering's squared. My remarks are short and already vetted."

There's a pause, the sound of him moving paper in the background, or maybe pouring a drink. I can't tell. He's always multitasking, even when he speaks like everything is a priority.

"She wants it to go smoothly."

It will. He knows that. He wouldn't have called if he didn't already trust it was handled.

"There's something else," my father says right as I think we're done, his voice flat and clipped in the way he reserves for things that aren't up for discussion. "I've arranged a meeting with Nikolai and his father next week at the Four Seasons. I'd like you to be there. We have some important things to discuss."

There's a second where the name doesn't land, not fully, and then it does, it comes with this strange heat that rushes up from the base of my spine like I've been caught doing something I wasn't supposed to. My fingers tighten slightly around the phone. Nikolai. Of course. The same Nikolai I spoke to for all of five minutes last night, whose voice I can still hear with a clarity that should honestly be embarrassing. The same Nikolai I spotted this morning across the quad, hands in the pockets of his pants. He'd caught my eye and nodded, and I'd nodded back, casual, unbothered—or at least I'd pretended to be, even though the look he gave me felt like an ellipsis at the end of a sentence I wasn't ready to finish.

I say nothing at first, because I'm trying to gauge just how much my father knows—or worse, how much of this has already been decided. I'm not stupid. He doesn't say things like "important meeting" without layers beneath the language. If this were business, he'd have sent an email. If it were political, he'd be posturing. But the inclusion of me, in person, in something scheduled between two men who operate like continents—that means something else. I just don't know what yet.

"Okay," I say finally, and my voice is smooth, practiced, the kind of tone you use when you want to leave absolutely nothing behind on the table.

"You'll receive the details soon. Don't be late."

"I won't."

The call ends, clipped and clean. I don't move as I sit there with the phone still in my hand, screen gone black, like I'm waiting for someone to undo it. Rewind. Rewrite.

Across the room, Thalia sets her pen down. She doesn't ask. She doesn't have to.

"He wants me at a meeting next week," I say. "...with Nikolai."

Her eyebrows shoot up and I internally kick myself because dang it, I forgot to tell her about seeing Nikolai at last night's gala.

She thankfully ignores that last part and instead looks at me with pity. "And you're going." She says it slowly like she's unsure. Like I've been given a choice to say no.

"Of course I'm going." My voice is too calm. Too even. "It's already on the calendar. Probably printed in serif font on monogrammed stationery. I'm sure there's a folder."

She doesn't smile. Good. I'm not in the mood.

I stare at the ceiling for a second, then lean forward, bracing my elbows on my knees like I'm trying to physically hold the moment in place. "You know what pisses me off?" I murmur, eyes still on the floor. "It's not that I have to go. It's not that my father snapped his fingers and, once again, I'm expected to play diplomat-in-training with a smile and a silk blouse." I look up. "It's *him*. It's the fact that he's here. That he just walked back into the world like nothing happened. Like he didn't vanish. Like I was some placeholder for a season and then suddenly inconvenient."

Thalia says nothing. She knows better than to interrupt when I get like this.

"I let myself believe it meant something. That those letters—that version of us—was real. Because it *was*. We didn't use names. We didn't talk politics. We just existed. For once, I wasn't a politician's daughter, or some perfectly postured future senator's wife. I was just … me. And he made me feel like that was enough." I laugh once, low and bitter. "And then he disappeared. Not a word. Not a reason. Just gone. And I let it go. I told myself it didn't matter because feeling something meant it mattered, and if it mattered, it could be used against me. So I locked it down. Like everything else." A pause. "He looked at me last night like none of it ever happened. Like I hadn't spent months wondering what I did wrong. Like I didn't wait for our house manager to hand me my mail like some pathetic cliché hoping for handwriting that never came." I shove my phone onto the nightstand like it burned me. "I am so sick of being expected to smile through every vanishing act. Every rewrite. Every man who gets to decide I'm convenient when it works for him and forgettable when it doesn't."

Thalia shifts, pulling her legs under her. "You still have the letters?"

I nod. "Bottom drawer."

She doesn't move.

I press my nail into my palm until I feel the sting. "I don't know what I'm walking into next week. I don't know who he is now. But I know who I was, and if he walks into that room pretending she didn't exist, I swear—" I stop myself. Breathe once. Then twice. Try to swallow the fury before it swallows me. "I don't know," I finish, quieter now. "I don't know what I'll do."

But I do know this, I haven't forgotten. And I'm not the girl he met in St. Petersburg. That girl thought she had time, that honesty was safe, that being seen was a gift and not a weapon. She wrote letters. I write outcomes. I know what I am now—a name, a brand, a walking strategy. I know how to hold a room without blinking. I know how to cut someone down without raising my voice. So if he thinks he's stepping into that meeting across from the same wide-eyed girl who let herself believe he was different? He's already lost.

I've played this game in heels sharper than most people's instincts, and this time, I'm not here to be chosen. I'm here to choose.

And if Nikolai is stupid enough to forget that, then let him. I'll remind him.

Beautifully.

Brutally.

And with a smile.

Chapter 3

Emilia

Today's the Chi Omega Alumni Brunch, which means the house is packed wall-to-wall with women who know exactly how long to hold a smile and exactly when to turn it off. It's a ladies-only affair, full of pearls, legacy donors, and those delicate little white gloves only worn by the kind of women who fund their daughters' philanthropy trips like it's a tax write-off. The dining room is glowing—soft chiffon drapes over the windows, floral centerpieces placed with surgical precision, and enough citrus-scented air freshener to make the foyer feel like a luxury day spa.

Clara's in her element. Frenzied, flawless, one mascara flake away from a full breakdown. I watch her from the back hallway as she snaps directions at the catering staff while simultaneously fixing a chair angle with her foot.

And then I see her.

Veronica Langford.

My mother arrives like she always does—ten minutes late and perfectly composed, as if her entrance is the real beginning of the event. Her heels barely make a sound on the marble, but somehow, people notice. They always do. Pale pink Chanel, hair smoothed to glossy perfection, diamond studs that flash every time she tilts her head like she's listening. She doesn't look for me right away. She never does. When her eyes finally land on me, it's with a kind of recognition that feels clinical, like spotting a familiar painting hung slightly off-center. She approaches without hesitation, but not with warmth.

"Emilia," she says, her smile already in place for whoever might be watching.

"Mother," I reply, stepping forward just enough to let her air-kiss land next to my cheek, like always—never on it.

She gives me one glance, head to toe, and adjusts the neckline of my dress without asking. Just a quick tug, like fixing a crooked napkin.

"You look ... presentable," she says, voice smooth, eyes already drifting past me.

I force a smile. "And you look exactly how I expected."

She hums at that, faintly amused but not really listening. She never is. One last glance to make sure nothing is out of place—on me, not on her—then she turns toward someone else, already halfway gone.

I don't watch her walk away. I've seen it too many times to bother.

"Her face hasn't moved since she walked in," Thalia murmurs, sipping her mimosa like it's medicinal.

I don't have to ask who she means. My mother's across the room in blush tweed and controlled elegance, holding court with the alumni board like she's still running the chapter, and maybe she is, just with better lighting.

"She pays good money for that kind of paralysis," I say, watching as she laughs at something no one else finds funny.

Thalia hums, eyes still on her. "It's impressive, honestly. You both have that same walk, slow, deliberate, like everyone's already wasting your time."

I glance at her, one brow raised. "Say that again and I'll sabotage your almond milk supply."

She smiles. "Worth it."

I check the room, then flip her off. She taps her glass lightly against mine.

"Classy, Madam President."

I smile back, all teeth, all polish. "Fake it till the checks clear."

We both lean back as a woman in pearls starts correcting a server about citrus wedges, and the performance hums back to life around us like it never broke.

The brunch, as expected, is elegant chaos. The kind that's been dressed up in white linen and hydrangeas, pretending it isn't unraveling by the minute. Clara's itinerary is already off—speech order shuffled, brunch service running ten minutes behind, and someone's gluten-free entrée somehow ended up in front of an alumna who's now halfway through a croissant she'll later insist she never touched. No one says anything directly, of course. They just whisper, sharply and audibly, in a way that makes sure the right people feel the mistake without ever having to name it.

I let it play out. Clara insisted on running point and I let her, because that's what delegation looks like in a house like this—power masked as trust. She's sweating behind her smile, flipping pages in a binder that's suddenly useless, nodding like everything's fine. No one believes it, but they appreciate the effort.

I don't move to fix anything. That's not my role today. Not until it actually matters.

Near the mimosa bar, I pass Brandi and her mother, Amanda Withers—local news anchor, three-time Chi O alum of the year, and walking proof that you can bleach a smile into permanence. Amanda's voice cuts through the air like a champagne flute shattering on tile.

"Did you see the Sinclair girl's dress?" she asks someone. "Tight as a wetsuit and half the length."

"She said it's custom," her friend replies, tone dripping. "From a designer in Miami."

Amanda's mouth curves. "Miami doesn't do designer."

A few seats over, Mrs. Carver—whose daughter married into some old New York money and now hosts a podcast about "generational elegance"—leans toward Veronica Langford like she's dropping classified information.

"I heard the Devereux girl is transferring," she says. "Apparently, she got caught with a Beta in the library after hours. His family's furious. He's pre-med."

My mother takes a delicate sip of tea. "If they didn't want scandal, they shouldn't have sent him to Bancroft. The entire school runs on sexual tension and overpriced therapy."

"I miss this place," Mrs. Carver sighs, wistful and deadly. "Do you remember when we got our house GPA back up after the cheating scandal?"

My mother nods. "Three girls got quietly dropped. The rest were given a scholarship luncheon."

"Ah, accountability."

I keep walking.

Willa and one of the sophomore girls are posted near the pastry table, half-listening to Ava's aunt talk about her third engagement. "He's in shipping," she says, "but he's very discreet. I can barely find him on LinkedIn."

Ava gives her aunt a look. "That sounds normal."

In the corner, Thalia's cornered by Mrs. Carmichael, whose daughter graduated with honors but now sells luxury pet vitamins on TikTok.

"She's building a brand," the woman says. "It's niche. Direct-to-consumer is the future."

Thalia nods slowly. "So is therapy."

I slide next to her just in time to interrupt what was definitely about to become a TED Talk on monetizing dog supplements.

"Time check," I murmur.

Thalia blinks. "Please tell me we're leaving."

"Ten more minutes," I say. "Then I fake a family obligation."

"Thank goodness. I can only take so many speeches about the 'golden years' from women who threatened to cut each other's curls with sewing scissors."

Clara, ever punctual even in crisis, approaches with the closing remarks printed in 14-point font and panic in her eyes. "Emilia," she says, "can you take over the final toast if Mrs. Whitmore keeps talking? We're going to lose the kitchen window for cleanup, and I still haven't found the junior committee girls for photos."

"Already handled," I say. "Thalia sent them out for coffee. They should be back in minute."

Clara stares. "You're scary."

"I'm on top of things."

She exhales and disappears again.

I rise as the mic is passed, the clink of stemware soft under the swell of polite interest. The room shifts toward me like it always does—trained, expectant. I smile the way I was taught: calm, camera-ready, warm enough to pass for sincerity.

"Tradition," I begin, voice even, glass raised, "is a word that gets used a lot around here. We tie it to banners, to brunches, to house songs we pretend to remember the words to."

Laughter—soft, controlled. The kind that doesn't mess with Botox.

"But if we're honest, tradition isn't always pretty. It's not supposed to be. Sometimes it's heavy. Sometimes it gets in the way. And sometimes, it reminds us exactly why we keep showing up."

I pause, let the silence settle. Across the room, Clara's gripping her place card like it might save her from drowning.

"This house has shaped a lot of women. Some who've followed every rule. Some who rewrote them. And some who were smart enough to act like they didn't care either way."

That gets a few smiles. One alumna coughs into her napkin.

"We've learned from all of them. From the ones who led, and the ones who quietly survived. From the women who came back to speak, and the ones who never looked back."

A few heads turn at that. I don't give them time to linger.

"So to the alumni—thank you for showing us what strength can look like. And to the girls still here, still figuring out what power feels like—don't worry. We'll make sure the next generation has better stories to whisper."

There's a beat of nervous laughter, a ripple across the table. I smile. Then I drop it.

"To tradition," I say, letting my voice shift just slightly. "And to the girls who know how to drink through it."

The room goes still. Just for a second. A few of the older alumni blink. Someone gasps softly into her champagne. My mother's lips flatten into a perfect, bloodless line. Across the table, Thalia smirks like she's been waiting for it all morning.

I raise my glass, take the smallest sip, and sit back down.

The applause comes late, but it comes.

She's moving before I even sit.

My mother glides across the floor like she's on rails, expression unchanged but eyes sharp enough to cut through glass. She stops beside me without lowering her voice. "That was reckless," she says quietly.

"No," I reply, lifting my glass to my lips. "That was honest."

"You embarrassed yourself."

I turn to face her fully, calm and composed. "Only if anyone here still thinks brunch is about honesty."

Her jaw tightens and her lips flatten to that practiced, painted line. No emotion. Just control.

Behind her, Clara rushes in like she's sensing blood in the water and trying to mop it up with a clipboard.

"It was memorable," Clara says, too fast. "Unexpected, but strong. Really … impactful."

"Unprofessional," my mother snaps, eyes still on me.

"Unscripted," I say. "There's a difference."

Clara goes quiet. Her eyes flick to me, then to my mother, then back again. She knows not to pick a side, but she's smart enough to want to.

I stand slowly, straightening my skirt one last time. Thalia's already behind me, watching, silent, glass in hand.

"I'm going to change," I say.

My mother arches one brow. "Excuse me?"

I meet her gaze, still smiling, sharp now. "I have a soccer game to catch," I say. "You know—your *other* daughter's game."

That's it. No raised voice. No exit music. Just the truth.

Her face doesn't move, but something in her eyes flickers—tight, fast, and gone.

Thalia finishes her drink in one clean sip. "Iconic," she murmurs under her breath.

We don't wait for a response. We just turn and walk, the sound of our heels cutting clean through the stunned hush behind us.

Upstairs, we move quickly, dresses off, sneakers on. My hair goes up. Thalia throws on a sweatshirt and pulls her curls into a high knot.

We're gone in five minutes.

No goodbyes. No explanations.

We slip out the side door just as the kitchen staff starts clearing champagne flutes and someone at the mimosa bar says, *"Did she really say that?"*

Yes, I did.

And I meant it.

The SUV is waiting just past the Chi Omega gates, parked like it belongs there. Keller opens the back door before we reach it, while the other—Ruiz—the quieter of the two—is already seated in the front passenger side. Michael nods as we climb in. He doesn't speak. He never does unless it matters.

The door closes behind us with that quiet, final thud that signals we're off duty, at least from the part that involves brunch speeches and legacy smiles. The AC hums to life. Leather cools beneath the backs of my legs. The noise from the house—the clink of glassware, Clara's voice trying to repack the morning into something salvageable—fades like a door's been shut between me and the performance version of myself.

Thalia drops into the seat beside me with a groan and peels off her shoes like she's casting off a curse. She stretches out, legs tucked under her, braid loose and falling over her shoulder. "She almost combusted," she says after a beat, not looking at me.

I don't need to ask who she means. "I'll hear about it later."

"I could practically see steam coming out of her ears." Thalia smirks. "Her eyes were screaming."

From the front seat, Ruiz shifts slightly. Doesn't turn around. Doesn't say a word. But I catch it in the mirror—the tiniest lift at the corner of his mouth. Just a flicker. And then it's gone.

I stare out the window. "Do you think I went too far?"

Thalia snorts. "Please. You said what half that room's been swallowing since 1997. You just did it with good lighting and a perfect center part."

I let the silence stretch for a moment. Let the road open in front of us, tree-lined and familiar. Bancroft's brick arches are already behind us, shrinking in the distance.

"She didn't even flinch," I say.

"That's what makes it worse," Thalia replies. "She didn't flinch, she calculated. You gave her something she can't spin, so she'll hold onto it until it's useful."

I nod once. She's not wrong.

"I almost didn't say it," I admit quietly. But I've reached my max limit with this family. My family.

"But you did."

"Yeah," I say, exhaling slowly. "I did."

Thalia doesn't respond. She just reaches for the water bottle at her side and takes a long sip like that ends the conversation. Maybe it does.

I pull out my phone. A text from Grace sits at the top of the screen. It's a picture of Coach Noah in all his glory. I show Thalia, and she lets out a low whistle. "That man makes my ovaries hurt."

I roll my eyes and squint at the photo. Blonde hair. Skin kissed from too many hours out in the sun. Wearing shorts that show off his leg muscles. This man definitely doesn't miss leg day. "Just your type."

She hums. "So damn true."

I turn to look out the window as the buildings blur by and slowly the scene changes to farmland and suburbs. I let out a breath I didn't know I was holding. It's almost as if the DC area has been slowly suffocating me.

-

The soccer complex is all chain link fences, uneven parking lines, and the smell of sun-warmed grass and concession stand popcorn. It's not polished. It's not curated. It's real, in the way nothing at Bancroft ever is. Michael pulls up to the drop-off zone, the SUV idling quietly as we step out into the sun.

The wind is softer here. It carries with it the sound of people yelling directions, whistles blowing sporadically, and the echo of cleats pounding against turf that's more dirt than grass. Thalia tugs her hoodie down over her hips and slides on a pair of aviators like she's trying to blend in.

Caroline spots us first, waving from the sidelines with one arm while balancing a Gatorade and tote bag in the other. She's wearing a loose tee and joggers, her hair in a high bun, skin tanned from too many hours out here without shade. She looks every bit the soccer mom. Harper's mom. Grace's best friend since preschool. A completely different version of a mother than the one I grew up with—present, welcoming.

"Look who it is," she calls, smiling as we approach. "I didn't know you were coming today."

"Grace asked me to," I say, pulling her into a one-armed hug. "You holding up?"

She shrugs. "Two team moms are fighting over something stupid, and someone's kid just puked in the bushes. But we're surviving."

"That sounds worse than last time."

"It is."

And then I hear it.

"Em!"

She's not running, but there's momentum in her step—ponytail bouncing, a small smile on her face. Her cheeks are flushed from warm-ups, a little sunburned on the nose, freckles dusted across them like someone scattered cinnamon on purpose.

She looks like a version of me, if I'd grown up softer. Her eyes are the same pale green—unmistakably Langford—but where mine are usually lined and calculating, hers are open, unguarded. She has our mother's chin, our father's jawline, but somehow none of their coldness. None of their control.

I wrap my arms around her like muscle memory. She smells like sunscreen and whatever vanilla-scented body spray she and Harper probably doused themselves in. Her arms tighten around my neck.

"You came," she breathes, like I didn't text her two days ago.

"Of course I did," I say into her hair. "Wouldn't miss Coach Noah, right?"

She pulls back, grinning. Her eyes sparkle. "I'm sure Thalia's thrilled to see him." She throws a knowing look in Thalia's direction.

Thalia, sunglasses slipping down her nose, smirks. "You better finally introduce me. It's been a while since I had a man in my life."

I elbow her, harder than necessary. "Hush, babe. There are little ears present."

Thalia rolls her eyes. "I'm not the one cussing. And she knows what I mean. Right, Gracie?"

Grace nods solemnly. "Yeah, Em. I'm fifteen. Not a kid anymore."

I glance toward the field. "You should head over there."

"Yes, ma'am," she says, giving me a mock salute before jogging off, already shouting something about warm-up drills, already lost in her world again—completely, unapologetically hers.

I watch her go.

Caroline nudges me. "How've your parents been?" She says it so casually, like my father isn't the Vice President of the United States.

"Busy," I say. "Always busy." Because what else am I supposed to say?

She nods like she understands. "Did Grace tell you about the upcoming school formal?"

I whip my head toward her. "She did not. When is it?"

"Next month." She pats my arm. "I'll text you the details, sweetie."

The nickname is more affection than I've gotten from my own mother in years.

Thalia flops into a folding chair and pulls a La Croix from her bag. "Alright," she says, popping it open slowly, "let's see how many goals this girl scores today."

"Two," I say, eyes already following Grace as she weaves through drills on the sideline.

The game starts with the kind of control that only U16s can manage. Grace is on the left wing, crouched slightly as the ball kicks off. Her jersey clings like it was made for her, the light blue catching the sun just right.

She moves fast. I hear her call for the pass.

Thalia has her knees pulled up in the folding chair beside mine, sunglasses still on but constantly sliding down as she glances over them. "Okay, she's good. She's definitely been practicing."

"She's kind of a beast."

"She plays like Lindsey Heaps."

I glance at her, intrigued. "Since when do you study soccer?"

She shrugs, sipping. "I know things."

From across the field, someone's dad yells a beat too loudly. Grace steals the ball, darts between two defenders, and sprints toward the goal like her cleats are on fire. She doesn't score—the keeper gets lucky and blocks it with her shin—but Grace doesn't flinch. She just spins away, recovers, and resets like she already knows the next chance is coming.

I lean back and glance at Caroline, who's sipping from a water bottle like she hasn't sat down since sunrise.

"You think they'll come?" I ask quietly.

She doesn't look up. "I've known your family for years, Emilia." She pauses. "If they wanted to come, they would."

"I know," I say, even though I wish I didn't.

A few minutes pass. Grace gets the ball again. This time, she doesn't hesitate. She angles left, fakes right, and shoots—clean, fast, unexpected. The ball hits the back of the net like it belongs there.

Thalia lets out a half-gasp, half-laugh. "Holy crap."

Grace turns and points at us. At me.

"One goal down!" she yells across the field.

I cheer louder than anyone on the sidelines. Probably too loud. But she's my sister.

Caroline leans in. "As long as she has you, I think she'll be okay."

I nod, throat tight. "I'm not going anywhere."

And I mean it.

Grace is mid-celebration, flying down the sideline like the final whistle is just the start of something bigger. Her socks are falling down, her ponytail is coming loose, and her cheeks are flushed with that unfiltered kind of pride. She high-fives three teammates, then walks to the bench for final instructions from her coach. Coach Noah.

Thalia eyes him from beside me, deadpan but impressed. She mutters, "It's actually illegal to look that good coaching youth sports."

He's standing just beyond the center line, clipboard tucked under one arm, hands on his hips, eyes flicking between his players and the parents. Late twenties, maybe thirty. Tall. Lean, not bulky. His joggers are black, his Ashburn FC shirt clings in all the right places, and there's a whistle around his neck and a towel slung over one shoulder. A faint five o'clock shadow shadows his jaw.

He laughs at something one of the girls says, and I expect it to sound coached. It's not. It's low. Real. The kind of laugh that people lean toward without meaning to.

Thalia shifts again. "That's illegal."

"Stop undressing the man with your eyes."

"I didn't say anything." She lifts her hands like a saint.

"You didn't have to. I know you."

Then his gaze lifts—sweeps the sideline—and lands on us.

Before I can say anything, Grace jogs over and grabs my hand, tugging without slowing down. "You have to meet Coach Noah," she says, like she's introducing me to royalty.

Thalia is practically vibrating with glee.

By the time we stop, he's already turning, towel still on his shoulder, eyes flicking from me to Thalia—and pausing a little too long on Thalia not to notice.

"You must be the sister," he says, extending a hand that's warm from the sun but steady. "You and Grace look alike."

"And you're Coach Noah."

He smiles slightly. "That's what they call me."

Thalia jumps in, extending her hand. "I'm Thalia."

Coach Noah's mouth curves slightly. "Nice to meet you, Thalia." He says her name like he wants to remember the sound.

Thalia bites her lip. I suppress a groan.

Then he turns to me, voice suddenly sharper, more professional. "Do you mind if I get your number?"

My brows lift, and he quickly adds, "Just in case I need to reach someone for Grace. Your parents are hard to get a hold of, and it'd be nice to have someone who's actually related to her, not just an assistant."

"Sure," I say. "That makes sense."

I rattle off the number. He taps it in, no smirk, no pretense. Just a quiet nod when he's done.

"Thanks," he says. "And thanks for coming. I know you don't live close."

I pause. Then, "Anything for Grace."

He glances at Thalia again, who's now looking at her phone.

"I should wrangle them," he says, but doesn't move right away. "It was good meeting you."

He says it more for Thalia's benefit than mine. Still, I answer, "You too, Coach."

Then he turns and walks back toward the field.

Thalia stays quiet until he's out of earshot, then she exhales slowly, adjusting her sunglasses like it's punctuation. "Well," she says, "I will definitely be coming to Grace's games more often."

I laugh. Thalia is the uncomplicated one. The one who lives for a good time. The one you bring for backup when the world starts burning. The one who does no strings attached with a list longer than most.

"That man can do me three ways to Sunday."

I grimace. "Jeez, Thalia."

She looks at me with zero remorse. "What? I'm a twenty-one-year-old woman. I have needs."

I don't say anything. Just watch Grace and her team gather for their post-game huddle. When she finally leaves the field, we head toward the car. I give Caroline a quick hug, thanking her for picking Grace up and getting her here. Then all three of us—Grace, Thalia, and me—slide into the back of the SUV as Michael pulls away.

-

The drive to the Langford estate takes only twenty minutes, but the moment we pull into the driveway, I can feel the tension seeping back in. Home. But not really. This is just one of their many houses—the one I grew up in during summer breaks and winter holidays.

No, no. Trent and Veronica Langford couldn't be bothered with raising a child, let alone two. I was sent to boarding school at eleven, right before puberty hit. Before that, it was private school, nannies, tutors, the whole shebang.

Fortunately, Grace was never sent away. My parents changed their tune. Not because they learned how to parent—hardly. But because they needed to maintain the illusion of being doting, involved. Instead, they let the paid help raise their youngest while sending their eldest away to be molded by teachers who demanded obedience and silence.

Thalia's head rests against the window as she peers up at the house. "I don't miss this place."

Michael stops the car, and Grace bolts out, already complaining about the sweat clinging to her back and needing a hot shower. I don't stop her.

Rose, the house manager, steps out from the front door, a perfectly poised smile stretched across her face. It's fake. I've known Rose my whole life and her smiles are obligations, not warmth.

"Nice to see you, Miss Emilia." Her eyes sweep over me, taking in my shorts and t-shirt. A rarity in this house, in this family. Disdain flickers across her features, but she schools it quickly. My mother trained her well.

"You haven't changed, Rose." I smile, but it's not real. And she knows that.

She ushers us inside. The house is too quiet, the kind of quiet that makes your skin itch. It's not peaceful, it's staged. Even the lighting feels curated. Warm enough to suggest comfort, dim enough to conceal the truth: no one is comfortable here.

Dinner is already plated when we're shown into the "casual" dining room, which, in true Langford fashion, looks like elbows on the table might trigger a security alarm.

My mother is already seated, posture uncannily straight, lipstick untouched on the rim of her wine glass. She doesn't greet us. Just glances up, scans, calculates, and returns her gaze to the center of the table as if our arrival requires no acknowledgment. My father isn't here yet. I doubt he'll eat.

He'll appear long enough to remind us he's important. Color me shocked if he shows at all.

Footsteps pad down the hall. Grace rushes in, kisses our mom on the cheek, and slides into her seat. Her cheeks are still flushed from the game, her hair damp and curling from a quick shower. She's in a hoodie and barefoot. Casual. And thank goodness for her, because the rest of us look like wax figures.

Thalia sits on my left, watching the room like it's a courtroom, waiting to see who speaks first. Spoiler: it's not going to be me.

Grace breaks the silence, loud and unaffected. "Mom, did Caroline text you recently?"

"How many times have I told you it's improper to refer to someone older than you by their first name?" My mother's tone could cut glass.

Grace pauses, fork halfway to her mouth. "She told me to call her Caroline. Said 'Mrs. Lang' was reserved for her mother-in-law."

Mother's smile is thin. "How dignified of her."

I cut in, tone flat. "Not everyone is like you, Mom."

A beat of silence follows. Everyone weighing how sharp they're willing to be in return.

Then Mother hums. "Yes, and that's why we're Langfords and they're not."

No one answers that. Because—what in the world?

My father arrives fifteen minutes late. No apology. Just enters, adjusts his cufflinks like he's still mid-conference call, and sits. He nods once at Grace, then begins eating. Says nothing to the rest of us.

Dinner somehow continues. Salmon. Risotto. Microgreens. A meal for champions, if champions only nibbled.

"I told Coach I want to start as center midfielder next game," Grace says between bites. "He said okay. Just like that. Didn't even question it."

Veronica lifts her glass, sips without swallowing right away. "When are you going to stop this little hobby of yours?"

My stomach turns. "It's a sport," I say. "She has the ability to go pro."

"Mm." She doesn't look at me. "That's not something Grace will do."

I open my mouth, but Grace beats me to it. "Why not? I've been playing for years. I love it."

It lands like a stray elbow to the ribs.

I feel the shift before I even react. Veronica's fork pauses. Trent's shoulders tighten. Thalia goes still.

I set my fork down, not because I'm finished, but because I'm ready.

Mother smiles. Brittle. Practiced. "Darling, sports are for people too dumb to do anything else. That's not you."

Grace says nothing. But I see it, the way her face changes. The loss, the disappointment.

"We're not saying you can't do soccer," Trent adds, adjusting his cufflink like that's the emotional part. "It's just not an acceptable career."

"It never was for me," I say, licking my fork. My eyes land on my mother's. Her expression sharpens.

"That's a generous rewriting," she murmurs. She hasn't touched her food.

"You signed me up for media training at ten," I continue. "By twelve, it was etiquette classes. At thirteen, I was skipping dances to attend fundraisers. You wanted polish. I gave you polish."

"And look how capable you are now." Her smile cuts. "It served you."

"Did it?" I ask, quieter. "Or did it just serve you?"

The silence that follows is immediate. And hard.

Grace frowns. "Wait... So you never got to play anything?"

I shake my head. "Nope."

"I thought you hated sports."

"That's cray cray," she adds.

"Agreed," Thalia chimes in.

Veronica's gaze flicks toward her, sharp and fleeting.

Trent sighs. "You had every opportunity, Emilia. If you wanted something—truly wanted it—you could've come to us."

"When?" I ask. "Between school, tutoring, debate, and posing for campaign mailers? When exactly was I supposed to figure out who I wanted to be?"

"You're being emotional," my mother says.

I lean back. "No. I'm being honest. But I get why you'd confuse the two."

The tension coils around the table like a too-tight scarf. Grace glances between us, gears turning. She's finally starting to see them clearly. And then, like someone flipping a switch, Veronica sets down her glass and shifts tone.

"So," she says smoothly, "has anyone seen the new proposal for the Langford Foundation's youth scholarship expansion?"

There it is. The redirect. The elegant burial of an inconvenient moment.

Trent picks up the cue. "Still in draft. I've asked the policy team to tighten the eligibility language."

Veronica nods. "Good. That needs to be consistent across all comms."

And just like that, we're back to faking it.

-

Dinner ends the way it always does in the Langford house—unmistakably quiet. The kind of quiet that could make a pin drop sound like an alarm.

Grace is the only one still eating, or more accurately, picking at her food. She's hardly touched her plate. Her gaze has been fixed downward more often than not. For a moment, I think she might be upset until I catch the glow of her phone under the table. I smirk, relieved. She's being a normal teenager.

Father doesn't notice. He's too busy pretending we're a normal, functioning family. A few documents are laid out next to him—he couldn't even leave work in his office. And Mother? She's probably feeling her Xanax kick in. Wine and pharmaceuticals. The perfect cocktail for checked-out parenting.

I rise slowly, tossing my napkin onto my plate. Thalia follows a beat later, her eyes flicking to mine in a silent ask: *Are we leaving?*

"Dinner was lovely," I say, just loud enough to sting if anyone's paying attention. "As always."

Veronica finally looks up. Her eyes are glazed. Her smile is soft but hollow, the socialite's version of sincerity. "Let's schedule lunch next week. Just us."

I offer the barest nod. "Let me know what works for you."

Before anything else can be said, Grace stands from the table and pulls me into a tight hug. "I'm really glad you came," she murmurs into my sweatshirt.

I hug her back, whispering into her ear, "I'm just a phone call away. Don't let them get to you. Soccer is cool."

She pulls back, grinning, and I wink. Then she turns to Thalia. "See ya, Thal."

"See you at the next game, Gracie girl."

Grace disappears up the stairs.

I start to turn, but my mother is already standing. She reaches out, placing a hand on my shoulder—light, precise.

A touch that's not affectionate, just a quiet reminder of the name I carry.

"Don't forget about lunch," she repeats, softer this time.

"I won't," I say, meeting her gaze, but I don't mean it the way she thinks I do.

She lets go first.

By the time I reach the front door, it's already open. One of the agents—Ruiz—stands waiting, familiar and silent. He nods once and opens the back door of the SUV.

The car is warm inside, softly lit, the engine already running. Thalia slides in beside me, and the door closes with a padded thud that feels more like containment than comfort.

We don't speak as the house fades behind us. It still glows in the windows, picture-perfect and utterly false, like a campaign brochure printed in gold.

I lean my head back, eyes closing briefly. Then finally: "That was a dumpster fire."

Thalia doesn't respond right away. The hum of the tires fills the silence between us. "Yeah," she says eventually. "It was."

"I wish I could walk away from all this," I murmur, eyes still closed. "Not just for a day. For good. The foundation. The press events. The posture. I'm tired of pretending it doesn't make me want to scream."

Thalia shifts beside me, one knee up, ankle crossed. "You wouldn't be the first legacy girl who wanted out."

"But I'd be the first who actually did it."

"That's why it scares them," she says quietly. "Because they know you could."

I don't answer her. I just stare out the window at the road ahead, the trees folding in around it like they're trying to offer cover.

Chapter 4

Emilia

It's Sunday. Supposedly a reset. A soft start. A deep breath after the chaos of the week.

Instead, I'm sitting cross-legged on the Chi Omega living room floor, surrounded by thirty sorority sisters with sheet masks, cucumber water, and enough estrogen-charged chaos to suffocate a small country.

Spa Sunday.

A self-care themed bonding experience that I, apparently, approved during a chapter leadership planning session when I was drunk enough to think it sounded "wholesome" and "on brand." Yay, drunk me. She's always making decisions I regret sober.

The room smells like someone spilled eucalyptus and ambition. Clara's gone overboard with the diffuser again, and now the entire living room feels like the inside of an expensive candle. Girls are scattered across floor pillows and couches, half in sheet masks, half in conversation, fully in performance mode. Spa Sunday—a house tradition dressed up as self-care but functioning more like open mic night for whoever's been holding onto the juiciest intel since Thursday.

Thalia is beside me, her legs stretched out, trying to pick a nail color like it's a high-stakes decision. Brandi is halfway upside down in a beanbag, scrolling through her phone with the exact expression of someone who just found a dead body or a deadline.

Brandi doesn't even look up from her phone when she says, "Have you seen the *Bancroft Ledger*? They're reporting a hot, new transfer student."

That's all it takes.

Poppy and Riley—still in sheet masks, still mid-face steam—scramble across the rug like bloodhounds on a scent. Brandi doesn't move, just angles her phone down so they can see the screen.

"Holy *crap*," Riley breathes. "That guy is next-level hot."

Brandi hums in agreement. Doesn't say anything, just starts passing her phone around like communion.

Clara perks up from the diffuser corner. "Wait—he's *British*?!"

Thalia lets out a dry laugh. "That's the rumor."

Ava holds the phone up like she's reading aloud from scripture. "Front page. Literally. 'Unconfirmed reports say the Poli Sci department has welcomed a tall, unnamed transfer student with a voice like imported whiskey and a face that could disrupt a midterm curve.'"

Someone actually whistles. Like, genuinely.

I keep my face neutral, my grip on my glass steady. I don't need to see the photo to know it's him. I already saw it. Confirmed it.

Max.

I knew the second Brandi said *transfer*. The second the word *British* hit the air. I've known since he walked into Comparative Policy on the first day of class, late but not apologetic, and answered a question like he was already ten lectures in. No one was mad. We were too busy trying to understand how someone could make *"public sector reform"* sound illegal in twenty-five states.

Brandi turns her phone so the rest of us can see.

The photo's grainy and clearly taken from across the quad, but it doesn't matter. Max is mid-step, wearing gray joggers and a black t-shirt, the kind that clings in ways you don't talk about out loud. His backpack's slung low on one shoulder, and his head's turned just enough to make it look intentional. Like he heard the camera. Like he *knows*.

The caption underneath: *"Ladies, a gift from across the pond. No name yet. Joggers confirmed. Developing story."*

There's a beat of silence before the room explodes in gasps, cackles, a literal slow clap from somewhere near the snack table.

I sip my lemon water. "He's in my class," I say, casually.

Every head swivels.

"What." Riley's already halfway across the rug, sheet mask dangling. *"Since when?"*

"Comparative Policy," I say. "He's been there since this past Monday"

Clara's staring at me like I just revealed I've been harboring a secret royal. "Does he *talk?*"

I nod once. "Yeah. Not much. But when he does…" I let it hang, then shrug. "You'll know."

And they would. Because when Max talks, the room goes still. Not out of awe, not intentionally. It just … happens. Like gravity tilts toward him for a second and everyone forgets what they were supposed to be thinking about.

It's not just the accent. It's the way he says things like he's editing them in real time—deliberate, measured, unbothered. Like he doesn't need the room's attention, but knows he'll get it anyway.

I haven't made eye contact with him since the first day. Haven't said a word. We crashed into each other in the courtyard. He caught me by the arm, said *"You alright?"* like he meant it, while my security detail made a full-fledge scene. So embarrassing.

"Hate that he's already famous," Thalia mutters, still scrolling through the post.

"Famous and not even trying," Brandi says. "Which is honestly worse."

I lean back against the couch and close my eyes.

He hasn't done anything wrong. Not really. He's just … here. And somehow, that's more than enough.

-

Monday mornings at Bancroft always feel like walking into a moving train and pretending you were there the whole time. The quad is already alive, swarming with too many people for how early it is, everyone dressed like they're headed somewhere more important than they are. Girls walk three across, arms linked, iced coffees sloshing in one hand, tote bags swinging from the other. Boys hover around the edges of their orbit like extras, half-awake, half-aware, tugging sweatshirts over wrinkled shirts and pretending the world isn't watching. Even the air feels caffeinated—clipped footsteps, laughter that's just a little too loud, like someone's trying to convince the day not to collapse on top of them. No one here starts slow. The week kicks off at full volume, and if you hesitate, you get swallowed.

By the time I step into the Comparative Politics lecture hall, the lights are already on and Professor Kerr is writing on the board with the posture of someone who's taken personal offense to the state of global governance. His handwriting is as illegible as always—jagged capital letters like he's trying to stab the concept of proportional representation into our heads before nine a.m. There's a folder tucked under one arm, corners bent, pages sticking out at angles, and the permanent scowl of a man who definitely spent the weekend reading five international op-eds and losing sleep over Belgium.

I move toward my usual seat—second row, far left—because it's close enough to signal that I care, but not centered enough to get called on. The desk is cool under my hands, my coffee still hot, the lid slightly loose, and I settle in with the quiet click of my laptop opening and the faint scrape of my chair pulling in. I've just started scrolling through my notes when I feel someone move into the seat beside me—not behind, not diagonally, but close enough that I catch the scent of clean laundry and something warm I can't name.

I don't look, but I know.

Max.

He says nothing at first, just exhales as he sits, the kind of calm, composed breath of someone who's never rushed a day in his life. A notebook thuds softly against the desk, followed by the click of a pen—deliberate, slow, like he's making a point without saying anything at all. Then, finally, his voice.

"Morning."

It's quiet, almost too casual, and yet the syllables are threaded with that accent—not sharp, not theatrical, just enough to draw attention without trying. British, maybe, or something near it. It does strange things to simple words.

I don't look over. I nod once and reply, "Morning," just as evenly, my eyes still on the screen, the word catching slightly in my throat but not enough to show.

He's never sat next to me before. Always somewhere behind, off to the side, part of the room but not near enough to disturb it. Now, I can feel the space between our elbows, small and electric, the way two magnets hover before they meet. He opens his notebook, starts writing in quick, angled strokes that make me feel like I should be doing something more important than rereading the same sentence in my notes three times.

Professor Kerr launches into lecture without a greeting—he rarely bothers with pleasantries—and calls on a girl in the third row before he's even finished his first sentence. She stammers something about closed-list electoral systems, and he flattens her answer with a look so withering it should be copyrighted. There's a tension in the room, a low-grade buzz of collective discomfort, and Max doesn't flinch once. He underlines a phrase in his notebook. I see the word *representation* in the corner of my eye, and the loop of his R is so sharp it looks like it could slice paper.

He shifts slightly in his seat, crossing one ankle over the other, completely at ease. "This your favorite class yet?" he murmurs, not loud enough for anyone else to hear.

I finally glance at him, just once, just a flicker of eye contact that feels more deliberate than it should. "It's definitely top five in dramatic monologues."

That smile. It flickers in the corner of his mouth like something he isn't fully letting out, not a grin, not performative, but real. Brief. Then it's gone.

A few minutes pass. He answers a question about mixed-member systems so cleanly that even Hearst doesn't have the heart to lecture him for it, and when I glance over again, he's already moved on, writing something down, tapping the back of his pen against his knee in a slow, thoughtful rhythm.

I turn back to my screen. Try to focus. But the weight of him next to me—not in a heavy way, just solid—is harder to ignore than I'd like. His presence feels deliberate. Not intrusive, but not accidental either.

When class finally ends, the scrape of chairs and low murmurs rise around us, the rustling of backpacks and group project complaints starting up like clockwork. I start to close my laptop, reaching for my coffee, when Max speaks again, this time with more intent.

"Hey."

I look up. He's still facing forward, but his voice is quieter now, like this part isn't for the room.

"If you're not already studying with anyone," he says, pausing just enough to make it feel like a question, "we should go over the readings sometime. Before midterms."

It's not a line. It doesn't even sound like he's trying. Just … offering. Simple. Direct.

I consider it. Not because I don't know what to say—I do—but because I want to watch him wait for the answer.

"Alright," I say, finally. "Sure."

He nods once, a small flick of approval, like he expected that but still waited for confirmation. "Can I get your number?"

I hesitate just long enough for it to feel intentional. Then I reach for my phone, type it out, hand it to him.

He enters his own without looking at the screen. Muscle memory. Confident fingers. No fumbling. "I'll text you," he says, standing.

And then he's gone, slipping into the crowd like it doesn't matter that something just happened—something small, quiet, unassuming.

But I stay in my seat for another minute.

Because maybe it did.

My phone lights up just as I step outside. The Chi Omega group chat has entered stage five crisis mode.

Clara: *URGENT: Halloween party theme still not finalized. SAE is pushing for "Heaven & Hell." Thoughts??? Also, who's designing the flyer? Can we decide by noon?*
Poppy: *That's a no from me. Too on the nose. Also, tacky.*

Sloane: *I vote yes if we make it sexy.*
Clara: We need a vibe that's dark but elegant. Something Chi O can post about.
Me: *We'll settle it at tonight's meeting. Don't lock anything in with SAE.*
Clara: *But I already—*
Me: *No. Tonight.*

I cut across the quad toward Danvers Hall, the sharp morning sun catching on windows and water bottles alike, heading to my next class: International Law with Professor Layton. If last week taught me anything, it's that this course isn't designed for the casually curious; it's meant to separate the serious policy students from the ones just chasing a title to slap on their summer internship resume.

Charlotte Klein is already in the front row, perfectly composed in a cream blouse and pearl studs so small and expensive they probably have their own trust funds. Her mother's a fixture in D.C. legal circles who's on retainer for at least half the capital's political dynasties, and Charlotte makes sure no one forgets it. She also happens to be Delta Gamma's Social Chair, a role she seems to believe carries the weight of a diplomatic appointment.

I didn't see her in class last week, which means she must've just returned from the Maldives, based on the filtered dispatches from her Instagram.

Two seats behind her sits that guy again—Dylan Reid, if I remember right. The one who offered a two-minute monologue last week that somehow managed to include zero relevant facts and three completely unrelated quotes. I half-expected he'd drop the class after that, but apparently, he's back for more.

Professor Layton begins without preamble, launching into lecture like we're already ten minutes behind.

"Today we're examining how institutions maintain influence without direct enforcement power," she says, pacing in front of the whiteboard with the energy of someone who deeply resents weak metaphors and unpaid interns. "We'll start with the IMF, then the UN Security Council, the WHO, and the ICC later this week."

There's a quiet scramble as laptops open and fingers start flying across keyboards. Layton doesn't wait.

"Someone," she says, scanning the room, "tell me the primary tool the IMF uses to exert control over developing economies."

Charlotte's hand is in the air before he finishes the sentence.

"Conditional lending," she answers crisply.

"Define it."

She straightens a little, voice sharp and clear. "Loans issued with required structural reforms, like budget cuts, trade liberalization, or changes to labor policy in exchange for financial support."

Layton nods once. "And the primary criticism?"

A guy a few rows down leans back like he's delivering the second half of a scripted duet. "That it prioritizes market stability over human needs. Often at the expense of social services."

"Correct." Layton turns and writes on the board in wide block letters: **INFLUENCE WITHOUT FORCE**.

"The most powerful institutions," she says, tapping the word 'force' with his marker, "rarely need to raise their voices. They just shift the rules until the outcomes feel inevitable."

I jot it down. That sentence has midterm question written all over it.

Halfway through the lecture, my phone buzzes once inside my bag. I ignore it. Probably Clara again—she's been on a slow descent into madness over font choices for our event signage. We're planning the biggest party of the semester with all the composure and coordination of a group chat full of manic interns and passive-aggressive emojis.

Layton assigns a reading for next week—something heavy on neoliberal critique and light on nuance, just the way she likes it—then dismisses us right on time, no wrap-up, no sentiment.

As the class filters out, I sling my bag over one shoulder and step into the aisle. Charlotte turns toward me, her voice smooth and practiced.

"Are you leading Halloween coordination?" she asks. "I heard your name mentioned in our house."

I raise an eyebrow. "I am. Why?"

"Just curious," she says, smiling, tight and bright and obviously not just curious. "Delta Gamma's throwing a party this year."

I smile back, cooler. "Of course you are. It's tradition, right?"

There's a pause. Not silence, exactly, just a shift in air pressure, the kind that says we both know what we're really talking about.

"Well," I add, "hopefully it's a better theme than glitter or Grecian cosplay this time."

She doesn't answer. Doesn't need to. Her smile stays right where it is, fixed and polite and thoroughly sharpened. Because in Greek life, everything is said, even when it isn't.

And at Bancroft, everyone knows the real conversations don't start until the doors close.

-

By the time I step into the café at the student union, the place is pulsing with noise. Not chaos—not yet—but that curated, high-energy buzz that always hits right after second block. Students shoulder their way through the line for iced matchas and overpriced paninis, a few professors grab quiet seats near the windows like they're observing a different species, and the rest of us navigate it all like it's second nature.

I head straight to the front of the line with a nod to Kenzie behind the register—Chi O legacy, still fighting to get on the event planning committee. She waves me through like it's protocol, which it is.

I grab my order—iced matcha, turkey wrap, no sides—and weave through the crowd toward the corner booth I always claim on Mondays. It's a power move without trying to be one. People know where to find me. They also know not to interrupt.

Thalia beats me by thirty seconds and is already stretched out like she owns the seat. She peels the lid off her latte and squints at the foam. "You look like you were just cross-examined," she says.

"Comparative Politics," I reply. "With Layton."

She winces. "Ooh, I heard she's tough."

Across the café, I catch sight of Charlotte Klein just as she enters, flanked by two girls I recognize from Delta Gamma's Instagram and one vaguely familiar brunette who I'm pretty sure transferred from UVA and has been trying to rebrand herself ever since. Charlotte walks like she knows every camera is pointed her way, even when there's no lens. Beige wrap coat, patent flats, hair in that overly-curled blowout that screams "I pretend not to care". She doesn't scan the room. She expects the room to notice her.

They make a slow circuit past the front counter, and of course—of course—their path cuts right past our booth.

I don't look up immediately, but I feel it. The slight pause in her step, the almost-smile. The tension between greeting and ignoring. She settles for the middle, a tight nod in my direction. "Langford," she says.

I raise my cup. "Klein."

Her gaze flicks to Thalia, who doesn't look up from her phone.

One of Charlotte's girls whispers something, not loud, but definitely meant to be heard. Something about "SAE taste levels".

I smirk. "Tell your exec chair we still have the receipts from last year's 'Heaven & Hell' disaster."

Charlotte's smile goes tight. "We were being ironic."

"Sure," Thalia says. "Nothing screams irony like glitter pitchforks and a fog machine in a fire hazard zone."

Charlotte doesn't reply. Just pivots gracefully and glides off toward the far window with her crew in tow, all giggles and shoulder brushes, pretending that conversation didn't happen.

As soon as they're out of earshot, Poppy appears, sliding into the booth with a tray and zero patience. "I hate her."

"She hates herself more," Thalia mutters. "She just dresses it better."

"She also just posted a poll asking if DG should go with 'Angels After Dark' or 'Royal Sin' as their theme."

I nearly choke on my matcha. "Tell me that's satire."

"It's Charlotte."

"So no." I unlock my phone and open a new draft in Notes.

Chi O x SAE: Masquerade Noir
- Palette: Black, gold, burgundy
- Dress code: Elevated cocktail + masks
- Visual: Gothic baroque with modern edge
- Music: Anything but frat basement trash
- Photo setup: Projection + string lights + velvet backdrop
- No glitter. No flames. No wings.

I send the draft to the exec chat.

Me: *Proposal for tonight's vote. Masquerade Noir. Keep it sharp. No one's leaving looking like a backup dancer for Hades.*
Clara: *Let's discuss*
Poppy: *We're not negotiating with sparkle terrorists.*
Sloane: *I'm already sketching options.*

I tuck my phone away and take another sip of matcha, eyes flicking back toward Charlotte's table. She's laughing now, too loud, too forced.

Let her perform.

We're building something better.

-

My phone buzzes again as I'm halfway through my wrap.

I glance at the screen, expecting Clara's latest revision or a meme from Sloane. But it's neither.

Preston: *Hey.*

Three letters. Like we're old buddies and not exes. Like we didn't implode in slow motion two months ago on the sidewalk outside the summer gala. Like I didn't catch him texting another girl from my bed.

Thalia clocks the shift in my face before I say anything. "What?" she asks, mid-sip.

I angle the screen toward her.

She stares for a beat, then lets out a dry, unimpressed breath. "Absolutely not."

I don't answer him. I just lock the screen and drop my phone face down on the table.

"You gonna read it?" Poppy asks, eyes flicking between us.

"I did," I say. "That's all it deserves."

"Let me guess," Thalia says, tone turning sharp. "He misses you. He made a mistake. He's just now realizing what he lost."

"Honestly?" I shrug. "I don't care."

And I don't. But I do wonder why now. Why today. What triggered the sudden burst of regret. Or ego. Or both.

Another buzz. I flip the phone over.

Preston: *Just saw your name on the invite list for that Capitol fundraiser this weekend. You going?*

I stare at the text for a moment longer than I should. He knows I'll be there. He also knows damn well who I'll be with, or more importantly, who I won't.

Thalia leans over again. "Want me to send him a gif of a dumpster fire?"

"No," I murmur, tapping my reply.

Me: *My father is the VP. Does that tell you if I'm going or not? Now keep scrolling.*

I hit send.

No typing bubbles. No follow-up. Just clean, final silence.

Thalia snorts under her breath, clearly impressed. "You should get that framed."

"I should," I say, popping the last bite of my wrap into my mouth.

Poppy leans in with a sly smile. "Man, I love a good ex-banishment. Very you."

"It's not even the text," I mutter, brushing crumbs off my fingers. "It's the audacity. The recycled 'hey' like we haven't already buried that corpse twice."

Thalia sighs dramatically. "We need to burn some sage before the party. Clear the air. Banish ghost-of-boyfriends-past energy."

"You'd need a bonfire," I mutter.

"Careful," Poppy adds, "SAE might take that literally."

A few girls from Tri Delt walk by, all matching blowouts and crop tops, mid-laugh over something that's probably not funny. One of them glances our way. Poppy lifts her cup in mock cheer. They look away.

The rhythm of the café has shifted now. More people are trickling out, rushing to class, meetings, or rehearsals, the mid-morning lull setting in.

Thalia glances at her phone and groans. "Dang it. I've got that study group thing in ten minutes for Behavioral Genetics. My professor likes to do random pop quizzes like we're still in high school."

I raise an eyebrow. "Didn't you say you were going to drop that class?"

"I was. Then I remembered I like my GPA, and I need this extra elective to graduate on time."

She starts gathering her stuff, shoving her laptop into her bag with zero precision. Across from her, Poppy drains the last of her drink and checks her own messages.

"I've got to meet the Bancroft Voice editor in fifteen," she mutters. "Apparently, they want a quote about Chi O's 'campus leadership' for their Greek Life feature."

That's the first I'm hearing about it.

I blink. "And they picked you?"

She grins. "I'm charming when I need to be. And Clara's banned from press after last spring's philanthropy interview meltdown."

"Right," Thalia says, standing. "The quote where she compared charity to 'emotional capitalism.'"

Poppy shrugs. "She was trying to be deep. Instead, she started a Reddit thread."

They both step away from the booth in tandem. Thalia tugs her coat on. "You good?"

"I'm heading back to the house," I say, already scooping up my cup. "Going to pretend the world doesn't exist for at least twenty minutes."

"Love that for you," Poppy says.

"Text if Clara starts spiraling again," Thalia adds.

"Only if it's meme-worthy."

They disappear into the crowd, and I take one last look at the window seat before weaving through the café and back out onto the quad.

The air's cooler now. The clouds thicker. My phone is quiet. And for once, I don't need it to say anything, because a quiet Chi O common room, a locked bedroom door, and a moment without the world pressing in? That sounds perfect.

-

The walk back to the Chi O house is short. Campus is still buzzing—a few tour groups clogging the path near the Admissions Lawn, a cappella rehearsals echoing out of the Performing Arts wing like we're in a musical no one asked for. I keep my head down, earbuds in with nothing playing, just enough to give the illusion I'm busy. Unbothered.

The house is quieter when I step inside. Most of the girls are in class or scattered across campus. No sign of Clara, which is a blessing. The common room smells like fresh lemon cleaner and whatever diffuser scent Ava snuck in that technically violates fire code but no one wants to ban because it actually smells good.

I head upstairs and unlock my door, slipping inside without a sound. It clicks shut behind me, soft, final.

This is mine. The one place no one else touches. The curtains are drawn halfway, letting in a moody stretch of early-afternoon light. My bed's still unmade from this morning—a rarity—but I don't fix it. I don't need to perform here. Not now.

I drop my bag, peel off my jacket, and stretch out across the mattress. My phone lands beside me. Face up. Silent.

I let my eyes close for a second. Let the weight of the morning settle across my chest. Classes, text chains, Charlotte's smugness, Preston's convenient nostalgia. The pressure of everyone expecting something from me. Always.

I breathe.

My phone buzzes once. Just a soft vibration against the blanket. I glance over, expecting another update from Clara. Instead, it's a name I don't expect to see.

Max: *Know any good coffee shops around here?*

Not "what's your favorite". Not "where do you go". Just know any. Neutral. A little out of the blue. Which, somehow, makes me trust it more.

I answer before I can think twice.

Me: *You looking for coffee or a hole in the wall joint with character?*

Both, probably. But let's see what he says.

Max: *Both. Bonus points if no one asks for your name.*
Okay, so he's paying attention. Or maybe he just hates baristas. Could be either.
Me: *There's a place down Main. No sign, menu on a chalkboard, indie music. They stare until you order.*
Max: *Sounds judgmental.*
Me: *It is. Their coffee rivals Starbucks though. Pretty legit.*

And I do kind of want to see what he does under the weight of uncomfortable silence and a chalkboard menu written in invisible ink.

98

The Arrangement

Max: *If I showed up around 5:30, would you be there?*

I pause. Not because I'm unsure because I know how this goes. Someone asks for your time, and you give them an inch, and suddenly you're someone's political girlfriend or a resume checkpoint or a story they tell their roommates like you're just another tour stop.

But Max doesn't feel like he's trying to use the moment. He's just ... holding it open.

Me: *I could be.*
Max: *You want company?*

Jeez. That's a question that knows it's a question.

Me: *Depends who's offering.*
Max: *Guy from class. Decent handwriting. Makes good eye contact.*

I actually laugh. Once, out loud, into the space of my room.

Me: *Vague. But I've accepted worse.*

Which is absolutely true.

Max: *I'll take that as a yes.*
Me: *I didn't say yes.*
Max: *But you didn't say no.*

He's good. Not in the practiced way. Just ... calm. Certain. No bluffing. Just letting me decide where this goes.

I watch the light shift across the ceiling. It's that weirdly quiet hour on campus where everything gets soft. Everyone's either napping or pretending they're not behind already. This could be nothing. A coffee. A distraction.

Or not.
Either way, it's mine to choose.

Me: *Don't be late.*
Max: *I won't be.*

I toss the phone to the other side of the bed.
And try not to think about how I'm already looking forward to 5:30.

-

The place doesn't have a name on the front, just a dark green door and a crooked sign in the window that says OPEN in those magnetic letters you can buy at Target. I don't even remember how I found it. I came once and then kept coming. By myself. With Thalia. With Poppy. With study groups. It's not fancy. Just good coffee, quiet tables, and a bathroom that's always out of soap … and paper towels.

The menu's still the same—smudged chalk on a black wall, a short list of things I've mostly tried. I got a latte last time. Basic, sure, but it did its job. Now I'm standing here again, reading it like the words might rearrange themselves if I wait long enough.

I'm about to speak—maybe a latte again, maybe just water—when someone steps up next to me, close enough to feel, not close enough to crowd.

"Big decision?"

The voice is low. British. Familiar.

I glance over, eyebrows raised. "You're early."

His mouth twitches like he's not sure whether to own it. "Didn't want to be late."

He's in a black tee and joggers again, like he didn't think too hard about it, but of course he did. His hair's slightly tousled, and his expression? That easygoing kind that makes it feel like he's been here before. Like we do this every week.

"You picked the place," he adds. "Figured it had to be worth showing up on time for."

I roll my eyes, but it's light. "I did you a favor."

He hums. "I owe you one."

Behind the counter, the barista gives a pointed look that says we've had enough time.

"Caramel macchiato," I tell her. "And the orange almond biscotti."

Max steps up, barely blinking. "Same. Minus the biscotti."

I shoot him a look as we move aside. "You're missing out."

He lifts one shoulder, grinning. "Can't commit to a cookie that breaks your teeth."

We drift toward the back. I don't have to look to know he's following; there's no question about it. I drop into the high-top near the corner, elbow immediately reminded of the wobble I always forget about. Max sits across from me, sliding into the seat like this is familiar.

"You always bring people here on first meetings?" he asks.

I break off a corner of biscotti. "Only the ones who ask nicely."

He smirks. "So just me."

"Lucky you."

He watches me for a second, then does a slow sweep of the room, like he's checking it for exits or secrets. The place smells like espresso and cinnamon and that lemon cleaner they overuse every afternoon. Someone in the corner booth has headphones in and a full stack of color-coded flashcards spread across the table. It's not a loud place. That's the point.

"You know," I start, leaning on my palm, "you're already kind of a thing on campus."

He blinks. "A thing?"

"Campus-famous."

He huffs a short laugh. "Why?"

"You were on the Ledger. Gossip column. Picture and everything."

He groans under his breath. "No."

"Blurry shot of you walking across the quad. Caption said, and I quote, 'A gift from across the pond. Developing story.'"

He groans louder this time. "Please tell me you're joking."

"Oh, I wish. It was wildly dramatic. They confirmed joggers. No name. No backstory. Mystery. Scandal. Apparently, that's all it takes."

Max leans back, laughing softly. "Glad to know I made an impression by existing."

"You really did."

His eyes flick up to meet mine, a little more direct now. "And what did you think?"

The question catches me off guard, and judging by the way Max is smirking, he knows it.

I hold his gaze and sip my drink. "I thought you knew exactly what you were doing."

He doesn't answer right away. Just lifts his cup slightly in a slow, unbothered toast.

We both drink.

"I mean," I add, setting mine down, "you did ask for my number after one class. That's bold."

He shrugs, casual. "I had a good reason."

"For coffee."

"For conversation," he corrects.

I arch an eyebrow. "Is that your thing? Conversation?"

"Only with people who make it interesting."

There's no heat in it. No pressure. Just a fact.

We fall quiet for a moment. Not awkward, just a pause, like we both know we've passed the part where small talk matters.

"So," I murmur, "tell me something real."

Max leans in slightly. "Real like what?"

"Whatever you don't usually lead with."

He looks down at his cup, tapping a finger against the lid once, twice. Then his eyes lift again. "I move a lot. Never really stay in one place long. This is the first time in a while I've tried to."

That's it. Just that. No dramatic pause. No detail.

And I don't press, because I get it. Not the moving part, no. I grew up in the D.C. area. Some will say that's cool, and maybe it is, but it's also suffocating. But I understand wanting to finally settle.

"That sounds like the kind of thing you leave off your admissions essay," I murmur.

He grins. "Didn't leave it off yours?"

"Mine was about clean water access and civic trust," I deadpan. "Super fun."

He laughs, and I let it hang there, the warmth of it, the ease. And for the first time in a long time, I don't feel like I need to steer the conversation. I just let it be.

Chapter 5

Emilia

This meeting is a mess.

Clara is pitching a "haunted garden aesthetic" like she's producing a Vogue spread, Sloane keeps interrupting to say we're all on crack if we think the budget can handle twelve industrial fog machines, and someone—probably Brandi—just floated the idea of synchronized dancers in corpse paint. Poppy's trying to keep the mood from combusting. I'm sitting at the head of the table with my notes open, highlighter uncapped, and absolutely no clue what anyone just said.

I'm thinking about Max, and I hate that I'm thinking about Max.

It was coffee. One drink. One hour. He wasn't even flirty, which somehow made it worse. He just sat there, calm, steady, that barely-there smirk like he knew I wasn't used to quiet people getting under my skin. He listened. Like actually listened. Not the fake kind where they nod and wait for their turn to talk. He asked things, and I answered without even thinking about why.

And now?

Nothing.

No follow-up. No "hey, that was fun." No second ask. It's like crickets. It's only been an hour.

Which is fine. It's fine. I didn't need it. I didn't expect it. I'm not the kind of girl who gets thrown off by guys who ask her to coffee and then vanish into the void. Except apparently now I am, because here I am, sitting through a party planning meeting like I don't secretly keep glancing at my phone every twenty minutes like a total idiot.

Dang it.

I should be focused. We've got a million moving parts, half a dozen rental deadlines, and one freshman intern who keeps pitching "sexy pilgrim" as a viable costume category. But instead, I'm thinking about some guy I've known for all of five minutes and another I've known forever but not really.

Because then there's Niko.

Which, yeah, great. Let's add that to the mental traffic jam.

I talked to him at the gala. Briefly. But that was all it took, because he remembered me and I knew he would. He said my name like it was familiar, like he'd already been expecting to see me again, like we weren't standing in the middle of a ballroom surrounded by donors and photographers and my father. And he looked different. Harder. Sharper. Like whatever softness I imagined when I met him back in St. Petersburg had been filed down and put away.

And now, in three days, I'm going to be sitting across from him in a private room at the Four Seasons while our families play power chess, and I'm expected to keep my crap together and be useful and not, under any circumstances, act like I still think about that first time we met. Which I don't. Not really. Just ... enough to be annoyed about it.

My phone lights up next to me—not Max.

Of course not.

It's just a calendar alert. *Volkov Meeting–Thursday 5:30PM–Confirmed.*

Confirmed. Like I ever had a say.

Poppy nudges me under the table. "You good?"

I nod once, too fast. "Yeah. Just distracted."

"You never get distracted."

"First time for everything."

She stares at me like she knows. She doesn't. Not really.

I flip the page in my binder like it means something. Across the table, Clara is still talking. Sloane has started braiding her hair like we've hit a full breakdown. Someone laughs too loud at a joke I didn't hear.

And I sit there, composed, still, smiling when I need to, while inside my head, it's just Max, silent and gone, and Niko, waiting and way too close.

And all I can think is how I really don't have time for this farce.

-

We're eating dinner late tonight, and for some reason, I'm not bothered by it. Because by the time I walk into the dining room, it's loud in the best way. The music's too low to be danceable but too loud to ignore, and the air smells like garlic butter and cheese. Girls are gathered around the table, plates loaded with chicken piccata, lemon penne, and pignoli cookies. Yum.

Thalia's already in her usual spot, hair still pinned from her last class of the day, her laptop barely closed. I slide in beside her just in time to catch Poppy mid-rant.

"—and then this idiot has the nerve to text me from her apartment," she says, waving her phone like a weapon. "Like I wouldn't recognize the backsplash in her kitchen. It's marble. Her family owns three wineries, and she Snapchatted the remodel last month."

"Nooo," Daphne says from across the table. "Not the backsplash."

"The backsplash," Poppy repeats, stabbing a piece of chicken. "And you know what he said? 'It's not what it looks like.' As if that sentence has ever been followed by anything that wasn't exactly what it looked like."

Eliza leans over. "Is this the same guy you loaned your G-Wagon to when he said he 'left his wallet in Georgetown'?"

"The one and only," Poppy mutters.

"Babe," Kenzie cuts in, half-laughing. "That man drives a used Lexus and wears sport coats with elbow patches. You knew what this was."

"I thought he had character."

"You thought wrong."

Ava, chewing loudly on a cookie, mumbles, "We need a vetting system. Like a background check, but for hookup reputations."

"There is one," Leigh says. "It's called group chat confirmation. If three or more of us have dated him and survived, he's eligible."

"Unless he plays lacrosse," Tinsley adds, without glancing up. "Then he's automatically disqualified."

A few groans ripple down the table.

"We're still going to the game Friday, right?" Nicolette asks. "Even if it's just to heckle South Atlantic's goalie. I heard he's dating a DG now." She looks towards Eliza.

Eliza raises an eyebrow. "We broke up four months ago. I'm healed."

"You sure?" someone teases.

"She showed up to formal in a red dress knowing damn well I was going to wear red. It was all over my Instagram story." She takes a breath. "I'm over him. I just don't like his rebound."

Laughter breaks out again, louder this time, echoing off the wood-paneled walls.

Marist is on her phone, flicking through an internship spreadsheet like it's a mood board. "Is it unprofessional to ask if the DOJ takes legacy referrals?"

"Only if you're subtle," Thalia murmurs, dry. "Otherwise, it's just networking."

"I swear," Elise mutters from down the table, "if one more senior in Econ says they're 'pivoting to political tech', I'm applying to pastry school out of spite."

Brandi claps once. "Honestly? A Chi O–run bakery would kill."

"We'd serve espresso and high-level gossip," Ava adds.

"Frosted cookies with text like 'He Said We Weren't Exclusive'."

I sip my Pellegrino, content to let the room spin around me—voices overlapping, jokes landing sharp and fast, the warmth of it all masking the sharp edge underneath. Because no one here ever really relaxes.

But sometimes?

They come dang close.

-

I skipped all my classes today. Not because I needed a break. Not because I'm overwhelmed or spiraling or any of the things I'd be expected to admit in a house full of girls who schedule self-care like it's a seminar credit.

No. I just didn't want to go. It has nothing to do with seeing Max again.

Which is how I've found myself standing barefoot in front of my closet, in nothing but a sports bra and shorts, hair pulled back, eyes burning from staring at silk, satin, and chiffon for the last twenty minutes. Dozens of dresses hang in neat, color-coordinated rows. Custom. Borrowed. Hand-selected. All useless. None of them feel right.

Friday's just another political meeting. That's what I keep telling myself. Just another roundtable with overpriced water bottles and people who know my name without knowing anything about me. Especially Nikolai. But still, the thought of showing up in something too boardroom makes my skin crawl.

Someone walks past my room. I don't turn. The hallway creaks, and a few seconds later, I hear her voice.

"Em?"

I glance over my shoulder.

Thalia's in the doorway, coffee in one hand, her Chi O sweatshirt falling off one shoulder like she rolled out of a Vogue spread. Her eyes scan the mess—the half-unzipped garment bag on the bed, the trail of hangers on the floor, the shoe boxes scattered like a panic attack with a designer label. She bursts out laughing. Actually laughing. It's rare. A little jarring. She doesn't usually crack that loudly.

"Jeez," she says. "Is this a breakdown or a rebrand?"

I sigh. "I'm not sure yet."

"Aren't you supposed to be in class?"

I wave her off and turn back to the closet. "Didn't feel like being mansplained about voter turnout today."

She crosses the room and flops onto my bed like it belongs to her, which, to be fair, it sort of does. Her coffee sloshes but doesn't spill. Magic. Or muscle memory.

"So what's with the closet massacre?"

"I need something to wear for Friday."

"Ah," she says, dragging the syllable out. "The mysterious Langford event with Nikolai and his father."

"Which I know nothing about," I mutter, yanking a navy sheath dress from the rack, inspecting it, and tossing it onto the no pile. "Just that my dad insisted I be there with him in something appropriate."

"You've got two dozen dresses here that scream 'appropriate'."

"Exactly," I say, pulling another dress—this one charcoal with shoulder pads. "They all scream. I need something that … whispers."

"Jeez," Thalia mutters. "You're dramatic when you're vague."

"I just don't want to show up looking like a congressional intern."

"Then don't."

I turn to her. "It's not that simple."

Thalia lifts her coffee. "It never is with you."

I exhale. "It's just a meeting."

"Sure it is."

Thalia's quiet for a moment. Too quiet.

I glance over just in time to catch the shift in her eyes—the way her focus sharpens, lips parting into a slow, dangerous grin.

She sits up straighter. Then stands. "We're going shopping."

I blink. "What?"

"You heard me." She's already tossing her coffee in the trash bin by my desk. "You've officially lost it, and I refuse to let you walk into some vaguely ominous Langford-Donor-Industrial-Complex meeting looking like a lobbyist's intern."

"I'm not even sure what I'm dressing for—"

"Exactly." She throws open my closet again and starts flipping through dresses like she's appraising stock options. "And that's the point. When in doubt, look better than the question being asked. You need something clean, bold,

110

expensive, but not flashy. Something that says, 'I'm not here for decoration, but you'll remember what I wore'."

"I have clothes like that."

Thalia turns, holding up a pale gray sheath dress with one hand and a look of unfiltered pity with the other. "You have potential like that. Not results."

I scowl. "That's rude."

"It's effective," she replies, already pulling open my bottom drawer for shoes. "Now put on actual pants. We're going downtown. We're not walking into Saks like you just bailed on your classes."

"You're being intense."

"I'm being right."

And she is. Because maybe I don't know what this meeting is yet. Maybe I don't know why I've been summoned, or what the stakes actually are. But I know better than to show up feeling unprepared.

And with Thalia?

Prepared is never optional.

It's the default.

-

We're barely ten minutes into the drive when Thalia's already texting her personal stylist to "pencil in a consultation window" and pulling up three boutiques on her phone that don't even have public-facing inventory. Apparently, last-minute wardrobe crises are where she thrives.

We arrive in Georgetown, because of course we do, and the car barely comes to a full stop before Thalia's already halfway out the door. Her sunglasses are oversized. Her tote bag is structured like a weapon. She walks with the kind of purpose that makes store associates snap upright and whisper into their earpiece.

The first store is all smoke and mirrors—sleek black walls, ambient lighting, associates who greet you like you've already disappointed them. The kind of place where the price tags are hidden, and everything on the rack is designed to make a statement you didn't ask to make.

Thalia picks up a cream shirt with hand-beaded detailing around the collar. "This looks like something your mom would wear to a charity luncheon she doesn't believe in."

"Exactly what I don't want to be," I mutter, thumbing through a row of dresses that range from aggressively structured to offensively matronly.

We leave fifteen minutes later. No purchases. No regrets.

Store two is better. French. Vaulted ceilings. Floor-to-ceiling glass displays with one dress per mannequin, like fashion exhibits in a museum. The sales associate offers us champagne before we even speak.

I try on a slate silk number with a high neck and an open back. Thalia winces before I've even fully stepped out of the dressing room.

"You look like you're about to accept a foreign ambassador's resignation."

"It's not that bad."

"It's everything wrong with 'polished'. It says, 'I'm here to be admired, not heard.'"

I sigh, tugging at the fabric. "It's comfortable."

"So is invisibility."

We finish the champagne and leave.

By the time we step into boutique number three, we're bordering on morally offended. Thalia's scrolling through her phone like she's about to pull rank on someone's client list, and I'm three minutes away from telling her I'll just wear black and call it a protest.

But then we see it.

It's not even on a rack. It's on a dress form, positioned like it's guarding the entrance to a secret society. Midnight blue. Tailored within an inch of its life. Structured shoulders. A soft V-neck with a twist at the bodice. The fabric folds in a way that draws the eye without shouting for it. There's power in the silhouette. Intention in the hemline. Understated armor.

We both stop.

"That one," Thalia says, pointing. "That's the one."

"I haven't even tried it on."

"You don't need to. You can feel it."

And she's right. I try it on anyway because I have to, and it fits like it was made to answer a question no one's asked me yet.

When I step out, the associate's eyes go wide. She starts saying something about the cut, the designer, the limited run. I don't hear it. Because for the first time since the meeting was scheduled, I feel ready. Not dressed. Ready.

We step out of the boutique with the garment bag in hand, the kind of silence between us that only exists when something is settled, decided, done.

Or so I think.

Until Thalia says, "Now we fix your hair."

I stop. "Excuse me?"

She doesn't even look at me. She's already pulling out her phone. "Don't fight me. You've been wearing it the same way since boarding school, and this meeting is not a boarding school speech and debate banquet."

"It's clean."

"It's predictable."

"I like predictable."

She stops walking. "You like control. But your hair is the last thing you haven't re-evaluated since you were fifteen. It's time."

I open my mouth. Close it again.

She books the appointment before I can come up with a decent argument.

The salon she picks is in the West End. Minimalist interior. Gold-rimmed mirrors. Staff that speak in tones just below a whisper but carry enough attitude to make you second-guess your own facial bone structure.

The stylist—Adrien, of course it's Adrien—combs through my hair with a kind of reverence like he's been personally offended by its past choices. Thalia's perched on the edge of the styling bench near the next chair over, sipping her espresso like we're at a private screening.

"So," she says, drawing the word out. "How nervous are you about Friday on a scale of one to full-blown palace coup?"

I tilt my head as Adrien starts sectioning. "I'm not nervous."

She raises a brow. "Liar."

"I'm not," I repeat. "I'm … curious."

"Curious is just pre-anxious."

I glance at her in the mirror. "Are you diagnosing me or projecting?"

She shrugs. "Little bit of both. You deflect like it's an Olympic sport."

Adrien snorts under his breath. "Hold still," he murmurs, clipping a section.

Thalia keeps her gaze on me, chin resting on her hand now. "You don't even know what this meeting is about."

"Neither do you."

"Exactly. Which is why I'm worried."

"You're always worried."

"I'm always right."

Adrien gives her a look. "She's not wrong."

"Et tu?" I mutter, earning a smirk from him.

There's a lull for a few seconds as he works a gloss through my hair—something subtle that smells expensive and promises shine without weight.

Thalia breaks the quiet first. "Do you think it's about your dad?"

"Isn't everything?"

"I mean … really about him."

I look away from the mirror. "I don't know."

"But you're preparing like it is."

I don't answer. Because what am I supposed to say? That there's something sitting under my skin, buzzing like static? That I can feel, deep in my gut, this meeting is a trap?

Thalia would tell me not to show up. To ghost my own parents. And as much as that sounds dangerously appealing, it's not something a Langford does.

As my father would say, *A Langford keeps their promise.*

Thalia watches me for a second longer. "Well. At least you'll look stunning when the world burns."

Adrien lifts a hand. "Correction. She'll look expensive."

We both laugh.

And for a second, it feels normal. Just two girls. One chair. A stylist with no patience for mediocrity. No texts. No expectations. Just a little evolution under the lights.

-

The windows are down. Not enough to mess up the blowout, but just enough to let the city in—the scent of pavement still clinging to the heat, the murmur of traffic like a heartbeat beneath us. The town car moves smooth through West End, gliding past bistros and boutiques that blur together in shades of beige and brass.

Thalia leans back against the leather seat, her feet crossed at the ankle, one manicured hand resting on her phone like it's just for show. "I still think you should've gone with the burgundy," she says, half-turning toward me.

"It made me look like I was auditioning to be a senator's wife."

"You are the VP's daughter."

"Exactly why I didn't need to lean in."

She tilts her head, amused. "The midnight was the right call."

I glance down at the garment bag folded between us. It still feels too much. Or maybe just too real, like it means something's actually coming.

Outside, the light flickers between gold and shadow as we turn toward Dupont.

"You remember Eva Sinclair's Halloween party sophomore year?" I ask out of nowhere.

Thalia snorts. "Please. The one with the fog machine and the fake Versace ice sculpture?"

"She claimed it was hand carved."

"She also claimed her boyfriend was from Italy. He was from New Jersey."

I laugh, twisting in my seat to face her. "Didn't she end the night crying into a bottle of Veuve?"

"Correction: sobbing into it. Called it her 'emotional cleanse'."

The driver slows at a red light. The city pulses around us.

"You ever think about how much of our lives has been performance?" I ask quietly.

Thalia doesn't respond right away. Just stares out the window. "I think about how much of it we learned before we even knew we were performing."

I nod.

We drive in silence for a minute—the kind that isn't uncomfortable, just heavy with shared memory.

Then she says, "Friday's going to suck, isn't it?"

I pause. "Yeah. I think it might."

She exhales. "At least you'll look expensive while it does."

I smirk. "You're such a brat."

"I'm the brat who got you out of your closet spiral and into that dress."

She's right. As usual.

We don't say anything else for the rest of the drive.

-

By the time we get back to Chi O, it's a full-blown midweek mess inside.

The front door swings open to someone yelling from the kitchen about burning garlic bread, and there's a bra draped over the banister like it paid rent there. The scent of heat-damaged hair and cinnamon candles smacks me the second we step in.

Thalia sighs like she's walked into a spa. "Oh how I've missed this chaos."

Ava's halfway down the stairs in slippers and a towel turban, holding a makeup bag in one hand and yelling, "Who stole my eyebrow pencil?"

"I think Clara borrowed it," someone shouts from upstairs.

"Clara has microbladed brows!"

"Then she borrowed it for sport!"

Thalia sidesteps a pile of tote bags and drops the garment bag onto the bottom step like it's the last thing holding her spine together. I shrug out of my coat and hook it over the newel post, because I know dang well if I hang it up properly, someone will still knock it onto the floor by morning.

"You want dinner?" she asks as we head upstairs. "Ava said she was making pasta. I said we already had carbs today, and she threatened to cut me with a nail file."

"I'm not hungry."

"You're lying."

"I'm tired."

"Fine. Emotional carbs only."

I kick open my bedroom door, toe off my shoes, and drop my phone on the nearest surface like it offended me.

Thalia stands in the doorway for a second, arms crossed, head tilted. "You feel better?"

I glance at the mirror and the dress hung neatly on the hook by the closet. The hair still holding. The girl in the reflection still sorting herself out.

"Yeah," I say. "I do."

She nods once. Then turns and disappears down the hall with a simple, "Good. Don't get weird about it."

Door clicks shut behind her. And I exhale like I've been holding my breath all day.

Chapter 6

Emilia

I didn't sleep. Not really.

Four hours, maybe. Just enough to blur the edges, but not enough to feel human. I've been in and out of shallow dreams since around 3 a.m., most of them useless fragments of nothing—noise and faces that don't mean anything. I don't even remember closing my eyes, just the hum beneath my skin that hasn't let up since yesterday.

Now it's 7:22 a.m., and I'm awake for good.

The house is starting to stir with the occasional creak of floorboards, the low thump of someone closing a bathroom drawer down the hall. No group chat explosion from Clara yet, which feels like divine intervention.

I stare at the ceiling for a second, letting the quiet hold a little longer than necessary. Then I reach for my phone, thumb hovering over my calendar even though I know exactly what it says.

Four Seasons, 5:30 PM.

I have just under ten hours.

Ten hours until I walk into a hotel conference suite in D.C., wearing a dress I didn't choose lightly, with my hair perfectly arranged and my nerves dressed up in pearls. Ten hours until I find out why my father insisted on this meeting and what the heck it actually means.

I exhale. Sit up slowly. The sheets are tangled, the room still dark, the early fall light just starting to edge its way through the curtains. I run a hand through my hair, already trying to mentally catalog what I need to do between now and then.

Shower. Steady. Smile.

And figure out what in the world I'm walking into.

-

The kitchen is already half-alive when I walk in—cabinets banging, someone's phone buzzing on the counter, the faint hum of the dishwasher drying last night's wine glasses.

Poppy's in her usual morning fit—oversized hoodie, shorts, hair in a bun that's pretending not to care. She's toasting a bagel with one hand and texting with the other. She looks up when I reach for the coffee. "You're up early."

"So are you."

"Yeah, well. Brandi left the bathroom light on again and I thought we were being interrogated by Homeland Security."

I smirk behind my mug. "Drama queen."

"Says the girl who once fake-cried her way out of Econ for three weeks."

"Strategic communication," I murmur.

Poppy eyes me for a second, then shrugs. "You doing anything tonight?"

I hesitate. "Nope," I say casually. "Just laying low."

"Jealous," she says, dragging cream cheese across her bagel with surgical precision. "I have to go to that pre-law mixer in the courtyard. It's basically just an excuse for Clara to use the phrase 'professional networking' while serving charcuterie from Costco.''

"Sounds riveting."

"You should come," she offers. "Give them something pretty to stare at while they pretend to know what civil code is."

I shake my head, sipping slow. "I've got stuff."

She shrugs. Doesn't push.

It's what I like about Poppy. She talks too much, but she listens enough to know when not to.

The conversation shifts. She starts ranting about a professor who gave her a B+ on a paper she clearly wrote in an Uber. I let her talk, nodding when I need to, laughing when it feels right. But in the back of my mind, the time keeps ticking. And I'm the only one in the room who knows what 5:30 really means.

-

The Four Seasons has always made me feel small. Not because of the chandeliers or the staff who remember your name without ever making eye contact, though that never helps, but because this place has been part of my life for as long as I can remember, and never once has it felt like mine.

I was six the first time I came here. It was for one of my father's campaign dinners, the kind where I was dressed in velvet and told to sit still, to smile, to say "thank you" like it was a rehearsed line and not something I meant. I remember the way my shoes pinched, how the napkins were folded like origami I wasn't allowed to touch. I remember falling asleep in my mother's lap while a lobbyist explained something about oil pipelines. And I remember waking up to her brushing my hair behind my ear, whispering, "Sit up, baby. Someone important is coming."

Someone important is always coming.

Tonight is no different.

It's 5:23 when I step out of the car. Not early, not late. Just like I planned. My hair is curled and pinned back behind one ear. My heels click as I walk through the revolving doors, not loud enough to draw attention, but certain enough not to be ignored.

The doorman tips his hat, and I nod in return. No smile. There's no warmth in my expression. Just something neutral, unreadable, which is exactly what I want.

Inside, the lobby glows with low light and polished surfaces, the scent of lavender lingering faintly in the air like a memory someone keeps refreshing. The bar is busy. Men in pressed suits sip from heavy glasses, their voices low and purposeful. I don't pause, but I feel their eyes follow me the way they always do. One of them catches mine for a second too long. I meet it without flinching. I don't smile. I don't need to.

"Ms. Langford?" a voice calls out, gentle and practiced.

I turn.

The woman behind the desk is all professionalism, hands folded, expression composed. She gestures toward a hallway. "They're waiting for you."

Of course they are.

I follow her past a row of closed doors, the carpet soft beneath my heels, the kind of silence that feels staged. When she opens the last door, I don't hesitate.

My mother is already seated, her posture flawless, hands folded neatly over the edge of the table like she's posing for a magazine cover she didn't have to audition for. My father stands as I enter, brushing a dry kiss across my cheek, and it's only then I feel it—the stiffness in his shoulders, the calculation in his smile. It's a look I've only ever seen when he's about to offer something expensive as collateral.

I expected Nikolai. I was told this dinner was a soft diplomatic gesture, a casual meal to acknowledge relationships being formed, nothing official, nothing binding. A nod. A courtesy.

I didn't expect to see the man seated at the head of the table. I didn't expect to feel the shift in my chest the moment he looked up.

He doesn't stand. He doesn't need to. His presence speaks before his voice does. His suit is flawless, the color of wet ink, tailored so precisely it looks molded to him. His cufflink flashes once under the candlelight. He lifts his glass as if I've just arrived for a final act he's already watched a hundred times.

"Emilia," my father says, gesturing toward the empty chair between him and the stranger. "You remember Nikolai, of course. And this is his father, Alexei Volkov."

Volkov.

The name slices clean through the air like a hidden blade, like something too sharp to notice until it's already under your skin. I keep my expression calm because I've been trained to, but inside something tightens, curls, burns. The name means something. I've heard it whispered through sealed doors, seen it tucked between headlines that never made the front page. Volkov isn't just a name. It's a warning disguised as legacy.

My gaze flicks toward Nikolai, and I see it in his face, the truth I never bothered to ask for. He watches me steadily, saying nothing, not because he doesn't know what to say, but because he knows I've already put it together. All the moments suddenly realign—the palace in St. Petersburg, the gala two weeks ago, the coffee shop, the classroom, the way he always seemed a half-step outside the rhythm of everything else. The familiarity I couldn't explain. The silence I didn't question. He knew. From the first word, the first look, he knew, and he said nothing.

I sit because it's what I'm supposed to do. Because the theater of it requires that I don't make a scene before the script is finished. The glass in front of me is full. The menu already folded and pushed aside. We are not here for dinner.

The silence stretches for a moment, heavy and waiting, before Alexei Volkov sets his glass down and speaks, his voice low, smooth, and terrifyingly composed. "This is not a negotiation," he says, his words soft enough to almost be mistaken for kindness. "It's a conclusion. A moment we have been building toward for years."

Years? What the ever-loving crap does he mean by years?

My father doesn't look at me. He stares at the white tablecloth like it's easier than facing the reality of what he's done. My mother, on the other hand, looks directly at me, expression serene, as if this is nothing more than an update to my calendar.

I already know what's coming. I feel it rise like smoke behind my ribs. I brace.

"You and my son," Alexei continues, "will be married."

No preamble. No softness. Just a stated fact.

The air leaves my body slowly. Not with shock—I'm past that—but with something else. Something deeper. The kind of betrayal that has a long echo. The kind that makes you feel stupid for not seeing it sooner.

I don't speak. Not yet. I glance again at Nikolai, who hasn't moved. He sits with the ease of someone who never had to lie to win. He's just been waiting for the right moment to let the truth reveal itself.

I try to breathe. Try to find the part of me that still believes I can claw my way out of this. But every version of the exit leads back here.

Alexei doesn't smile, not really, but something about his face shifts, the satisfaction of a man who's just crossed the finish line and knows no one else saw the race even start.

"This alliance," he says, like the word means anything clean, "binds our families. The Langford name gives us legitimacy. Ours gives you protection. Permanence. Immunity."

"Protection from what?" I ask, and I hate the way my voice catches.

My father finally looks up. His eyes are tired. "From consequences."

"And what do I get?" I ask, still calm, still pretending.

"You get to be untouchable," Alexei says, gently now. "You get to keep your sister safe."

And there it is.

Grace.

Fifteen. Soft-hearted. Brilliant. Still thinks I can fix anything. Still calls me when she can't sleep. Still trusts that I'd burn down the world before I let anyone touch her.

The ground tilts, but no one notices. Or maybe they do, and they just don't care.

I look at my mother. Her wine glass is raised halfway to her lips.

"What happens," I ask her quietly, the words catching in my throat like splinters, "if I don't sign?"

She hesitates. Just for a breath. A beat. Then, she smiles, tight, tired, practiced. "At least he's good-looking."

My hands curl into fists in my lap before I can stop them. I don't feel the pain. I'm too full of it already. "He's the damn Russian mafia," I say, and it doesn't come out like a scream, but it cuts harder than one.

My mother's face doesn't flinch. My father exhales like I've made things inconvenient. And Nikolai? He finally moves, not toward me, but toward the center of the moment. He doesn't apologize. He doesn't look ashamed. He just waits. Still and deliberate, like he's always been part of this story. Like he was never anything else.

And maybe he wasn't.

Maybe I was the only one who believed otherwise.

No one responds to what I said. Not my father, who's still pretending this is just another one of his meetings. Not my mother, who's dabbing at the corner of her mouth like she just remembered her lipstick. Not Nikolai, who looks at me like he's waiting. For what, I don't know.

And that's what does it. The silence. The ease. The certainty in the air that I'll fold the way they've always expected me to.

Because I always do, don't I?

I play the part. I wear the clothes. I know which fork to use and which lie to tell and when to hold my tongue in rooms where no one else does. I've made myself indispensable to my father's image, sculpted myself into something sharp enough to matter, but not threatening enough to question. I've excelled at it—played the daughter, the prodigy, the presence that makes men nod and say she's impressive as though that word doesn't carry its own chain.

But in this moment, something inside me splinters.

Because for all my sharp edges, all my perfect posture and perfectly calculated silences, I never saw this coming. And that scares me more than the alliance. More than the name Volkov. More than what marrying Nikolai might mean.

I didn't see it coming.

And that means I've been playing checkers in a game that's always been chess. I've been so busy proving I can sit at the table that I forgot who owns the damn board.

I blink, and my throat feels raw. The problem isn't just them. It's me. Because deep down, I *knew* there were things I wasn't being told. I've always known, but I didn't press. Didn't push. I thought I could stay above it, orbit the worst of it, skim influence off the top without ever getting my hands dirty. That I could survive in the game without belonging to it.

And now?

Now I'm the pawn they're using to end it.

I grip the edge of the table to keep myself still. My fingers ache. My pulse drums behind my teeth. Because this moment, this dinner, isn't just about betrayal. It's about proof. Proof that no matter how good I am, how careful, how polished or poised or valuable I've made myself, they still see me as a girl to be traded.

A girl who exists for strategy. For alliances.

A girl who doesn't get to say no.

And the worst part?

A small, sick part of me wonders if they're right. If this is who I've always been. Not powerful. Just useful.

Something flashes in my chest—fury, grief, humiliation. But underneath it all, something worse:

Recognition.

I've spent my whole life becoming exactly what they needed.

And now?

Now they're cashing in.

I don't know how long the silence lasts, just that it swells between us like something alive. My hands are still in my lap, curled so tight I can feel my nails pressing into my skin. No one says a word. Not my father, not my mother. And certainly not Nikolai, who sits like he's been carved from the same stone as this table, silent, unmoved, watching me like he's been watching this moment unfold since the day he first learned my name.

I look at him now—really look at him—and something inside me cracks wide open. Because I remember his face before it wore this stillness. I remember the boy in that palace hallway, five years ago, when we were both too young to know what we'd become. Or maybe he already knew. He was quiet then but not cold. He smiled, barely, like he was unused to company. He asked me where I was from. I never asked him the same. I didn't need to. He didn't want me to. But I remember the way I felt when I looked at him, like he didn't belong in that place either.

I was wrong.

I turn to him now, and my voice is low, sharp, all edges smoothed only by restraint. "You're okay with this?"

He doesn't look away. Doesn't blink. Just meets me head-on like he knew I'd ask it. "I didn't know who you were in St. Petersburg," he says, quiet but steady. "Not then."

The words land, soft but heavy, because I know what's coming next. "But after," I murmur, almost a whisper. "You knew."

"I did," he answers.

The overhead light dances between us, but the warmth doesn't reach. It never did.

"How long?"

Nikolai doesn't flinch. "Years."

Of course he did. Which meant he knew who I was when we were writing letters back and forth. When I opened myself up to him.

The air feels thick in my lungs, like it's been poisoned with the realization that every interaction since then—every glance, every silence, every word he didn't say—was part of a play I didn't know I was cast in. I think of the way he looked at me across the ballroom two weeks ago, like he remembered something, like he was calculating how much of me still matched the girl in the abandoned room.

"You knew what this dinner was," I say, eyes narrowing. "You knew what your father wanted."

He says nothing.

"So you just let me show up and find out like this."

Another beat of silence. He doesn't apologize. He doesn't even shift in his seat. "I didn't ask for this," he says finally.

My mouth twists. "But you didn't stop it either."

"No," he says, and it's the most honest thing in the room.

I don't realize I'm shaking until I reach for the stem of my glass and feel the tremor. I set it back down before I can do something impulsive. Like throw it against the wall.

"I was never supposed to be a person to you," I whisper. "Just a name on a list. A box to check. Langford: acquired."

His jaw tightens, just slightly. But it's the first tell I've gotten from him all night.

"You weren't a box," he says, and it comes out raspy.

I let out a breathless, bitter laugh. "That's rich, coming from the guy who's been sitting on this secret for how long while my life was handed over like a campaign donation?"

Nikolai's voice lowers, but there's an edge now, a strain I haven't heard until this second. "You think I had a choice in any of this?"

"No," I snap. "I think you had options. And you took the easy one."

That lands. He blinks once, slow. Still composed, but no longer unreadable. There's something there now. Regret maybe. Or shame. Or worse—justification.

"I did what I was told," he says finally.

"So did I," I bite back, "and look where that got me."

We stare at each other across the table, across the divide of everything we used to be—and everything we'll never be again. The room is empty save for us.

I don't know what breaks the moment. Maybe nothing does. Maybe it just collapses under the weight of what neither of us is willing to say out loud.

But one thing's clear: He won't fight for me. Because he never had to.

I don't remember getting into the car. I don't remember telling Michael where to go. I only remember the way my hands wouldn't stop shaking once the doors closed, and the way the silence settled around me like a tomb.

I pull out my phone.

Call Thalia.

She picks up on the second ring.

"Meet me," I say, and my voice is hoarse, wrecked, cracked open. "Wine bar off Fifth. I need—, I need something that burns."

She doesn't ask questions. She never does.

The bar is lit like a secret—low amber lighting, leather seats that swallow you whole, and a bartender who pours like he knows you're not drinking to socialize. It's the kind of place where conversations don't echo. Where the wine tastes expensive because it has to justify the things you're about to say out loud.

Thalia's already there when I walk in, sitting in the back booth, tucked into shadows like she's waiting to be recruited into something illegal, her boots up on the empty space beside her and her jacket slung like a dare across the armrest. A bottle of wine's been opened. Two glasses already poured. She doesn't smile when she sees me. Doesn't wave. She just looks like she's trying to figure out how bad it is before I even sit down.

I take the glass. I don't even say hello.

She lets me have the silence. That's the thing about Thalia. She knows how to wait for the words I don't want to say.

After the first sip, I set the glass down and stare at the rim. "I'm being pawned off."

There's a beat. A pause, just long enough for the wine to settle and the meaning not to.

"Okay," she says slowly. "Is this metaphorical, emotional, or geopolitical?"

"No," I say. "It's a contract."

Her eyes narrow, the joke dying on her lips. "What?"

"A marriage contract," I say. "Signed tonight. My father. Another family. The whole legacy-and-security pitch. You know. Old money cosplay."

She blinks. "Wait. Hold on. Back up."

I look up at her.

"To who?" she asks, her eyes narrowing in suspicion.

"Nikolai."

She snorts. "The same guy you wrote letters to? The one you saw at the gala?"

I don't say anything. Because... nailed it.

She stares at me. "Is that such a bad thing?"

I know what she's getting out. Nikolai. The same Nikolai I wrote letters to for over a year. The boy I fell for before I even realized I was falling. The one I told things I've never told anyone else, not even Thalia.

"He's a Volkov."

No flicker of recognition. Of course not. Why would she know? Thalia deals in lobbyist dirt and cabinet secrets, not syndicate networks.

I watch the moment it dawns, not because of what she knows, but because of what she doesn't. "Wait..." she begins, the gears turning in her head. "Isn't that Russian?"

"Bratva," I nod. "One of the most powerful criminal syndicates in the world."

Thalia blinks once, then goes perfectly still. Her spine straightens. Her glass stays frozen mid-air. "You're joking."

"I wish I was."

"No, Em, that's—" She cuts herself off. "That's not just ... power. That's the damn mob. That's bodies in rivers and whole elections rigged and—why would your father—?"

I cut her off before she can spiral: "Because the Langford name is bleeding out," I say. "Because the ethics probe cost him allies. Because marrying me off to a criminal empire somehow makes our family relevant again."

She sets the glass down with a sharp *clink*. "He signed a marriage contract with the Russian mafia?"

"Keep your voice down," I snap. "He said it was already arranged. He said I should be honored."

Her voice drops, cold and low. "And you?"

"I signed."

"Why?"

"Because they played the Grace card."

Thalia doesn't breathe.

I press on, because if I stop I'll never get through it. "He said if I refused, they couldn't guarantee her safety." I don't elaborate, because what more can I say?

Her voice is barely audible now, but it cuts like glass. "He threatened your sister to force your hand."

I nod.

She leans back like the force of it is physical. Like something inside her has broken open and she's trying to hold the edges together. Then, more carefully: "Did you know?"

I pause. "No. I didn't know he was part of the Bratva."

She looks at me. "You need to get out, Em." Her voice is hushed now, hollowed out. "And you need to make it fast."

I laugh, but it's shallow. "You know how this game works. You only leave in a bag or through illegal means."

Thalia doesn't speak. Her knuckles are white against the edge of her glass.

I look at her, eyes burning. "He knew who I was for years. Didn't mention a thing. No heads up."

The silence explodes around us.

Thalia slams her glass down. Thankfully it doesn't break. A few people around us stare. The bartender watches from across the room, his eyes glaring into the side of Thalia's head. I turn my attention back to Thalia, her face is flushed with anger.

"No," she says, voice shaking. "No. Screw that. Screw him. Screw your father. Screw anyone who thought this was okay."

"I didn't have a choice."

"I know. That's why I'm angry."

We sit there—two girls raised in glass houses and taught how to smile through war—now cracked, now splintered, now staring down the face of something darker than politics ever warned us about.

"This isn't alliance," she says finally. "This is ownership."

I nod. "I want out."

"I know."

"And I'm not walking into this blind."

"No," she says. "You're not."

We then begin to plot.

-

Niko

I pace the length of the room, then check my phone for the fifth time. Max was supposed to call with an update. He's usually right on time. Precise. Efficient. Annoyingly dependable. But lately, he's been … distracted. And I know exactly why.

What started out as a job has suddenly become something else entirely. I expected him to report on Emilia—who she was with, where she was going, who she bumped into at a events—but not the way he's been talking about her. Not with that edge in his voice. That twitch in his silence. He talks about her coffee order like it matters. Mentions the way she keeps a pen between her fingers when she's thinking, like that's intel worth recording. He calls her Em, like he's earned that kind of closeness.

It pisses me off more than it should.

I never call her that.

Emilia. That's her name. It always has been.

And I've practiced saying it—alone, under my breath, in moments I'll never admit to—ever since the day I found out my father had brokered my future like it was a poker chip. Since he dropped her name like it was supposed to be a peace offering, a gift, some politically expedient trade that tied blood to power and called it family.

But the thing is, I already knew her name. I knew it after the night she introduced herself in St. Petersburg. Sixteen years old. Sharp as broken glass. Pretty, yeah, but that's not what made me stop. What made me remember her. It was the way she stood there, perfectly still, in a wing of a palace she wasn't supposed to be in, and didn't flinch when she saw me. I never told her my last name, and maybe that makes me a coward. I didn't want her to shut down like most people do when they find out who I am. Who my family is. It's a curse.

And when I saw her again at the gala—five years later, older, fiercer, so lethal in that dress—I realized something that settled deep and unwanted in my chest: suddenly, the idea of marriage didn't seem so constrained. Not to her at least. Call me selfish, I don't care.

Again, I check my phone.

Not even a full minute has passed.

What was Max doing?

I crack my neck from side to side, tension bleeding through my spine. Then I reach up and undo the top button of my shirt, like it'll help me breathe. It doesn't.

Tonight was a train wreck, to put it bluntly. My father played it like a script he'd already memorized—cordial, calm, smug as anything. And I? I sat there like a soldier who didn't know whose war he was fighting. I didn't say a word when the contract hit the table. Didn't move when Emilia looked at me like I'd put the knife in myself. Because I didn't know what to say. Not yet. Not when everything that mattered was still buried under the weight of my mother's murder, the truth I've spent years piecing together, and the empire I've been raised to inherit and plan to dismantle.

My phone vibrates once. Finally.

Max.

I swipe to answer, pressing the phone to my ear as I turn toward the window. Beyond the glass, the forest is still, the last light caught in the branches.

"She's still at the bar," he says, his voice low, careful, like he's not sure if I'm already mad or just starting. "Same booth. Downing wine like it's a contest."

"Who's with her?"

"Thalia. That's it. Em's—" he stops. Corrects himself. "Emilia's not saying much. Just sitting there. Zoned out. You know the look."

Yeah. I do.

"She check her phone?" I ask.

"No."

I move to the bar cart, grab the glass, and finally pour the scotch.

"She pissed?" I ask, though I already know the answer.

Max exhales, and I can hear the pause in his breath, like he's biting back something he doesn't want to say. "She's seething, Niko."

Good. Let her seethe. Let her rage. She deserves to. For once, I need her to. If she'd taken it with a smile, I would've known I'd backed the wrong one.

"You should've told her," Max says, voice dropping. "Before tonight."

I let the scotch roll over my tongue before swallowing it down. "Yeah," I mutter. "I know."

"She looked betrayed."

"She was."

"You didn't say a word."

"I didn't know if I could."

That's the truth of it. Because if I opened my mouth, I might've told her everything. About my mother. About the list. About the plan to take my father down before he turns me into him. About how I don't want her as a pawn, I want her as my partner.

But I can't give her that yet. Because if she's not strong enough to choose me when everything's still broken, she'll never survive what comes after.

"She's not going to make this easy," Max says.

"She's not supposed to."

"You trust her?"

"I trust she won't stay quiet."

I look out the window again. The moon is out now, hanging just above the trees, its light cutting across the ground.

"She's going to hate you," Max mutters.

"She already does."

And it kills me that I can't explain why that matters.

Because if she hates me, she's still thinking about me.

And if she's still thinking, there's still a chance.

A long, cold, bloody chance. But a chance all the same.

-

Max

I should walk away the second I see her coming.

I know I should. I should pivot, duck behind the sculpture garden, pretend to take a call, cross the quad in the opposite direction, anything to avoid what's about to happen. But I don't. Because some messed-up part of me—the weak part, the part I've kept buried under orders and duty and silence—wants to know what it feels like. Just once. Not to watch her from a distance. Not to filter her life through transcripts and surveillance photos. But to be close. Really close.

Close enough to hear her laugh. To see how she moves when she doesn't know someone's watching. To breathe the air around her and let it fill my lungs like I have a right to it.

And then she collides with me.

Hard.

Not on purpose, but enough to make her stumble and for her security detail to jump like I've just fired a shot. Her shoulder clips my chest, and she lets out this sharp little gasp of, "Crap—sorry—" before she even registers what's happening. Her hand lifts, instinctively reaching for balance. She doesn't have to. I've already caught her.

My hands land on her arms like they've been there before. Firm, steady, practiced.

Because they have.

Maybe not in real life. But in my mind? A thousand times. In dreams I never asked for. In day-old fantasies I push back down before they can take root. Since the beginning of summer when Niko asked me to track her. Watch her. Learn her. I've spent so long pretending I don't care that I've almost started to believe it. But I do. And it's a problem.

Back at the coffee shop, I told her I transferred for the change of scenery. She looked at me like she knew I was lying, not completely, just enough. She didn't press. That's what kills me. She could've, but she didn't.

And then, just as fast as she hits me, the entire mood shifts.

"Ma'am, step back."

Keller's voice cuts in, sharp and clipped. Too sharp. Too fast. A second later, Ruiz moves in behind him, already halfway to drawing his sidearm like I've pulled something more dangerous than being in the wrong place at the wrong time.

She stiffens, not with fear, but confusion. Annoyance. Her eyes dart, not to them, but back to me. Like she's checking to see if I'm the threat or if they're just overreacting. I raise my hands without thinking. Years of instinct kick in. Body loose, posture easy, smile on. It's the same one I've used to get out of more than a few messy situations.

"Uh … bad time?" I ask, even though I already know the answer.

"She's under protection," Keller snaps, like I don't know her entire detail's rotation schedule, preferred ammo, or who flinches when they lie. I probably trained with half of them in London before they ever stepped foot on U.S. soil.

She steps out from behind them.

Every inch of her is fire. It doesn't even take effort. She moves with command—shoulders squared, chin lifted, like she's used to being surrounded by power and isn't impressed by any of it.

"She didn't hit you," she hisses, sending Keller an annoyed look. "She brushed his arm. Calm down."

Then she looks at me again. And something in me comes unspooled. "You good?" she asks. Like she's checking on me. Like I'm the one rattled. Like I matter.

"Better now," I say, and flash a grin that's half reflex, half heart attack. I see her eyes flick to it—the dimples, the charm—and for a second, I think maybe she sees me.

The real me.

And then I turn and walk away. Because if I don't, I'll say something real. Something stupid. Something honest. And that's not allowed. Not here. Not in this game. And definitely not when she belongs to him. Not yet. But it's coming. And I can't be the one to screw that up.

Now it's weeks later, and I'm sitting in this beat-up Honda that smells like sweat, old fries, and bad choices, watching her through the windshield while she slowly, silently falls apart in a back booth at the wine bar. Thalia's talking, filling the air like it'll stop the bleeding. Emilia's still. That same stillness I saw the first day we met, the kind that hides chaos under the surface, the kind that warns you not to get too close.

I haven't blinked in three minutes.

All I can think is: she can't ever know.

Not about me. Not about Niko. Not about what we're really doing.

She thinks I'm just another guy in her class, a friend, charm cranked to a dull hum. Which is the point.

She doesn't know I'm watching. Listening. Tracing every move. Every connection. Laying out the map from the inside.

This started years ago. Before her. Before I knew her name.

I used to think Niko was making her up. Some perfect girl he invented to throw his father off. Another story to buy time. But then she walked into the story, and she was real. Worse, she was better than real. Smarter. Sharper. Not what I expected. Definitely not what he expected. Which made everything more complicated.

Niko and I aren't close in the way people think, but we understand each other. We grew up inside the same machine—taught to follow orders, inherit power, swallow guilt and call it loyalty. The Bratva molded us into what it needed: sons who would serve.

We both decided not to, which cost us dearly, with my father and with his mother.

So when he told me the plan to dismantle it all from the inside, I said yes. No questions.

But then his father forced his hand. Marry or lose everything. So Niko gave him a name.

Emilia. The eldest daughter of Trent Langford, VP of the United States.

From the outside, it looked like a bluff. Like another stall tactic. But I saw it for what it was. A choice, and not one he wanted to make.

He never meant to bring her into this. She was supposed to stay untouched. Unknowing. Outside of all of it. But he couldn't fake it with anyone else. Wouldn't.

So now she's part of the plan, not because she signed up for it but because he couldn't imagine doing this beside anyone else.

He's still trying to protect her. Still trying to thread the needle—play the heir, burn the empire, keep her safe. But he's not going to be able to do all three. And when it breaks—when the first crack shows—she's going to feel it.

And if she finds out what this is? What we're doing? She'll walk. Or worse, she'll look at him and not see the man, just the blood.

And that's when it all falls apart. Not the plan. Him.

The truth is, I wasn't supposed to feel anything. Just track her movements. Report patterns. Feed intel to Niko and stay close enough to monitor but not close enough to matter.

But I do matter now. At least in my own head. And that's the problem.

I still remember how her voice sounded when she apologized. Like it actually meant something. Like she didn't know I'd been following her shadow for months. And I hate it. I hate that I liked it. I hate that it cracked something open inside me I've been trying to keep locked in since the day my father died, and I swore I'd never be used the way he was.

But mostly? I hate that I only want her.

Her.

The girl who's off-limits. The one who's taken. The one I'm watching for someone else. And the worst part? I think she'd understand if I told her the truth. And that might just be enough to ruin me.

…My phone buzzes.

I tear my eyes off Emilia just long enough to glance down at the screen, thumb hovering.

Sebastian: *FYI. Callie from that rooftop bar is asking where you've been. Wants to know if you ghosted.*

Of course she does.

I stare at the message, the words barely registering before the annoyance kicks in. I can't even picture her face anymore. Blonde, maybe. Or was that her friend? It doesn't matter. She was pretty, loud, easy to smile at, easier to leave. One of those nights I half-remembered but logged anyway because it looked normal on paper. One more notch on a résumé I used to be proud of. One more girl I let see a version of me that wasn't real. Not the way it is now.

I lock the screen without responding.

Because the only girl I'm thinking about is sitting inside, back straight, shoulders tight, her glass of wine still untouched and her eyes distant in the kind of way that guts me. And I'm not that guy anymore. I'm not the player. Not the flirt. Not the safe, easy maybe that Callie and girls like her get.

Emilia changed that.

Without even trying.

And that scares me.

Because she's not mine. Because she never will be. And because I want her anyway. More than I should. More than I can admit. More than I've ever wanted anything clean. And so I do what I've always done when something real starts to burn—I look for something easy to pour the fire into.

I bring up my messages, scroll to her name, and send off a text without second guessing myself.

Me: Are you free Friday night?

I stare at the screen for a second. Not because I care about the answer, but because I already know that whatever it is, it won't be her.

And maybe that's the only way I'll survive this.

Chapter 7

Emilia

I don't want to be here, not after last night. I know everyone here. Or at least, I'm supposed to. That's the unspoken rule of the Capitol Hill fundraiser: you shake hands with people you already have dossiers on. You smile at men who once made jokes about your father's voting record. You wear heels that make your ankles scream because optics matter more than circulation, and you never, ever show up unprepared. This is my mother's arena—all crystal glassware and artfully-arranged orchids, laughter that sounds like strategy, and elevator pitches disguised as compliments. And I've walked these floors enough times to know the difference between donors, diplomats, and the daughters dragged here to keep up appearances.

Yep, this is definitely her world.

I used to trail behind her as a kid, clutching a tiny bag and trying not to wrinkle. By the time I turned sixteen, I could spot the weak links in a room like this faster than most staffers. By nineteen, I knew which donors were full of crap before they opened their mouths.

I don't love it, but I know it, and knowing it is survival.

So when I walk into the Hamilton Room, nothing surprises me. Not the men in tailored suits clapping each other on the back like they don't spend their mornings leaking to the press. Not the wives in champagne-toned sheath dresses, air-kissing over flutes of sparkling wine that isn't quite French enough to impress them. Not the speeches that'll start in forty-five minutes about economic resilience and bipartisan cooperation while everyone claps like they're not secretly planning each other's downfall.

It's all so familiar I could scream.

And then I see him.

Max.

Standing near the edge of the room, next to the auction table, looking completely at ease. Like this is just another Thursday. Like he was born in a room like this—or, worse, like he couldn't care less that he wasn't.

For a second, my brain just stops. He's in a dark suit, open collar, hands casually tucked in his pockets like he doesn't notice how hand-picked everything is around him. No name badge. No plus-one ID. Just Max looking like he belongs when I know for a fact that he doesn't.

Because this isn't a campus event. This isn't the coffee shop. This is the Capitol Hill Fundraiser. And Max? He's Comparative Politics Max. Coffee shop Max. The guy who will randomly text me memes. The guy who shrugged when I asked if he was planning to apply for summer placements. The guy who said, "Nah, not really my scene."

And yet here he is.

In the middle of my scene.

I narrow my eyes as I watch him. Waiting for the part where he notices me. Waiting for him to look out of place. To fidget. To crack a joke. But he doesn't. He sips from a glass of something expensive, head tilted slightly, scanning the room like he's clocking people, not wondering why he's here.

And suddenly, I don't know who he is. But I want to.

I weave past the small cluster of staffers and lobbyists, heels silent on the marble, eyes fixed ahead like I have somewhere to be, and I guess I do now. I don't even realize I'm walking toward him until I'm almost there. He's turned slightly away, watching a congressman gesture too dramatically about something, but I can see it in his profile— the smirk tugging at the corner of his mouth, the same lazy confidence he wears to class like a favorite hoodie. But here? Here it feels … different. Sharper. Cleaner. Studied, maybe.

His head turns, like he senses me before I speak. His eyes meet mine, and his smile appears slow, like it's blooming rather than snapping into place. Like he's genuinely happy to see me.

"Langford," he says with that gravel-soft voice that makes women go weak in the knees. That makes me pause because I'm still caught up in the way he sounds when he speaks.

"Max," I return, trying to keep my tone flat, neutral, a little amused, like I haven't just short-circuited internally trying to figure out how the hell he's here.

"You look like you've seen a ghost."

"More like a glitch in the matrix," I murmur. "What are you doing here?"

He shrugs, like the answer is so obvious it's barely worth saying. "Didn't want to miss the silent auction. I hear there's a signed portrait of the Secretary of Agriculture up for grabs."

I raise an eyebrow. "Is that your way of saying 'I'm not telling you'?"

He just grins. Neither confirms nor denies it.

And that's the moment I feel it—the subtle shift under my skin. Because for weeks, Max has been background noise. Safe. Casual. The guy who fades in and out of campus life without a trace. But now, standing here in this room where people's presence means something, I'm starting to wonder if he was ever background at all. If I've been looking at him wrong.

"This is a hard room to get into," I say, watching him closely.

His eyes flick to mine again, something unreadable in them. "So I've heard."

I want to press. To ask who got him in, who he knows, why he's acting like this is all normal. But I don't. Because that would mean admitting that I care. That I noticed. That I'm still noticing.

Instead, I take a sip of my drink and glance over his shoulder—and my pulse stutters. The color in my face drains. My eyes narrow into slits.

Nikolai. The man responsible for turning my whole world on its axis. Not that my world was turning in the right direction, but at least I had some semblance of control. But not anymore.

He's making his way across the room with that same coiled ease, the kind that makes people move without realizing they've stepped aside. His suit is charcoal again. His shirt black. His presence unmistakable. And I hate that he looks good.

Max turns slightly, following my gaze, and the moment he sees Niko, his entire posture shifts—subtle, but not subtle enough for me to miss it. Shoulders still loose, but his eyes tighten. Like he's bracing for something.

Of course he is.

Nikolai Volkov is impossible to ignore even when he's silent. And when he's walking toward you like you owe him something? You don't blink. You don't breathe. You wait.

He stops beside me, close enough that I feel the edge of his jacket brush against my wrist.

"Emilia," he says, calm and unreadable, like this is just another event. Like we didn't sign a contract last night that tethered our names together in the quietest, most suffocating way possible.

I shift half a step back before I can stop myself. "Didn't realize this event was on your calendar," I say coolly.

"I go where I'm needed." Why the hell would he be needed here? Oh right, my father...

"And here I thought I would only have to see you when necessary."

He smiles faintly, pointedly ignoring my sarcasm before looking around the room. "Some would say this fundraiser is ... necessary." He looks back at me and it takes every part of me not to slap him, and he knows it. The son of a gun is playing me at my own game.

I glance sideways at Max. He hasn't said anything. He doesn't need to. He's watching Nikolai with the kind of stillness that says he's not surprised to see him. Not startled. Not curious. Just aware. Familiar, even. And that hits wrong. It lands in the pit of my stomach like a bad headline I haven't read yet.

And then something flickers behind Max's eyes. Not fear. Not guilt. Just calculation. He meets my gaze with that easy expression I've seen dozens of times across lecture halls and coffee shop tables, but now it feels too easy.

So I ask the question. Simple. Direct. A line in the sand. "Do you two know each other?" My finger moves between them.

The air stretches tight. There's a beat of silence. Then another. Niko says nothing. Just watches.

Max shrugs once, like it's not even worth thinking about. "Never met."

147

And something in me rattles. Because I know what I saw. I saw recognition in Niko's eyes. I saw Max's posture change the second Niko entered the room. I felt the weight of it, the way people who've been circling the same secret space always feel when they collide in public.

But Max lies. Effortlessly. Calmly. With that casual, lopsided smirk like he's never held a secret in his life.

And I don't know which part hits harder—the fact that he lied, or how good he is at it.

I let Max's answer hang between us—*Never met*—and maybe I believe him. Maybe I don't. Either way, I don't press. Not because I don't want to, but because in a room like this, pressing too hard gets remembered. And I already know what it feels like to be watched.

So I nod once—slow, almost amused—like I'm not trying to decode the flicker of tension that passed between him and Nikolai like a silent exchange they'd both agreed not to explain.

"Well," I say lightly, lifting my glass in an invisible toast. "This has been quite … enjoyable. I'll see you in class Monday."

Max just dips his chin. No apology. No smirk. Just that low-level calm he always wears when he's withholding something.

But I'm used to people holding their cards too close. I was raised on it.

I step back just enough to pivot toward Nikolai. He's still standing too close. Still watching like he's trying to read something in my expression, something I'm not giving him.

"You clean up," I say, eyeing the lapel of his suit, my voice going down an octave. "Guess this is what Bratva formalwear looks like."

He almost smiles. Almost. "I came to be seen," he says. "Is that a crime?"

I love the way he uses the word crime like that's not the theme of his world. The Bratva are crime incarnate.

"Only to me," I murmur. Because yes, him being here, in my world, is a crime against ME.

His gaze sharpens slightly, not at the words but the edge beneath them.

I don't give him a chance to respond. I turn and head towards the other side of the room, to put some space between me and Nikolai. But I barely make it ten steps before my name is being called, this time in that tone. The one that means I'm being hunted, socially speaking.

"Emilia." Clara's voice cuts through the noise like a blade wrapped in velvet.

I turn and there they are—my girls, my committee, my personal Greek chorus. Clara's in the lead, champagne in one hand, trouble in her eyes. Poppy's grinning like she already knows too much. Sloane's behind them, arms crossed, expression so bored it might be a weapon. Thalia brings up the rear, eyes locked on me like she's already clocked my blood pressure.

Clara doesn't even wait. "Okay. You have approximately three seconds to explain why you were just playing conversation chicken with both of those walking wet dreams."

I blink. "What?"

"Max," she says, like I'm an idiot. "That Max. Comparative Politics Max. Hot, British Max. The man has been the lead character in the Bancroft Ledger gossip column for weeks, and now he's suddenly at this event? Talking to you?"

She says you like she can't believe he would talk to me.

"Comparative Politics isn't that scandalous," I mutter.

"He has cheekbones that could cut federal funding," Poppy says. "That is scandalous."

Sloane lifts a brow. "And then there was the other one."

149

I say nothing.

"You know," she adds. "The one who looks like he kills for fun."

I want to say that he does, I'm sure of it … that's what the Russian mafia does … but that would cause issues for me. So instead I say, "His name is Nikolai." But it's flat and feels wrong on my tongue.

Clara's eyes go wide. "You know his name?"

Thalia makes a soft noise behind me—amusement, I think.

Poppy fans herself with a cocktail napkin. "This is giving Bridgerton but with hotter men."

"He's nothing," I say, reaching for Thalia's drink and taking it without asking. "Both of them. Just random run-ins. Max goes to class. Nikolai … loiters." My life. This place. He's always around when I least expect it.

Clara narrows her eyes. "Random men don't loiter at Capitol Hill fundraisers unless they're paid, planted, or politicos."

"Or," Sloane adds dryly, "you're secretly starring in a very sexy espionage subplot and haven't told us yet."

Wouldn't that be the dream.

That's the thing about these girls. To them, a dream would be marrying a guy who can continue funding their lavish lifestyles. But not just any guy. A hot one. But me? My dream is leaving it all behind. Maybe I'll marry a blue-collar worker. Someone who works hard, who's so far removed from this world they don't identify with either political party.

Thalia tilts her head at me. "You okay?"

I meet her eyes just briefly. She knows. She's the only one who knows. And she's watching me like she's waiting to see if I'll crack. I might.

"Peachy."

She hands me another drink anyway. It's fruity this time. Small mercies.

"Just saying," Clara goes on, "if either of them ends up on the Winter Formal invite list, I want a front-row seat for the fallout."

"I'm not inviting *anyone*," I mutter.

"Girl, you don't have to. They're already orbiting."

I sip slowly, watching the swirl of conversation and money and power spin around us, but my head's still back there with Max lying to my face and Niko watching me like I'm already his. I am, but only on paper. At least... that's what I keep telling myself.

I brush a strand of hair behind my ear and plaster on a smile. One that says I'm fine. Everything's fine.

Let them think it's all just gossip.

Because right now, that's easier than what it might actually be.

-

Waking up before the sun is never my plan. I don't care how disciplined or well-adjusted people pretend to be, if your eyes are open at 5:30 a.m. on a Sunday, and you're not getting paid for it, something's wrong. Because for me? Something is very wrong.

I've been tossing for hours. Staring at the ceiling. Rolling onto one side, then the other. My sheets are twisted around my ankles like I fought something in my sleep. Maybe I did. My own head, most likely. The past few nights keep rerunning like a bad episode, too loud in some places, too quiet in others. Every silence stretched out, every glance sharper than it should've been. Max showing up out of nowhere like it was nothing. Niko just ... there. My mother's expression so neutral I wanted to scream. And the contract. Signed. Final. Done.

I sit up slowly, legs swinging over the edge of the bed. The floor is cold. I don't reach for a robe. I don't do anything except sit there for a minute, palms on my knees, breathing like I'm trying to make oxygen stick.

There's brunch with my mother in a few hours.

Which—no surprise—is not something I'm looking forward to. It's not like I expected a heart-to-heart or an apology last night. But after the Four Seasons? After watching my dad hand me off like a party favor and listening to Alexei Volkov talk about his criminal dynasty like it was a Fortune 500 company? You'd think my mom might say something. Ask how I'm feeling. Offer even the tiniest scrap of humanity.

But no. Nothing.

She didn't speak to me after. Didn't call. Just casually walked out like she didn't watch her oldest daughter get sold off to a Volkov under the guise of "strengthening political ties". She didn't flinch. She never does. And that's maybe the most messed-up part—how normal this is to her. Maybe it is. My grandmother was like this as well. Bless her soul. Not.

I shuffle into the bathroom and catch my reflection. I look like the girl from the Ring. Hair matted. Eyes puffy. Skin pale, lips dry. There's a faint mascara smudge under one eye like the ghost of a girl who was trying to keep it together. I splash cold water on my face until it stings, not because I care how I look, but because I need to feel something other than this … dull, buzzing numbness.

Brunch is at ten at an exclusive cafe. Because of course it is. White linens, fresh tulips, servers who refill your water before you realize it's low. It's one of her places—the kind of restaurant where everything is staged but acts like it's effortless. The food will be overpriced and underwhelming. The conversation? Barely there. If we talk about the fundraiser, it'll be in soft compliments. If she brings up

Nikolai, I'll know it's strategic. If she doesn't, I'll know it's worse.

I towel off my face and dig through my closet. I pass the blush-toned sweater dress she once complimented, the cream blouse she bought me after I got accepted into the Policy Honors program, and instead I grab my oldest pair of jeans— soft from wear, frayed a little at the hem—and a long-sleeve black tee that's fitted but not fitted enough to look like I tried. I pull my hair into a clip. No makeup, just some balm and a swipe of something vaguely moisturizing. My gold, chunky hoops are the only thing that stay. She hates them, as they look way too casual.

Good.

Let her comment on it.

I sit down on the edge of my bed, phone in hand, but I don't check my messages yet. Don't want to see if Max texted. Don't want to check the Bancroft Ledger, or worse, my father's name in headlines. I just sit. Staring at nothing. Breathing. Trying to hold myself steady.

Because in three hours, I have to walk into a restaurant and pretend like I'm not furious. Like I'm not scared. Like I'm not still trying to figure out when I stopped being a person and started being a transaction.

And my mom?

She'll order coffee and something poached, like nothing ever happened.

-

Three hours later…

I didn't even bother with my hair.

What's the point?

It's barely 10 a.m. on a Sunday, and I'm heading into battle disguised as brunch—not the fun kind with bottomless mimosas and girls in floppy hats pretending to love each

153

other for Instagram. No, this is the Langford kind. The table-for-two with my mother, where the eggs are dry, the knives are metaphorical, and everything is said with a smile that doesn't quite reach the eyes.

The place is tucked off a side street near Dupont, all smoked glass and gold-trimmed signage, one of those "power brunch" spots where senators take their mistresses under the pretense of campaign strategy, and interns accidentally overhear classified information while refilling oat milk lattes. The kind of place where brunch costs more than my monthly coffee budget, and you're expected to know which fork to use even if you're just ordering a buttery croissant.

The hostess gives me a once-over like I've tracked mud onto the marble floors, her nose wrinkling at my jeans, and I'm tempted to tell her it's designer just to watch the twitch of panic behind her eyes. I don't, though. I let her assume I'm lost. Maybe a staffer. Maybe a mistake.

Then I drop the name.

"Langford. She's already here."

And just like that, the wind shifts. Her spine straightens. Her eyes widen. And suddenly I'm not the girl in casual wear anymore. I'm Emilia Langford, Daughter of the VP of the United States, Bride of Bratva Promises, Political Princess with a crown she didn't ask for and can't return.

She guides me through the dining room with the nervous energy of someone who's been told never to screw up in front of old money. The crowd is exactly what I expected: D.C. wives with weekly Botox appointments, campaign advisors nursing three-hour hangovers in linen button-downs, Ivy Leaguers in pastel polos arguing about global ethics while sipping imported tea they didn't brew themselves. Every table smells like fresh hollandaise and alcohol.

And there she is.

The Arrangement

Veronica Langford, queen of composure, sitting in the far booth like she owns the place, which, in a way, she probably does. Her blouse is cream, of course. Silk, pressed within an inch of its life. Not a hair out of place, not a wrinkle in sight. Her nails are that perfect, glossy shade of non-threatening pink. The kind rich women wear when they want to appear neutral, like emotional Switzerland in a world full of screaming opinions.

Her eyes flick up when she hears my name. One quick glance. Not enough to betray anything real. But just enough that I see it, the slight, involuntary flinch. She doesn't rise. Doesn't greet me. She just folds her menu and says, with all the warmth of a snowstorm, "You look comfortable."

I slide into the booth across from her, cross my arms lazily over the table, and shrug. "Thanks. This is what normal people wear."

Her expression doesn't crack. She just picks up her water, takes a sip, and says nothing. But I can feel it. The disappointment radiates off her like heat from a stovetop. She's probably mentally dressing me in something with pearls right now. Probably wondering how I turned out so uncooperative when she spent years shaping me into something presentable.

The waiter appears, chirpy and fake smiling like he's auditioning for a toothpaste commercial. My mother orders egg whites, no butter, no cheese, side of fruit, black coffee with almond milk. I ask for the flakiest, butteriest croissant on the menu and a cappuccino with extra foam. I say "extra foam" just to see her eyelid twitch. It does. Extra calories for the win.

She waits until the waiter's out of earshot before speaking.

"The Capitol fundraiser went off without a hitch, don't you think?"

I shrug, already tired of the performance. "Sure."

"Emilia."

I look at her, deadpan. "What do you want me to say, Mother? That it was magical? Flawless? The glittering crown jewel of elite D.C. society?"

She doesn't respond, but the purse of her lips says plenty. I keep going.

"You should give me credit, honestly. I was handed a contract that basically said sign here to surrender your entire life, and I didn't throw my drink on anyone last night. That's progress."

She exhales slowly through her nose—that tight, measured kind of breath that says she's counting to ten behind her eyes, trying not to crack her face open in public.

That's the thing about my mother. She doesn't do emotional. Not in public. Not in private, either, unless you count the time she got misty-eyed when we toured the Reagan Presidential Library. She's been playing the role of Political Wife for so long I don't think she remembers how to take the costume off.

"You'll adjust," she says finally, like it's just another wardrobe change. Just another event to prep for.

I stare at her. Let the silence thicken between us like syrup.

"I'm sorry, are we still pretending this is normal?"

Her lips tighten, but she doesn't rise to the bait. That's her game. No one gets to see her sweat. Not even me.

"I didn't know," she says quietly. "Not until the ink was already dry."

I don't know whether to believe her. But I want to. That's the worst part. I want to.

"Then why show up?" I ask. "Why stand there while Dad bartered me like I'm a condo in the Hamptons?"

She pauses, eyes trained on the silverware. When she speaks, her voice is almost too soft. "Because I've done it too, Emilia."

That makes me freeze.

"I was barely twenty-two when my father told me I'd be marrying a Langford," she says. "I didn't love him. I didn't want him. But I understood the assignment. I knew the kind of life I was being handed."

I stare at her. Not because I'm shocked, but because she's never said anything like this before. Ever.

"You think that makes it better?" I ask.

She lifts her gaze to mine. "No. But it means I understand what it takes."

"What it takes to do what? Be miserable and quiet for the rest of my life?"

She doesn't answer. She doesn't have to. The silence is the answer.

I sit back, the weight of it crashing over me like a second skin. My cappuccino arrives. I don't drink it. She picks at her fruit. Doesn't eat it. And for a long stretch of time, we just sit there in that shared, suffocating understanding that this is the path carved out for us, and heaven help the girl who tries to leave it.

Then, as the check lands between us, she reaches for her purse and says, cool as ever, "At least he's good-looking. You could do worse."

I almost choke. Because she said the exact thing the night I signed the contract.

"You're joking."

She shrugs, all nonchalance. "It helps."

I laugh, not because it's funny, but because the alternative is screaming. "He's the Russian fucking mafia, Mother."

"Language," she replies, like that's what worries her the most. My language. Not the fact that I'm being forced into bed with an international criminal.

And that's it.

That's the exact moment I know.

We are not the same.

-

A heavy knock startles me awake, the soft spill of golden light cutting across my face from the blinds. I push myself up slowly, the throw blanket tangled around my legs, hair stuck to the side of my face, skin warm from sleep that I hadn't planned on but clearly needed. The knock comes again, louder this time, followed by a voice I know better than I know my own reflection.

"Emilia?"

It's Thalia.

I groan, grab my phone off the nightstand. 6:47 p.m. Crap. I must've passed out after brunch with my mother—a brunch that sucked every ounce of energy out of me and left nothing but a simmering headache in its place.

I shuffle to the door barefoot and swing it open. Thalia stands there with a brow raised, wearing an oversized hoodie and a smirk that says she's been up and functioning for hours, unlike me.

"You missed the dinner call. Clara's threatening to submit a catering order form in Comic Sans just to make a point," she says. "Get your pretty little butt up."

"Ugh," I mutter, grabbing a hair tie off my dresser and looping it around the mess on my head without checking the mirror. "Comic Sans is a hate crime."

We make our way downstairs to the dining room, the scent of garlic and butter meeting us halfway like a soft ambush. The table is packed. Over a dozen sisters seated, half-eaten bowls of pasta in front of them, and a bottle of something sparkling, that's definitely not from our budget, being passed around like communion wine.

"There she is," Clara says with her usual brand of passive-aggressive cheer. "Nice of you to join us, Langford. We were beginning to think you died."

158

"I did," I reply, dropping into the open seat between Thalia and Sloane. "But I came back for the food."

Marist snorts into her water. Poppy nudges a bowl of salad in my direction.

We're mid-passing of the breadbasket when Clara slaps her hands down on the table. "Okay. Halloween party talk. Let's go."

"We already decided on masquerade," I say, not looking up from my plate. "Unless someone's here to argue with the woman who coordinated last year's Great Gatsby soirée and kept Sloane from setting the table linens on fire."

"That was one time," Sloane mutters.

"Still. A point stands," Thalia says, tossing a crouton into her mouth. "We're not debating theme again."

Poppy pulls out her phone. "We've got three confirmed vendors for lighting and masks, and SAE says they're handling alcohol and the DJ."

"As long as the DJ knows how to mix string instrumentals with Cardi B," Marist adds, deadpan. "Mood and mess."

Clara, in typical Clara fashion, opens her iPad and starts scrolling through the shared planning doc. "Budget's locked. Guest list capped at three hundred. No plus-ones unless you're screwing them or they're verified on social."

"Same policy as rush week," Tinsley says, like it's gospel.

"I'm going red," Ava pipes up. "Like full velvet, dramatic as ever. I want to look like the villain in a Shakespeare play."

"You always look like the villain," I say, sipping my water. "This is just themed now."

Laughter rolls down the table. The kind that says we're used to poking fun and being poked at. Everyone here knows how to take it, give it, twist it into something worth remembering.

"Any chance we don't use that weird signature cocktail recipe from last year?" Sloane asks. "I still can't drink anything with elderflower without gagging."

"Noted," Poppy says. "We'll pivot to blood orange and champagne. Better color. Less floral vomit."

I lean forward just enough to make myself heard. "Everyone needs a mask. No cheap glittery stuff. If I see a single bedazzled Amazon impulse buy, I'm pulling your drink tickets."

Clara points her fork at me like she's proud. "That's the spirit."

"Also," I add, glancing around the table, "if you're planning to bring someone, let me know. We're not repeating last year's incident where some freshman guy in a Rick and Morty costume threw up on the staircase."

"I still have the shoes I wore that night," Thalia says with a grimace. "Haunted."

The talk continues—dates, decor, playlists. Someone floats the idea of fog machines. Someone else wants a tarot reader in the corner. Clara shoots them down with a glance that says this isn't Coachella, it's a Chi Omega event. Every choice, every detail, every RSVP matters. As the planning drifts into debate, I settle back in my chair, watching it all unfold.

These girls—dramatic, entitled, ruthless, loyal—they're my circle, for better or worse. And as much as I've spent the last forty-eight hours feeling like my life is spiraling into something I didn't choose, here, in this room, I still have some say. I still run the show. And come Halloween?

They'll see exactly why Emilia Langford isn't just a name on a donor list.

She's the one who writes it.

Chapter 8

Emilia

The rest of October flies by in a blur of business. Between classes, midterms, and planning the Halloween party—which, let's be honest, has officially morphed into a full-blown masquerade soirée—I'm convinced I need a vacation. And probably a wine subscription. Definitely the wine subscription.

I've been very intentionally ignoring Niko and Max since the Capitol Fundraiser. Just because I'm contractually obligated to marry him doesn't mean I'm going to play nice. Because I won't. And he can choke on that silence for all I care.

Last weekend, I dragged Thalia, Ava, and Poppy out of the house for what I claimed was "fresh air". What I actually did was haul them to my little sister's soccer game in Virginia. Thalia was fine with the spontaneous detour—she likes chaos when she's not the one causing it. Ava and Poppy? Slightly less enthusiastic about spending their Saturday on a field surrounded by people who think wine is only for "special occasions". Blasphemers. I had to promise them a spa day after just to get them to shut up in the car.

Coach Noah was there again. I kept it polite. A little more reserved than last time. Not that he noticed, which is probably for the best. I'd hate for his picture to show up in the news tomorrow morning. Missing.

Most of my days have been spent at the library, head down, buried in my laptop, trying to drown out thoughts of murder. Or maybe just dismantling the system one corrupt institution at a time. That feels more doable. Less messy.

The library is quieter than usual for a Monday evening, but that doesn't mean it's peaceful. The low hum of laptops, the occasional rustle of pages, and the too-loud whispers from a study group in the back corner all blend together into the kind of background noise that's just irritating enough to keep me from completely zoning out. I've taken up my usual table near the window, the one with the best light and the least foot traffic, and I'm three pages into outlining my Comparative Politics notes when I hear a familiar voice.

"Well, well. Fancy seeing you here, Langford."

I don't even have to look up to know it's Wells Ballard.

I sigh through my nose, not bothering to hide it. "Wells."

He slides into the seat across from me without asking, wearing that stupid grin that's probably gotten him out of three cheating scandals and into at least five networking dinners.

"You always this friendly, or just for me?"

"Just you," I say, flipping a page. "Feel special?"

"I do," he says, unfazed. "Listen, I didn't want to bother you—"

"Then don't."

"—but I was wondering if I could borrow your notes from last week's lecture? Professor Layton was going off about Rousseau and I was … mentally elsewhere."

I glance up, arching a brow. "You mean hungover."

He shrugs. "Details."

I slide my notebook toward me, hand covering the top page. "I'm not your personal scribe, Wells."

He leans in slightly, smile still intact. "Come on, Langford. You're the smartest person in that class, and I'll owe you."

"You already owe me," I say. "For the time you copied my discussion points and presented them like they were your own."

"I gave you credit after the fact."

"On Snapchat."

"Still counts."

I roll my eyes and push the notebook toward him. "You have 48 hours. Don't spill anything on it."

He flips it open like he just won the lottery. "You're an angel."

I ignore his comment.

There's a beat of silence before he casually says, "So ... big Halloween party this Friday."

I narrow my eyes. "You mean the one Chi Omega and SAE are co-hosting?"

He nods, trying to look casual. "Yeah. Sounds like it'll be a good one. Masquerade, right?"

"Right."

"Any chance it's open invite?"

I raise an eyebrow. "You're fishing."

He puts a hand to his chest, mock-offended. "I would never."

"You're literally fishing. This is bait. And bad bait at that."

He grins. "Can't blame a guy for trying. Rumor is... it's going to be ... elite." He makes a gesture with his hand.

"Rumor's correct."

"Any chance you'll be wearing something scandalous and mysterious?"

"Any chance you'll be leaving now?"

He laughs, hands up in surrender. "Alright, alright. I'll see you Friday?"

I give him a non-committal shrug. "Depends on whether you return my notes in one piece."

"Deal."

And just like that, he's gone—notebook in hand, grin still intact, and every part of him smug with the illusion of winning.

I shake my head and return to my outlining, already regretting every second I just gave him. And knowing without a doubt he's not getting into the party. Not on my watch.

-

The ceiling is the same shade of off-white it's always been, but tonight it feels closer somehow, like it's pressing down on me in slow increments, daring me to acknowledge that I can't breathe as easily as I used to. I've been lying here for hours, not really sleeping, not really thinking, just existing in the limbo between fury and numbness. Every time I close my eyes, I see him—Nikolai—with that calm, unreadable expression and that voice that could slice through steel without raising its volume. And every time I open them again, I remember that I'm not free. Not really. Not anymore.

I roll onto my side, the sheets twisted around my legs, hair sticking to the back of my neck. My phone vibrates softly on the nightstand, and I reach for it like I always do—a reflex, a habit I haven't been able to break even after everything. It's not the group chat. Or Max. Of course it's not. He hasn't reached out, hasn't tried to explain, hasn't said a word since the fundraiser.

No. This message is from someone worse.

Mother: *Which do you prefer? White peonies with garden roses or white lilies with lavender sprigs?*

Attached are two images, filtered and manicured within an inch of their lives. The first is delicate, romantic—soft blush against ivory, like a bridal catalogue ad made sentient.

The second is colder, more sterile, the kind of arrangement you'd see at a politician's funeral or the lobby of a high-end divorce attorney. I stare at them for a full minute, trying to decide which one pisses me off more, and then type a reply with fingers that feel heavier than they should.

Me: *For what?*

The dots appear immediately. Of course she's waiting. She's always waiting, like a spider perched in the corner of a perfect, curated web.

Mother: *For your engagement party, of course.*

There's no "Just kidding." No "I hope you're excited" or "Let me know what you think". Just another decision already made for me. Another line drawn around me like a cage, pretending to be a ribbon. The words hit harder than I expect, not because they're surprising, but because they aren't. This is how it works. This is how it's always worked. My mother doesn't ask questions. She issues directives. She doesn't offer comfort. She offers logistics.

I drop the phone face-down on the comforter, grab a pillow and quietly scream into it.

And I wonder, not for the first time, what it would feel like to set it all on fire. To burn it all down— the pedigree, the alliances, the perfectly constructed web of power and proximity I've been raised to worship.

I flip the phone back over and stare at the lock screen. My reflection stares back in the dark glass.

And I think *screw this.*

I don't know what I'm looking for. Not exactly. But I know *who* might help me find it.

Knox.

I haven't seen him in months. Not on a campus at least.

I didn't know at first.

Knox was just … there. Part of the background noise that came with Thalia spending every waking second at my house. Her parents were breathing down her neck about her major again, asking if she was *done playing psychologist yet,* so she camped out in our kitchen like she paid rent, and Knox trailed along behind her.

He wasn't loud or flirty or trying to get my attention. He just kind of existed. Always around. Always on his laptop. Didn't say much unless he had something clever to drop into the conversation, which he usually did.

At first, I figured he was just one of those too-smart-for-his-own-good types. The ones who take apart printers just to see how they work or who somehow knows your SAT score even though you never told them.

But then things started to stand out. Little things. He never asked for the Wi-Fi password. His phone was jailbroken or whatever the term is now. He'd scroll past things on Twitter that hadn't even hit the news cycle yet. Once, Thalia joked about digging up dirt on a professor and Knox just said, "Too easy" and pulled up the guy's LLC filings.

He never called himself anything—not a hacker, not a genius, not even particularly interested. But I paid attention. Because it's what I do.

So when I walked into my dad's office and found him sitting at the desk, eyes locked on the monitor, fingers moving fast, I didn't need to ask what he was doing.

He was in.

I didn't raise my voice. Didn't ask questions. Just leaned against the doorframe and waited.

He looked up, tried to play it casual. Said he was curious. Just poking around. Called it "research". Something about a paper.

I didn't say a word. Just tilted my head. Gave him the look my mother taught me—the one that says I know what you're doing. Keep lying. I dare you.

He didn't. He closed the laptop. Quickly. Said nothing else.

And he knew—right then—that I could've ruined him.

But I didn't.

I just told him to stay out of my father's files. And to answer the phone when I called. Because eventually, I would. And when I did, he wouldn't get a choice.

Well. It's eventually.

I unlock the phone. My thumb hesitates over his name in my contacts. I haven't messaged him since March, but I never deleted his number. And maybe that says more than I want to admit.

I tap the message bar and type.

Emilia: *I need to talk. You still around?*

The typing dots appear almost immediately, like he's been waiting.

Knox: *Depends who's asking.*
Emilia: *Don't play cute. You owe me.*
Knox: *Thought you forgot about me.*
Emilia: *I don't forget anything. Especially not debts.*
Knox: *Same place. Tonight?*
Emilia: *No. Tomorrow.*

He doesn't argue.

Knox: *5PM. Don't be late. I'll send you the location.*

I stare at the screen a second longer, then kill the conversation and throw the phone back onto the bed like it burns. I don't know what I'll find when I talk to him, but I know what I'm hoping for—leverage. Answers. Proof that I'm not losing my mind. That this isn't just about an engagement. That there's something bigger at play.

But before that, before I can unravel this whole thing, there's tonight. The Halloween party. The appearance. The illusion. The version of me that still plays the game well enough to be invited back.

There's a knock on the door, and then Thalia pushes it open without invitation, a mask already placed across her eyes and a pair of heels slung over one shoulder.

"Time to get slutty, Madam President," she grins. "Halloween waits for no woman."

I don't move. Not at first, because even with everything going to hell in a handbasket, I still have a role to play.

Still have a mask to put on.

I sit up slowly, the weight in my chest coiled tight, and glance at the closet like it might give me permission to disappear.

Then I force a smile. "Let's raise some spirits," I mutter, clapping my hands together.

And for tonight, at least, I pretend.

But tomorrow?

Tomorrow, the unraveling begins.

I take one last look at my phone, still lit up with texts I have no intention of answering, and toss it face-down on the bed like I'm doing us both a favor. The buzzing stops. Coward.

Down the hall, the Chi Omega house is a circus on fire. Perfume clouds linger like battle smoke, glitter dusts the floors like someone assassinated Tinkerbell, and there's at least one scream every five minutes that has nothing to do with actual distress and everything to do with someone stealing a hair straightener.

It's Halloween. It's a masquerade. It's our biggest event of the semester co-hosted with Sigma Alpha Epsilon and held off-campus at some historic venue that looks like it was stolen from a movie set and doused in dry ice and overpriced cocktails. And as sorority president, I'm supposed to be thrilled. I'm supposed to be the picture of composed excitement.

But mostly, I feel like I'm suiting up for battle. Again.

The bathroom looks like Sephora exploded and nobody survived. Clara's on the counter in a satin robe, gluing on lashes while scrolling Instagram with one hand and messaging someone with impressive speed. Tinsley's sitting on the closed toilet, curling her hair and sipping straight from a mini champagne bottle like it's hydration. Ava's halfway through reapplying her eyeliner for the third time, and Marist is storming in and out, accusing everyone of stealing her necklace—again.

I catch my reflection in the mirror—makeup set, dark brown hair pulled back into a high pony, the dress fitting like a glove. The green velvet mask sits by the sink, still deciding who I'll be tonight.

Thalia appears in the doorway like a queen entering her court, already dressed, already glowing. She tosses a look my way. "Car's here."

"Let me guess," I retort. "Black SUV? Government plates? A driver who looks like he kills people for sport and has strong opinions about breakfast cereal?"

Her hesitates, "Keller's pacing. So … yes."

Keller. My ever-loyal, ever-furious agent who treats my social life like a war zone and my friends like potential assassins. He's probably already cursing me out under his breath for making him wait. Again.

I slip into my heels, smooth the front of my dress, and grab the mask. "Should we roll out before he has an aneurysm or after?"

"Let's keep him on edge," Thalia says sweetly. "Makes him feel alive."

We head downstairs, heels clicking like warning shots, and as we push open the front door, there he is. Keller. Dressed in his usual black suit with a comm in his ear and a permanent scowl like joy personally offended him once in 2007.

"Ladies," he greets us without looking at any of us directly, eyes still scanning the street like a sniper's about to take us out between the rose bushes.

"Aw, you wore your 'I hate fun' face," I chirp as I slide into the back of the SUV. "How festive."

He doesn't reply. He never does. Probably because he's contractually obligated not to tell the Vice President's daughter to go to hell.

Inside the car, the seats are still warm from my earlier rendezvous, the partition already up because Keller has a very low threshold for girl talk. I sprawl across the back like the reluctant royal they've made me, Tinsley immediately pops open another mini bottle and holds it out like a toast.

"To making memories."

"To questionable decisions," Clara adds, sipping something suspicious and neon.

"To the fact that Emilia's being escorted to a college party like she's headed to a NATO summit," Ava mutters, raising an eyebrow in my direction.

I lift my bottle. "May the ghosts be hot and the drinks stronger than my self-restraint."

Laughter cracks through the car, loud and wicked and familiar.

Outside, D.C. glows like it's ready for mischief. Inside, I shift the mask over my eyes and lean into the night like it owes me something. Because if I'm going down this path—tangled in secrets, politics, Bratva shadows, and an engagement I didn't ask for—I might as well look good doing it.

And maybe, just maybe, make a little trouble of my own.

-

The town car slows in front of the gate, black and glossy and conspicuous in a way that makes my skin crawl, not because I'm embarrassed, but because I already know what it looks like to everyone else. A girl in a designer gown stepping out of a government-issue sedan, escorted by a man who looks like he's here to intercept a foreign dignitary, not drop off a twenty-one-year-old at a college masquerade. I can already feel the eyes tracking the windows from inside the venue, whispering guesses, half-truths, assumptions. They don't need to guess for long.

Everyone already knows who I am.

I've never hidden it. Not when I was the daughter of a diplomat, trailing behind my father in Paris and Prague and St. Petersburg. Not when I was the senator's daughter, shaking hands at campaign fundraisers and pretending to like chocolate chip cookies at county fairs. And definitely not now as the Vice President's daughter, where every move I make feels less like a choice and more like a headline waiting to happen.

Keller steps out first. He doesn't scan the sidewalk dramatically or make some show of checking for snipers on the rooftops—that's not his style. He's calm, methodical, quiet. Like always. He's already given the all-clear by the time he opens the door for us, and I step out last, heels clicking against the pavement, gown fanned around me like armor spun from green satin and frustration.

"Ma'am," Keller murmurs, nodding once like we're in a briefing room instead of on a cobblestone street outside a masquerade venue.

I shoot him a look. "Keller, we've been over this. If you call me 'ma'am' again, I'm going to start calling you Mr. Buzzkill in front of your boss."

He doesn't smile, not with his mouth, but his eyes twitch at the corners, and that's enough. "Copy that," he mutters.

Behind me, the girls are already filing out. Clara adjusts her thigh slit like she's about to enter a ballroom scene, Poppy mutters about her clutch being too small for her perfume, Sloane checks the angle of her mask in the town car's window reflection. Tinsley fights with her heel strap, cursing softly under her breath. All of us glitter like something mythic under the moonlight. Like this isn't just a college party, but a coronation.

We walk the half block to the gates by choice, not because the car couldn't get closer but because I wanted this moment. To see it. To take in what we've pulled off. Months of planning, hundreds of group texts, more committee meetings than I care to count—it all led to this. And now, standing just outside the entrance, I finally let myself breathe it in.

The venue's an old estate turned private club with ivy climbing the stone walls, wrought iron archways threaded with golden lights, and trees lit from beneath like they've been dipped in honey. A soft bass thump hums from somewhere deeper inside the courtyard, warm and low, like a heartbeat. Everything looks exactly the way we planned it, just elevated. Like the space rose to meet us.

Chi O's been working on this since September. We picked the theme, the venue, the guest list. We booked the lighting team ourselves. Oversaw the bar licenses. Approved every detail from the color of the cocktail napkins to the playlist playing through those speakers. This wasn't just about throwing a party. It was about setting a tone. Raising the bar. Reminding this school—and every handsy frat boy in it—that Chi Omega runs things. We're not here for attention. We are the attention.

Clara falls into step beside me. "You're sure you don't want a security tag or something? Just in case some drunk poli-sci major tries to propose?"

"If anyone proposes to me tonight," I mutter, "I'm legally allowed to set them on fire."

Tinsley catches up, laughing. "Honestly? You'd look good doing it."

Keller clears his throat behind us, just loud enough to remind me that he's still there, still watching.

I glance back at him, smirking. "Don't worry, Buzzkill. I'll keep my arson hypothetical."

"I didn't hear anything," he replies, rolling his eyes.

That's the thing about Keller. He plays his role well, but he doesn't treat me like glass. He knows I'm not just a politician's daughter or some legacy brat with too much money and not enough sense. He watches, protects, assesses, but he lets me lead, which is more than I can say for most of the men in my life.

We hit the gate, and the moment we step inside, it's like walking into another world.

Velvet masks, darkened corners, champagne towers, low laughter, and whispered names. Everyone looks expensive, anonymous, dangerous in the way you only get to pretend to be when you know who you are underneath it. I let the mask settle over my face, feel the shift in my spine as it clicks into place.

Tonight isn't about being the Vice President's daughter. It's about being the girl who built this night with her own hands—the one they'll all remember when the night fades.

And right now?

I'm ready to be unforgettable.

-

Inside, the party is a fever dream.

The Arrangement

Light spills like melted gold across the hardwood floors, flickering off crystal chandeliers that probably saw the Prohibition and kept its secrets. The air smells like champagne and ambition—heady, sharp, alive. Every inch of the old estate house hums with energy, like the walls themselves are holding their breath.

People are everywhere—dancing, laughing, leaning too close in corners under velvet-draped sconces. Dresses cling like liquid, masks sparkle like secrets, and there's a pulse to the night that thrums just beneath my skin. This is the kind of party we dreamed up months ago in the Chi O dining room, iced coffees in hand and laptops in our laps. The kind that makes you forget things. Or remember them too clearly.

And for one fleeting second, I think I've won. The night is unfolding exactly how we planned—elegant chaos wrapped in designer heels and half-whispered gossip.

I thought I had a moment to breathe. To own the room. Just for a second.

But fate? Fate doesn't give a flying frick about my moment.

Because walking through the grand doors like he's stepping into a war he already won is Nikolai Volkov.

My fiancé. My own personal, six-foot-three problem in tailored black. Cold jaw, cruel mouth, and the kind of energy that silences a room without him ever having to raise his voice. He belongs here like shadows belong to candlelight, carved from the dark, impossible to ignore.

And he looks good. Too good. Dangerous and expensive and irritatingly composed.

My lungs seize. My spine locks. I shouldn't react—holy hell, I shouldn't—but my body betrays me before I can lie to myself. My heart jumps. My stomach flips.

He hasn't seen me yet, which is the only reason I still have control.

So I move—fast. Past the hors d'oeuvres, past the girls at the bar, past the sticky curiosity curling around my ribs. I need to breathe. To regroup. To get my footing before he—

I slam into someone.

Hard chest. Warm hands. That scent—a mix of musk and cedarwood.

"Crap," I whisper.

"We've really got to stop meeting like this." His voice is low, amused, like velvet wrapped around a smirk.

I look up and, of course. Max. Black suit, collar open. His mask is skewed just enough to show the edge of his smirk, and his eyes—blue and amused—don't miss a thing.

I don't even think. Don't wait. I grab his hand. "Dance with me."

It's out before I know I'm going to say it. Fast. Sharp. Like a lifeline thrown into water I'm drowning in.

He blinks, surprised—not at the request, but the urgency in it.

But he doesn't ask questions. He lets me tug him toward the center of the floor, where the lights soften and the music dips into something sultry, something smooth. The bass thrums low, the kind of rhythm that settles in your spine and makes promises it has no intention of keeping.

We slip into the space between couples—not too close, not too far—and I press my palm to his shoulder like it's a tether.

His hand finds my waist. Firm, yet gentle. "Everything okay?" he murmurs, just above the music.

I smile, but it doesn't reach my eyes. "Never better."

He watches me—really watches me—but he doesn't press. He just moves with me, easy, fluid, like we've done this a hundred times before. We haven't.

And for a moment, I forget about the man near the door with the knife-edged stare and the blood-colored past. I forget that Max is hiding secrets from me.

175

But even through all that, I let Max be the distraction I need. Even if it's only temporary.

The music slows into something molten and low, bass-heavy and dripping with heat. My fingers curl lightly into Max's shoulder, my other hand still linked with his, warm and steady, grounding me in a way I didn't know I needed until it happened. His touch isn't demanding. He doesn't steer me, doesn't lead. He just moves with me like he's been waiting to.

His thumb brushes over my knuckles, slow and casual, but it lights up my nerves like a live wire. His breath is close to my ear now, too close. "You sure you're okay?"

I should lie. Say yes. Say something flirty and unbothered. But I'm too caught in the way he's looking at me like I'm not a collection of responsibilities and legacies and titles I never asked for, but a girl worth noticing. Worth holding.

"I don't know," I say honestly.

And for a second, it's like everything else fades—the party, the noise, the weight of my name, even the fact that I'm legally engaged to the Bratva's heir. Max leans in, slower this time, eyes locked on mine, and the tension curls tight in my chest because this moment—this stupid, almost reckless moment—feels dangerous in a way I hadn't prepared for.

And then someone taps his shoulder. "Can I steal him for a dance?" The voice is breezy. Confident.

Clara. She smiles like she owns the room and probably believes she does. She's glittering and polished, and she looks at Max like he's a free drink with top-shelf appeal.

Max hesitates. I feel it—the weight of the choice—but I'm already stepping back and dropping his hand. "Go ahead," I say, managing a half-smile that doesn't reach anywhere near my eyes.

"Em—"

"I need to hit the restroom anyway," I say, already slipping away. "I'll catch you later."

I don't wait for him to follow. I don't glance back.

The hallway is quieter. Cooler. The bathroom's tucked behind a narrow archway, and I slip inside like it's a chapel and I'm looking for absolution. Inside, I grip the edges of the marble sink, stare at myself in the mirror, and try not to unravel.

The mask comes off first. Then the earrings. Then a deep breath that rattles around in my chest like it doesn't know where to land. My lipstick is still intact, my hair still smooth, but I don't feel pulled together even though I look the part.

Because no matter how hard I try to fake it, how many smiles I paste on, how many dances I choreograph to keep people out of my head, he's still here. Somewhere in this house. Breathing the same air.

Nikolai Volkov.

And I hate that I noticed the exact moment he walked in.

I fix the clasp on my dress, square my shoulders, reapply a quick swipe of gloss, and step out into the hallway.

And freeze.

Because leaning against the opposite wall, one foot braced against the plaster, arms crossed like this is all a game and he's already five moves ahead, is Nikolai. The mask he wore earlier is nowhere in sight. His suit is black-on-black, tailored within an inch of his life. He looks carved. Sharp. Unapologetic.

My stomach flips.

"What, are you lurking now?" I ask, forcing my tone into something biting, flippant. "Very on-brand."

His eyes drag over me slowly, deliberately. "Wasn't lurking. I was waiting."

"For what? Your conscience?"

His mouth twitches. "Funny. But no." He pushes off the wall, the movement fluid, predatory. "I was waiting for you."

The hallway is narrow. The air between us crackles like tension wrapped in velvet. I take one step forward, because I won't give him the satisfaction of backing down.

"Well, here I am," I say. "Let's hear it."

He studies me, eyes like storm clouds over ice. "You're good at pretending, Emilia, but not that good."

I want to curse him out, but I'm too focused on the way he said my name. "Pretending what?"

"That you don't feel anything when I walk into a room."

His words land like a strike across the ribs, and I hate how true they feel. I hate the part of me that still remembers the way he looked in St. Petersburg. The way he said my name like it mattered.

I lift my chin. "You don't get to psychoanalyze me like we're close."

"We are close," he says, stepping in until there's barely a breath between us. "In ways you still don't understand."

I swallow hard. "You knew. You knew about the arrangement. About me. And you said nothing."

"I couldn't," he says, voice lower now. "And if I had … would you have believed me? Or would you have run faster?"

I open my mouth, but no answer comes. Because I don't know. I really don't.

He leans in, his breath brushing the shell of my ear. "You can dance with every guy in this house, Emilia, but none of them will ever know the parts of you I already do." The finality in his voice coils through me, heat gathering low in my stomach. My thighs tense, my breath falters—and for a heartbeat, I let my eyes flutter shut and surrender to the ache of this moment.

But he's gone when I open my eyes. Back to the party, like he didn't just detonate something in my chest and walk away from the wreckage.

I stand there for a full minute, pressing my back against the cool wall and exhale slowly, letting myself feel everything I'm trying not to.

Because Max may be the escape.

But Nikolai?

He's the reason I need one.

-

That day in St. Petersburg? It wasn't just a meet-cute in a palace room. No, it was hours. A whole stolen afternoon, tucked away in some forgotten wing of a Russian estate that smelled like old velvet and power plays. I was sixteen—diplomatic passport, press-blowout, patent leather heels that made my feet ache—and already halfway to jaded. I didn't sneak off looking for anything, really. Just a break. Just a second to breathe without someone watching me like a stock they were waiting to cash in on.

And somehow, fate dropped him in my path.

He was already there when I found the room. Dark coat. Longer hair. A little wild at the edges, like no one had dared tell him how to behave. He was leaning against the window, staring out at the snow like it had wronged him personally.

"You're not supposed to be here," he said, glancing over, bored but curious. That accent—part London prep school, part something older and colder—coiled around the words like smoke.

"Neither are you," I said, refusing to flinch. I was sixteen, but I wasn't stupid.

He didn't smile. Didn't move. Just tipped his head, studying me like I was some kind of puzzle he didn't expect to like. "American," he said, referring to my accent.

"Emilia," I answered, because I didn't want to be known by my last name.

He nodded once. "Nikolai."

No last name offered either.

And we talked. For hours. About things that didn't matter and things that did. Politics. Boarding school. Why people lie even when they don't have to. I told him I hated the opera. He told me he'd broken a kid's nose once at school for calling his mother a whore. We didn't try to impress each other. There was no need.

At some point, I sat cross-legged on the floor, my heels abandoned, legs numb from cold marble. He joined me, his coat still buttoned, like if he took it off, he might unravel too.

"Tell me a secret," I said. "Something no one knows about you. No fake crap."

He didn't blink. Just stared at the high ceiling for a second before saying, "I don't want to be like him."

That was all. But I heard it. Felt it. That quiet, sharp crack of something raw and angry and true.

I could've matched it. Told him something deep. Something real. But instead, I said, "When I was thirteen, I told a Spanish ambassador that Rhode Island was a made-up state. I kept it going for weeks. Even drew him a fake map."

And he laughed, a real laugh. The kind that starts low in the belly and then keeps going until he can't stop.

We left that room with flushed cheeks and something unnamed humming under our skin. And before I disappeared back into the world of polished speeches and diplomatic pleasantries, he said, "Write to me." And then scribbled his address on a napkin. I never stopped to wonder why letters— why something so old fashioned, when a text would've been easier.

But now I understand. The things he confessed, the things he put in the letters—those kinds of things couldn't live on a phone.

So I did. I wrote for a year. Letters mailed to London in thin envelopes tucked with sarcasm and honesty and the kind of truths you only tell people who live far enough away to never use them against you. He always wrote back. Short, careful, always signed Niko.

Until one day, he didn't. No warning. No explanation. Just silence. The kind that feels intentional. Like I should have taken the hint.

And now?

Now, that boy is a man I don't recognize. A man who knew for who knows how long that I was being promised to him like a piece on a chessboard. And said nothing. Now, I look at him—tall, cold, impossibly composed—and I see a stranger wearing the face of someone who used to make me laugh so hard my ribs hurt. Who made the hard days brighter. And yeah, maybe I still feel that crackle in my chest when he walks into a room. But I'm not sixteen anymore. And I don't write letters to ghosts.

-

I didn't see Nikolai again after our ... bathroom encounter. Or maybe I just made a deliberate effort not to. It's hard to say when you've spent the last several years mastering the art of selective awareness. Out of sight, out of mind, right?

But I do see Thalia.

With Sebastian.

Heading up the stairs like it's nothing. Like he's not Nikolai's best friend. Oh yes, I did my own digging on the man in question. London's very own playboy here in D.C.

She catches my eye on the landing—that same pointed look she always gives me when she knows she's about to do something reckless. The look that says don't judge me right before she does something thoroughly unhinged.

181

I don't say a word. Just shake my head slowly. Not because I'm mad. I'm not. But concerned? Absolutely.

Not for her reputation—Thalia has never cared about that. Not even for her heart—she rarely hands that out.

But for her sanity.

Because if there's one thing I've learned from watching Thalia date, it's this: she has a type, and that type is men who smell like expensive bourbon and generational trauma. She goes for walking red flags with yacht money and trust fund delusions, then acts surprised when they self-destruct.

Sebastian's no exception. I just know it.

Chapter 9

Emilia

First thing I notice is how heavy my body feels, like I've been sleeping in someone else's skin.

There's glitter stuck to my cheek, a dull throb behind my eyes, and the faint smell of smoke and something sweet still hanging in the air. I'm just starting to piece myself back together when the door swings open.

Thalia walks in barefoot. Her dress is wrinkled, cheeks flushed, Sebastian's jacket slung over one shoulder like a trophy. Her hair's a mess. Heels hooked on two fingers.

That look on her face? Satisfied beyond measure.

She looks like she had herself a damn good time—and she's not sorry about it.

She pauses when she sees me staring. Before I can open my mouth—not that I had anything to say—she holds up a finger.

"Spare me."

I give her an innocent look. "You're a grown woman."

She smirks. "I am."

She tosses the jacket onto her bed, kicks off the night like it's a pair of shoes, and collapses into the blankets like she's reclaiming territory.

I watch her for a beat. Not because I'm judging—Thalia doesn't do shame, least of all the walk of shame. She walks into fire barefoot and comes out with better stories. She knows the game—knows how to win it, lose it, and still walk out like she meant to.

But Sebastian?

Sebastian's not a game. He's a warning label dressed in fancy clothes and smirks, too close to Nikolai to be anything but intentional, too polished to be harmless. And I'm not naive enough to believe he walked into Thalia's orbit by accident.

I don't say that, of course. She already knows. She knows who he is. She knows what he's connected to. But I also know Thalia. She'll play with the match just to watch it burn, and when it does, she won't flinch. She'll light another.

Instead, I ask, "Fun night?"

She hums, stretching. "Delightfully bad decisions. You should try it sometime."

I roll my eyes. I've had plenty of bad decisions to last a lifetime, though not the kind Thalia means when she floats through the door barefoot and satisfied, wearing someone else's jacket like a wink she doesn't need to explain.

Mine weren't wild or thrilling or worth telling stories about. There was Preston—the only one who ever made it past my walls, the only one I didn't keep at arm's length, the one I let believe he actually saw me. I gave him everything. Not just the soft parts of myself I usually keep buried, but the one thing I'd never handed over to anyone else.

He knew he was the first. I wanted him to. I wanted it to mean something.

And maybe it did, for a minute.

But it turns out being someone's first doesn't stop them from screwing someone else.

He cheated like it was nothing. No drama. No explanation. Just a shrug and a look that told me I'd made it all heavier than he ever meant it to be.

Before him, there were the others—if you can even call them that. A handful of guys with good teeth and slick smiles, all of them a little too eager, a little too rehearsed. They didn't want me. They wanted the idea of me. The access. The shortcut. The last name. They'd flirt like they meant it, then pivot the moment they realized who my father was. What's he like at home? Can you introduce me? And just like that, I wasn't a person anymore. I was a door.

So I stopped letting people close. I learned how to smile without offering anything. How to kiss without caring. How to vanish before things could stick.

Preston was the exception. The mistake. The one I thought might actually be mine. And then he reminded me exactly why I stopped trusting anyone in the first place.

So no, I'm not chasing guys for the thrill of it. I'm not looking to be undone by someone who barely knows my name. Thalia can have her delightfully bad decisions. I had one. That was enough. Or at least, it should've been.

But lately, my mind's been wandering, slipping into places it shouldn't.

Max with the easy smile and the warm hands, who bumped into me the first day of school and actually apologized like a decent human being. Max who remembered my coffee order and sat through Comparative Politics like he gave a crap, who texts like he means it but never pushes, who makes everything feel simple in a way I almost forgot was possible. He makes it feel easy to breathe. Like maybe I don't have to brace myself all the time.

And then there's Nikolai.

Nikolai who was never easy. Nikolai who wears a suit like sin and danger stitched it onto his skin. The boy I met when I was sixteen, who looked at me like he knew how the story would end and wasn't in a rush to get there. He made me feel awake in a way that was all sharp edges and fast heartbeats, alive in a way I couldn't explain, not even to myself.

He used to write me letters. Pages filled with wry jokes and sideways confessions, updates from abroad, little observations only I would understand. I'd read them again and again until the corners curled and the ink smudged. Then one day, they just stopped. No warning. No goodbye. Just silence. Now he's back like nothing ever happened. Like years didn't pass. Like the engagement means something other than control.

I want to hate him. I should hate him.

But my body betrays me every time he gets too close. And my heart—the stupid, traitorous thing—still skips when he says my name. I don't know what's worse: the part of me that still wants answers ... or the part of me that still wants him.

My gaze slides to Thalia's side of the room. She's already passed out, one leg kicked free of the blankets, her hair fanned across the pillow like a warning label that says do not disturb.

I slide back under my own covers, willing myself to sleep for just a little bit longer, but my head's still buzzing. Max, Nikolai, last night—it's like my thoughts have formed a committee and no one knows how to shut up.

I close my eyes, and just as I'm starting to drift, there's a knock at the door. It's so soft I almost don't hear it. But then it comes again. Then a third.

I groan and throw an arm over my face. "Seriously?"

I roll out of bed, careful not to wake Thalia, and crack the door open. Ava stands there, already dressed and annoyingly put-together, holding an envelope.

"This came for you," she says, offering it like it might bite.

I take it without a word, nod, and shut the door.
I crack the seal and slide the paper out.

Your presence is requested at the Volkov estate. 12 p.m.

That's it. No greeting. No signature. No explanation.

I stare at it for a second, like more words might magically appear. I turn it over. Nothing. I check the envelope. Shake it once. Empty.

That tight little pull starts low in my stomach.

Of course it's today.

Not even a full morning's notice. No heads-up, no details, no chance to say I already had plans, even if I did.

Because it's not really a request. It's a schedule. Mine, apparently.

I glance at the time. Just after 9. Three hours to get dressed, pull myself together, and prepare for … what, exactly? I have no idea who's going to be there, what they want, or why they couldn't wait.

My stomach lurches, and I barely manage to slap the letter onto my desk before I'm on the bathroom floor, knees crashing against tile, hand gripping cold porcelain, and everything I didn't want to feel clawing its way out of me.

I vomit hard, like my body's staging a revolt. Like it's finally fed up with me pretending I'm fine.

It's not just the alcohol from last night, though that didn't help. It's the letter. It's the name printed in perfect font. It's them. The Bratva. It's him. Nikolai. Another wave hits, sharp and sour. My throat burns. My eyes sting. My future is trying to crawl out of me.

Behind me, the blankets rustle.

"Em?"

Thalia's voice, rough and sleep-wrecked. A beat later, she's in the doorway. I hear her stop short, then sigh. "Okay, wow."

"I'm fine," I mutter, forehead against the tile. "Totally normal morning. Just casually throwing up my soul."

"Crap," she says, stepping in. "Do I need to call poison control or like ... a priest?"

I tilt my head just enough to gesture toward the desk. "Letter."

Thalia pads over, still barefoot, still wearing last night's makeup like war paint. She opens the envelope, scans the note.

I hear her scoff. "How nice of them."

"Right?" I say, weakly. "No warning. No time to prepare."

Thalia doesn't respond right away. She just stands there, rereading the letter like it personally insulted her. "Holy crap, they really don't waste time," she mutters. "Do you even know who's going to be there?"

"Nope," I say, sitting back against the wall, legs folded, hands shaking slightly. "Could be Alexei. Could be the entire cast of Sopranos: Bratva Edition."

Thalia drops the letter back onto my desk and walks over, crouching in front of me like I'm a bomb she's considering how to disarm. "Look, I could tell you to breathe and that you've got this and all that affirming crap, but instead I'll just say this: throw up, cry, scream into a pillow if you need to. But then you get up, put on something lethal, and walk in there like they're the ones lucky to be sitting across from you."

I let out a bitter laugh. "You should be the one marrying into the mafia."

"Too much commitment," she says, standing and stretching like she didn't just give a TED Talk on emotional warfare. "But I will pick out your outfit, because I refuse to let you show up looking like a hostage."

I groan and press my palms to my face. "This is so messed up. My life is so—"

"Yeah, yeah. You signed your life away," Thalia says cheerfully, already rummaging through my closet. "But you're going. And you're going to look hot. And terrifying. Like if they even breathe wrong, you'll slap them with a lawsuit and a martini glass."

Ha. I'd love to see their faces. Imagine that—me, marching into the Volkov estate with a cease-and-desist in one hand and a vodka soda in the other. To whom it may concern: go screw yourself.

Bratva being sued.

I'd be dead in less than twenty-four hours. Buried somewhere in the wastelands, no body, no news story. Just a missing girl and a quietly erased name.

Gone.

But sure, I'll wear lipstick and pretend I'm the threat in the room.

"Thalia."

She spins dramatically, holding up two sweaters. "Burgundy with the killer neckline, or black and suffocatingly hot?"

I stare at her for a second. "Burgundy."

"Atta girl."

-

Not gonna lie, the thought of the Volkovs having an estate in the U.S., let alone the D.C. area, never crossed my mind.

I always pictured them in Russia, somewhere cold and endless, a stone palace built on secrets and old blood. Something dramatic. Intimidating. Not tucked away in some leafy pocket of northern Virginia.

But apparently organized crime has gone domestic.

I sit in the back seat of a black SUV. Keller's behind the wheel, as usual—stoic, square-jawed, sunglasses on even though the sky's overcast. Ruiz rides shotgun, flipping through something on a tablet like he's bored of chauffeuring me everywhere.

Neither of them speaks. I don't blame them.

I've got one AirPod in, Coldplay coming through loudly. They know what that means. No chatter. No check-ins. Just drive.

The outfit I'm wearing feels stiffer by the minute, like the closer we get, the tighter everything fits. My boots dig in when I shift my legs.

I stare out the window, watching neighborhoods melt into stretches of gated driveways and manicured trees.

My fingers drum once against my thigh, sharp and rhythmic.

I hate not knowing what I'm walking into. I don't know if it's just Nikolai and Alexei or if I'm stepping into a full family lineup. I don't know if this is a test or a trap—or both.

11:47 a.m. Almost showtime.

I glance at Keller through the rearview. He meets my eye for half a second, gives a barely-there nod. Like he's saying, *you've got this.*

Ruiz doesn't even turn around, but I know he's clocked my tension from the moment I sat down. Probably marked the way my jaw's been tight since we left the house.

I exhale slowly, press my palms to my knees. It's just lunch. With people who could make me disappear. No big deal.

My reflection catches in the glass. I don't smile. I don't blink.

-

A man in all black steps forward as the SUV slows to a stop, dressed in tactical gear with a sidearm at his hip and the kind of expression that makes it immediately clear he doesn't like surprises—or company.

His eyes move to Keller and Ruiz, flat and unreadable, but there's a certain edge there, a flicker of something territorial, like he's already decided he doesn't trust them and has no intention of pretending otherwise. The pat-down is aggressive, almost performative, as if he wants them to know this is his perimeter, and they're already standing too close to the wrong line.

When it's my turn, I step out of the car, keep my posture easy, and offer him a small, deliberate smile—not friendly, but not defiant either—just enough to say I'm not here to make trouble unless you are.

He doesn't smile back. Doesn't speak. His gaze drags from the heel of my boot to the slope of my ponytail, slow and clinical, like he's trying to figure out where exactly I fall on the spectrum of threat versus ornament.

And while I'd love to say I didn't care, the truth is, I'm wondering the same thing. I hold the smile a second longer than I should, mostly because I have no idea what else to do with my face when someone with a gun is measuring me like he's trying to guess my price tag.

Before he can say anything—or worse, keep looking—a voice cuts clean through the air behind him.

"That's enough, Lev." A woman steps forward like she's walked this exact line a thousand times before and never once stumbled. It doesn't take more than a second to clock the resemblance: dark hair, sharp features, the kind of posture that says she hasn't been unsure of herself since the cradle.

Volkov, obviously.

Her eyes land on me, and if she's impressed, it doesn't show. There's no warmth in her gaze, no welcome—just a cool flicker of judgment, like I'm a late addition to a guest list she didn't approve.

Her chin lifts, the gesture small but sharp, and her voice is crisp when it finally comes. "Welcome, Miss Langford."

She turns and walks back inside without a word, and for a second, I hesitate, unsure if I'm supposed to follow or wait to be summoned like a dog.

Lev settles that quickly—he snaps out a hand, sharp and silent, a gesture that's not quite a command but leaves no room to argue.

So I move.

I catch up to her just as we cross into the house, stepping into what I assume is the living room, though the space doesn't feel like any version of living I've ever known.

It smells like money. Not new money—old. The expensive kind. Cold marble. Aged scotch. Leather that's been polished so many times it might as well be lacquer. It smells like silence and power and the kind of secrets people kill to protect. The lighting is low and golden, cast from a chandelier that probably cost more than my first year of college.

There are people already seated, and I feel their eyes before I find their faces, the quiet weight of being watched settling into my spine as I step further inside and try not to betray the fact that every instinct in me is screaming to turn around.

Alexei is the first face I find, and it's exactly where I knew it would be—centered, grounded, immovable—his posture straight, his expression unreadable, his smile the same calm, calculated thing he wore the day he turned my future into a transaction and told me I should be grateful.

He nods in greeting, a gesture that feels less like acknowledgment and more like possession. Seated next to him is a man I don't recognize but can't quite look away from, someone whose features stir something uncomfortable at the back of my memory—not recognition, not exactly, but a strange, stubborn feeling that I've seen him before, or maybe someone who looks like him.

And then my gaze finds Nikolai.

He doesn't rise, doesn't offer a greeting, doesn't even tilt his head. He just looks at me, slow and steady, and the moment our eyes meet, it's like the room tightens around us, like something invisible pulls taut and no one else seems to notice but me.

He's dressed simply—black on black, sleeves rolled, posture relaxed in that deliberate way that says he's in control without needing to prove it—and his face gives nothing away, not even the barest flicker of what he's thinking, though I know him well enough to see what isn't being said.

The woman from the door sits next to him. She doesn't bother with introductions, doesn't even offer the pretense of warmth, only a slight gesture toward the empty chair across from her, accompanied by a voice that is perfectly smooth and perfectly dismissive.

"Please, have a seat."

I lower myself into the chair slowly, like it might bite— or collapse or detonate—and out of the corner of my eye, I catch the faintest curve of a smirk tugging at Nikolai's mouth, like he can hear my thoughts in real time and finds them mildly amusing.

I bite the inside of my cheek to keep from groaning.

Then my gaze catches on movement off to the side—a figure sprawled too comfortably in a room this tense, all casual arrogance and unbothered charm—and when I finally look at him properly, he grins like this whole performance was staged for his amusement and I'm the opening act.

Sebastian.

Of course it's him.

He winks. Unapologetically. Like we've been in on this from the beginning. Like I'm already part of the game, and he's just waiting for me to realize I've been playing it blind.

Which, let's be honest—I have.

The Arrangement

I don't know him. Not really. But I know of him. Nikolai's letters painted enough of a picture. The infamous best friend. British. Reckless. Irreverent. The kind of man who sets fires just to see who runs toward the smoke. And damn it, just thinking that makes me realize he's the male version of Thalia.

And the second my face betrays the flicker of surprise, I feel it—that shift, quiet but unmistakable, before I even glance back.

Nikolai doesn't say a word. He doesn't need to. The tension rolls off him in measured waves—the barely-there tick of his jaw, the way his shoulders square, the way his eyes flick to Sebastian and then land back on me, colder now, unreadable, heavier in that way that makes my lungs burn.

I turn back toward the woman across from me—the same woman who greeted me at the door, still composed, still watching—and I wonder if she's finally going to say who she is or if she just assumes I've done my homework.

"I'm Irina Volkov," she says, like the name should carry enough weight on its own. Her gaze never leaves mine, and though her tone doesn't shift, there's something in the way she says it, like she's naming a role in a play I didn't realize I'd been cast in.

I nod once, acknowledging her words, unsure what else to do, and glance briefly at Alexei, then Nikolai, who hasn't moved, hasn't spoken, just continues watching like he's studying the way the air shifts around me.

Irina smooths an invisible crease from her skirt, then folds her hands neatly in her lap. "You must be wondering why we called you here on such short notice," she offers, and the words are said with such calm precision that it takes me a second to realize she's asking a rhetorical question. She pulls out an envelope from behind her chair and hands it to me. She then leans back, folding her eyes and remarks, "We thought it was time you understood what this engagement really means."

My gaze lifts slowly to hers, but I don't speak. Not yet. I want to hear it. All of it. Because it's about time I understood.

"Your marriage to Nikolai is, of course, a union in name," she reiterates. "But in function, it's something much more significant. It's access. Legitimacy. A bridge between two worlds—ours, and the one your father's built behind podiums and press coverage."

Alexei hums quietly, something that might be approval, but otherwise remains silent.

"Now," Irina continues, "we're not naive. We know the Langford name comes with its … complications. But it also comes with reach. And there's no one in your family with more reach than your father."

She looks at me carefully, watching for the first signs of pushback, but I stay still, my eyes pinned to hers.

"We want you close to him," she divulges. "We want his calendar. His meetings. His deals. We want to know what he's planning before he knows it himself."

My mouth parts slightly—just enough to taste the weight of the words—but still, I don't interrupt.

Because what the hell.

"You'll do this quietly," she explains. "Elegantly. He won't suspect. He already trusts you. That's your leverage. You'll smile. You'll play the daughter. You'll listen when no one thinks you're listening." If only she knew that's what I do now.

It's only then that Nikolai finally moves. His gaze meets mine for the first time since I sat down, and I can't read it—not fully. There's no pride in his expression, no sympathy either. Just a quiet, steady pressure behind his eyes that tells me whatever part of this he didn't orchestrate, he still condoned.

A slow, tight breath pulls through my nose. "And if I say no?" I question, and my voice barely cracks, but it does.

Irina smiles, faintly, but there's no humor in it. "You won't." And then she nods, just once, toward the envelope resting on the table in front of me, like she's inviting me to open a door I didn't know existed.

"Because it turns out," she continues, voice as calm and steady as it's been this entire time, "Trent Langford is not your biological father."

For a moment, I honestly think I've misheard her. There's this strange pause in my brain, like the words didn't land right, didn't make sense, didn't belong in this room, and then—before I can stop myself—I let out a quiet laugh. Not because it's funny, not really, but because it has to be a joke. Because she has to be joking. Because the alternative is impossible. Ridiculous. Insane.

But no one else is laughing.

Not Alexei.

Not Irina.

Not Nikolai, who hasn't even flinched.

And as the last shaky breath of that laugh slips from my mouth and dies in the air between us, I realize they're serious.

Deadly serious.

And that's when the sound of it—the truth—finally hits. Not like a slap. Not like a scream. But like a slow, crumbling wall giving way somewhere deep inside me, distant at first, then suffocating.

I blink.

My lips part. Close. Part again.

"You're lying," I say, but the words feel limp the second they leave my mouth, like they're not meant for her—they're meant for me.

Irina shakes her head. Not cruelly. Not smugly. Just like she's sorry I had to hear it this way but not sorry it was said.

"There's a DNA test," she says, voice low. "Trent ran it himself. Years ago. After you were born. He already knew he couldn't have kids the traditional way, not naturally. That's why your sister, Grace, was conceived through IVF." She pauses just long enough for it to sink in, then adds, like it's an afterthought, "Didn't you know?"

The question punches harder than anything else. Because no, I didn't. Of course I didn't. And it's in that moment, that exact second, that I realize just how deep the lie goes. How long they've been keeping this from me. How much of my life was built in the dark.

Across the room, Sebastian's gaze slips away, no longer smiling.

The man beside Alexei watches me with a sadness that confuses me, like he knows what it's like to have something pulled out from under your nose.

But it's Nikolai's silence that stings the most.

Because he knew. They all did.

I look down at the envelope, at the crisp edge of truth folded so neatly inside.

And for the first time, I understand exactly what kind of game I've been dragged into. They're not just asking me to betray my family. They're telling me I was never really part of it to begin with. And that alone should be enough to make me play along—the idea that my anger will tip me over, turn me into one of them. Like rage will turn me loyal. Turn me Bratva. But here's what they don't get: I don't owe my "father" a thing. Not loyalty. Not silence. Not obedience.

I could say no. Could ask for something in return. But the Bratva doesn't do bargaining.

And I'm not stupid enough to find out what happens when someone tries.

-

The SUV pulls away from the curb in front of the Chi Omega house, and I wait until the taillights disappear around the bend before slipping through the side gate without so much as a glance at the wide, glowing windows behind me. I keep my head down, my pace measured, like I'm just another student cutting through the alley for a smoke, not a girl who just walked out of the kind of meeting that shifts the tectonic plates of a person's life. I trade my heeled boots for worn sneakers hidden beneath the shed in the backyard, tie my hair tighter, and shrug on a hoodie that smells faintly of Thalia's perfume and cheap detergent. The Uber arrives on time, just like I planned, and I slide into the back seat without saying a word, the driver too numb to care and too seasoned to ask questions.

As the car winds out of the Greek Row bubble and toward the darker edges of the city, the world begins to shift. Brownstones give way to industrial skeletons, clean sidewalks turn cracked and weeping, and somewhere in the distance, a dog barks behind a fence that hasn't held properly in years. The warehouse we pull up to doesn't advertise itself, doesn't pretend to be anything but what it is—a rusted out, concrete-faced ghost of utility with one blinking light above the door and a keypad that scans your face before buzzing you in. Inside, the air is stale, electrified, tinged with solder and heat and the chemical breath of too many machines stacked on top of each other without care for ventilation.

Knox is already there, right where I knew he'd be—half-hunched over three monitors, sleeves shoved up to the elbows, hoodie wrinkled, and headphones wrapped around his neck like a war medal. He doesn't turn when I enter, doesn't need to; he knew I was coming. We arranged this yesterday, back when this was just about gathering leverage. Before I sat across from a room full of Bratva royalty and found out the man who raised me did so out of convenience, not blood.

He speaks without looking up, voice scratchy from too much caffeine and not enough sleep. "You look like someone stepped on your throat."

"Yeah, well," I mutter, pulling the hood off and dragging a metal chair across the floor, "you should see the people who did it."

That gets a glance, brief but sharp. I drop into the chair beside him, elbows on knees, fingers steepled in front of my mouth. I take a breath. Then another. "I need two pulls."

He finally swivels to face me, blinking slowly like he's rebooting. "Go on."

"First one's the Volkovs. Nikolai. His father, Alexei. A woman named Irina. Dimitri. And someone named Sebastian—British, younger, close to Niko. I want their holdings, assets, shell corporations, real estate portfolios, body counts. I want to know where they hide their secrets and where they dump the bodies."

He whistles, low, long. "So we're skipping background checks and going straight for the jugular."

"They're hiding something. A lot of somethings. And I've been pulled into it without a manual."

Knox leans back, the chair groaning beneath him, and studies me like I'm a line of flawed code. "And the second?"

"There is a man out there who fathered me, a man whose name I don't know, whose face I wouldn't recognize, but whose blood is in my veins. And I need to know who the hell he is."

Knox tilts his head, cracking his knuckles one by one before spinning back toward the keyboard. "Fuck, Langford. You never bring me anything easy."

"I don't need easy. I need the truth."

His fingers begin to move, tapping out strings of code that look like gibberish to anyone else but feel like poetry to him.

"This'll take time. Volkov won't be simple—he's likely insulated six layers deep in front orgs and diplomatic immunity. And ghosts like your dad don't like to be found."

I nod once, jaw set. "I'm not leaving until we start."

Knox doesn't argue. He just pulls up the first firewall and begins.

And for the first time in days, I feel like I'm doing something that matters.

-

Nikolai

The house is quiet now. Eerily quiet. Emilia left a few minutes ago. She didn't say anything. Didn't look at me. Just walked out, her head held high. But I know better. Her mind is spinning, calculating. Like a beautiful storm brewing.

Irina's footsteps echo down the hall, the cadence clipped and clean, like everything about her. She doesn't speak, but I know she's pleased with how it went. Pleased with the precision of the knife she drove between Emilia's ribs with that calm, smiling voice. To Irina, truth is just another weapon in the arsenal. Another tool to keep people small. Predictable. Bendable.

She's heartless, plain and simple—smiles like she's doing you a favor while she tears you apart. And Dimitri? Didn't say a word. Just sat there like a prop while his dead brother's wife ran the whole show. Coward. No wonder Max got out of dodge and went to school overseas for uni. I would've too.

I turn away before she can gloat, before that smug little smile turns into something nastier. I can't look at her and not picture what she might've said to my mother that fateful night—some quiet, cutting thing dressed up as civility, the kind of cruelty that doesn't need to raise its voice to land like a knife. I head down the hall, past walls that try too hard to look important. This place isn't even their real home—just a second house, a stateside front dressed in heavy frames and just enough polish to pass for respectable. The portraits lining the walls are all the same: stern men in suits, eyes too flat, smiles too tight, all of them screaming power without saying a word.

This house was built like a cathedral, but it feels more like a coffin.

My phone buzzes, low and insistent, and I fish it out of my pocket to see Max's name lighting up the screen. I let it ring twice before picking up.

"She's gone," he says without waiting. "Slipped her security, snuck out the back, caught an Uber to some warehouse on the edge of town. No signal inside."

Of course she did.

I drag a hand through my hair, slow, biting back a smile that shouldn't be there. Naughty girl. Always pushing, always testing the limits like she doesn't realize I built the map she's trying to outmaneuver. It's cute. Infuriating. Hot.

Max is still waiting on the other end, like he's not sure if I'm going to lose my marbles or start laughing. Truth is, I'm somewhere in between—because I should be pissed, should be barking orders, spinning this into control again. But instead, I lean back, letting my head tilt just slightly, and stare at the ceiling like it might give me the answer to why the hell she gets under my skin the way she does.

She's clever. Too clever.

And bold.

And absolutely going to get herself neck-deep in something she can't crawl out of if she keeps poking around the way I know she is.

"She inside yet?" I ask, voice low, almost bored.

"Yeah," he says. "No visuals past the door. Place is sealed. She's not answering her phone."

Of course not.

I hum, dragging a thumb along my lower lip, thoughtful. "Keep your distance. Don't let her see you."

Max hesitates—barely—but I catch it.

"She's not your problem," I add, voice going sharp around the edges. "Not unless I say she is." Then I hang up. No goodbye. Because the truth is, she already is my problem. Has been since the moment we crossed paths all those years ago.

I lower the phone slowly, the screen still glowing in my hand, and let my head fall back against the leather. The ceiling above me is cracked in one corner—small, harmless, a flaw that doesn't matter in the grand scheme of things. But now? Now it pisses me off. Just like everything else.

The girl is inside a warehouse chasing shadows, and I'm here, locked in a house I don't call home, choking on secrets and trying not to feel.

Across the room, Sebastian shifts in the chair he's been lounging in like he owns the place. I don't need to look to know what's coming. I can feel his smirk from here—lazy, sharp-edged, cut from the same fabric as every mistake I've made since this mess began.

"Daaamn," he drawls, the word low and almost sympathetic. "She's really in your head, isn't she?"

I say nothing.

He leans forward, resting his elbows on his knees, eyes glinting under the amber light. "I mean, I knew she'd get to you. But this? Watching you spiral in real time? It's honestly better than porn."

I finally turn to look at him, deadpan. "Fuck off, Seb."

He grins, slow and unbothered, like he's been waiting all night for that. Hands lift in mock surrender, but he doesn't back off—he never does. "Relax. I'm not judging," he says, voice dipped in something smoother now. "To be honest, I'd probably be falling apart too if I'd ghosted the girl I used to write love letters to and then found out she's the walking, talking middle finger of fate."

I clench my jaw and drop the phone onto the desk, hard enough to make a point.

Sebastian just whistles again, soft this time. "You didn't tell me she was Petrov's."

I didn't know either. Not until Irina came to me. This doesn't change anything though. Just makes her mine even more. "She wasn't supposed to be anything," I mutter. "Not to me."

"Yeah, well," he says, standing now, stretching like a cat who knows the dog's on a leash, "you're in deep now, brother. And she's not just someone's daughter anymore. She's yours—whether you admit it or not."

I don't respond. Can't.

Because the worst part?

He's right.

-

Emilia

The kitchen smells like cinnamon oatmeal and overpriced coffee grounds someone brought back from the farmer's market. Sunlight's pouring through the windows, soft and golden, the kind of fall morning that makes the campus feel romantic instead of exhausting. Chi O is alive again—not hungover, not crazy—just humming with low-grade energy. Catching up. Resetting. Pretending we're not all sprinting toward the inevitable collapse of Thanksgiving break and December finals.

Ava's perched on the counter, eating dried mango and scrolling through her phone with a scowl. "Is it too early to fake a family emergency so I can skip Friendsgiving?"

"You already said your grandma died this year," Clara calls from the other room.

"I didn't say *which* grandma," Ava shouts back.

I'm at the table with my laptop open and a cappuccino I didn't really want. I've got my planner laid out—neat columns of tasks, color-coded by urgency. I haven't touched any of them.

It's been two days since the Halloween party. Twenty-four hours since I found out that the man who claimed to be my father my entire life isn't actually my father. And less than a day since I walked into a back-alley warehouse and basically committed espionage.

I haven't heard from Knox.

I didn't expect to, not yet. But that doesn't stop me from checking my phone every hour like a psycho.

Across from me, Thalia's grading a stack of peer-review essays for her sociology class. Red pen in hand. Hair twisted up with two pencils. Glasses on. She looks intimidating, focused, effortlessly cool—and somehow still aware of me without even looking.

"Okay," she says, eyes on a paper. "What's with the coffee-stirring aggression?"

I stop stirring. "I'm thinking."

"You're brooding."

"There's a difference."

She finally looks up. "Is this about yesterday's meeting?"

I glance around. The kitchen's full of motion—girls flitting in and out, someone arguing with their mom on speakerphone, someone else in a hoodie labeled "property of SAE" digging through the pantry for Pop-Tarts. It's all normal. Easy.

And I am anything but.

"Kind of," I say.

Thalia raises an eyebrow. "Vague and suspicious. Nice. You working on the agenda for the chapter?"

"Mostly."

"I can finish it if you want."

"No," I say quickly, and Thalia raises an eyebrow. "I need the distraction."

That earns me a longer look, but she doesn't push.

"You know you can tell me stuff, right?" she says. "Like ... real stuff." She emphasizes the word.

I pause. "I know."

She holds my gaze for another beat, then nods and goes back to her papers.

But my stomach is still tight.

Because I do want to tell her. Not everything. Not yet. But enough. Enough to get this thing out of my head before it eats me from the inside. But if I confess everything that's happened over the past twenty-four hours, it becomes real. It becomes bigger.

And right now? I need it to stay quiet. Hidden. Mine.

So I click back into the chapter agenda and pretend I care about the item marked "sweater order deadline".

Across the kitchen, Clara says, "Do we know if we're doing a formal this semester?"

"We never do one in the fall," I answer automatically. "Too close to exams and too many people leave early."

"We could do a chill winter thing," Ava offers. "Like a cocktail night."

Thalia looks up again. "You offering to plan it?"

Ava blinks. "No. Just offering to show up in a backless dress and judge other people's dates."

"Cause that's a normal thing to do," I mutter.

And just like that, we're back to normal.

But my phone buzzes again, and even though it's just a PayPal notification from the t-shirt company, my pulse still spikes.

Because this time next week, Knox could have answers.

And I'm not ready for what I might see, or who I might see.

Chapter 10

Emilia

The lecture hall is freezing, the kind of institutional cold that makes every hoodie and puffer jacket in the room feel like it wasn't enough. Rows of students are draped in fleece, faces buried in laptops, half-listening while Professor Layton walks us through the implications of state sovereignty in regional conflicts.

It's just after 10 a.m. My coffee is already cold. My fingers are moving across the keyboard, but I couldn't tell you what I've written in the last ten minutes.

Because five minutes ago, I got the text.

Mother: *Engagement celebration confirmed. November 21st, 6 PM. Your attendance is not optional. I'll expect you Thursday evening for final fittings. Makeup artist already booked. You'll smile for the camera.*

Just like that. No preamble. No call. Just a command disguised as courtesy and an emoji she probably didn't even pick herself.

I haven't opened the message. I read it on the lock screen and shoved my phone face-down on the desk. But it's still there. Burning. Looming.

Two seats away, Charlotte Kleins sits. Her blonde hair is clipped up in some effortless twist, dark turtleneck tucked into plaid slacks, phone screen glowing just out of view under the desk. She types fast. Glances up. Smiles at Layton like she actually gives a crap about institutional reform, then goes back to texting.

I don't hate her. But I don't trust her either.

We've been in the same rooms since freshman year. Same major-adjacent circles. Same sorority functions, same leadership mixers, same donor events we had to dress up for and pretend we weren't bored to death by. She's always been pleasant. Polished. Calculated to a fault. The kind of girl who throws a birthday brunch at a country club and makes it look like a spontaneous idea.

She doesn't speak to me unless there's a reason.

Today, apparently, there is.

"Nice mask Friday night," she says under her breath, eyes still on her laptop.

I glance sideways.

"Sorry?"

"At the party," she says, tapping her keys like she's not even invested. "You wore that green velvet thing. It was dramatic."

"Thanks," I say tightly.

She pauses. "That guy you were with—he didn't go here, right?"

And there it is.

Not a question. A test.

I don't look at her. "There were dozens of guys, Charlotte."

I can feel the annoyance radiating off her. "The hot one. Tall. Wearing all black."

Ahh, Nikolai. Of course she noticed him. It's hard not to. I don't react, just blow her off with a quick, "Oh him. Yeah."

She waits, as if I'm going to tell her who he is. She looks at me expectantly. I roll my eyes, already done with this conversation, but I give her something. "He's a family acquaintance." I leave it at that.

Charlotte lets out a small, amused breath. "Right. Of course." She turns back to her screen, but the edge is still there. The curiosity. The suspicion.

Because she noticed. Not just me. Him. The way I moved with him. The way I looked at him. And even if she doesn't know who Nikolai Volkov is, she knows he wasn't just another plus-one. Not that I invited him. She knows something is off. And girls like Charlotte? They always come back for blood.

Professor Layton shifts topics—war by proxy, soft power plays, public diplomacy as performance. The irony is almost unbearable.

I pretend to take notes, but my mind is elsewhere.

The engagement party is happening in a few weeks. And I have no idea how to feel about that, or what people will say.

-

The booth at Saiphin Thai is loud and smells like delicious fried basil rice. There's a plate of shrimp rolls no one's touched, three half-empty Thai teas sweating through paper napkins, and Sloane telling a story that has Poppy halfway to losing her ever loving mind.

Sloane picks up her tea and rolls her eyes. "I'm not even kidding. He looked at me and said, 'You seem complicated.' Like that's supposed to win me over."

Poppy stabs at her noodles. "Did you stay or run?"

"I told him he seemed basic and asked for the check."

Thalia laughs. "You're doing the Lord's work."

"He's lucky I didn't forward the transcript to his mom," Sloane says.

Poppy grins and leans toward me, suddenly switching lanes like only she can. "Okay, but speaking of complicated — that guy at the party Friday. Tall, dark, and kind of scary hot? Wasn't he the same guy from the Capitol fundraiser?"

I blink, feigning ignorance. "What?"

"That guy from Friday night," she says. "Tall. Black suit. Quiet. Looked like he probably owns a watch that costs more than my car."

"Definitely didn't go here," Sloane adds. "Had that 'knows how to kill a man in his sleep' type of energy."

I pause with my chopsticks halfway to my plate. "What about him?"

Thalia keeps eating like she hears nothing.

"I just didn't realize he'd be at the party," Poppy says. "I thought he was Capitol-circuit only. Fundraisers. Donor galas. You know—old men in bow ties and strategic seating charts."

"I think he was invited through ... someone," I say carefully.

"So you know him?" Sloane asks, eyes flicking up.

"Kind of," I say, then turn to Thalia. "Pass the fish sauce?"

Thalia slides it over without a word. Her eyes widen as they flick to mine.

Poppy leans back, unconvinced but delighted. "Okay. Just saying. It was giving 'international arms dealer'."

Sloane hums. "Sexy though."

"I'd let him ruin my life," Poppy groans.

"He already ruined mine," I mutter under my breath, then take a sip of tea before anyone can ask me to repeat it.

Thalia coughs to cover a laugh. Poppy squints. Sloane raises a brow.

"Wait, what?"

"Nothing," I say, perfectly cool. "Let's talk about something more fun. Like your thing with the campus security guy."

Sloane gasps. "That was one time! And technically, I was locked out."

"Of your dorm," Thalia adds, "or your dignity?"

"She had his taser in her coat pocket the next morning," Poppy says helpfully.

We all dissolve into laughter again, just like that.

But I feel it. The tension under my skin. The text from my mother still sitting unanswered on my phone. The weight of knowing that in just a few short weeks, they'll all know what they're only hinting at now. That the joke won't be funny anymore when they see the ring, the headline, the man beside me.

But right now? We're still pretending.

And pretending is something I'm very, very good at.

-

The building at Grant and 6th still looks like it's in shambles.

No signage, no working elevator, just three floors of broken fluorescent lights and the kind of smell that says someone, somewhere in this place once tried to hide a body. Typical Knox. He's always had a flair for the post-apocalyptic. Digital savant with the emotional range of a damp napkin. I used to think it was an aesthetic choice. Now? I'm not so sure.

Knox texted me earlier, saying he had some intel for me. I'd be lying if I said I didn't jump up from my bed with glee. Fortunately, Thalia was not in the room when my display of excitement was shown.

The top floor door creaks open before I touch it. That's never happened before. And I don't like it.

Inside, the room's dimly lit by Knox's usual chaos of monitors—all glowing in quiet blue pulses like something alive and watching. Wires snake across the floor like veins. There's a stack of hard drives near the desk, a half-eaten protein bar stuck to the edge of a circuit board, and a long-cooled coffee cup someone should've thrown away weeks ago.

Knox is seated like always, hoodie up, back hunched, typing like the world's about to implode, which, at this point, wouldn't surprise me. But he's not alone.

There's a man standing in the corner, facing away from the monitors. Early forties maybe, lean but built like he trains for stress. He's wearing a navy blazer that's definitely tailored and boots that look way too worn. His hands are in his pockets. His posture is still. And from the second I step into the room, he's watching me like I'm a threat.

I glare at him before I even realize what I'm doing.

Knox doesn't even look up. "You bring the burner?"

"Yeah," I mutter, already on edge. "Want to tell me why this feels like the opening scene of a Netflix limited series?" I toss the burner phone onto the desk and nod toward the stranger. "Who is this?"

The man turns just enough to meet my eyes—no expression, just steady, predator-calm.

"Agent Rhys Mercer. FBI."

I stare at him.

Then at Knox.

Then back to Mercer.

"...You brought the feds into this?"

Knox finally peels his eyes from the screen, stretching his neck like he's just now realizing I might be pissed. "Look, I wasn't planning to. But I found something. Something I couldn't handle alone."

"Oh, really?" I say, jaw tight. "And what part of 'please help me dig into this screamed, 'bring in the FBI'?"

"I didn't do it for fun," Knox snaps, unusually sharp. "This isn't like when I hacked your father's files, Emilia. This is ... different. Bigger. Dangerous. I ran your guy's name, Volkov. I traced it. And it didn't just lead back to him."

The word father has me staggering a bit.

He flicks his trackpad, and a screen lights up. A web of shell corporations, wire transfers, legal entities. Some of the names I recognize—vaguely—from political fundraisers and trust documents I wasn't supposed to see. Others I don't. But I see the pattern.

At the center?

Langford Family Holdings.

My father's name. Or shall I say, Trent Langford's name.

Over and over and over again.

My stomach does a slow, cold flip.

Knox clicks again. A folder flashes on the screen.

Project Daggerfall.

"Encrypted six layers deep," he says. "It took everything I had to even peek at the metadata. It's Langford-signed. It's routed through a Volkov proxy firm. And it's buried under layers of national defense paperwork I'm not even legally supposed to know exist."

I stare at it. The folder. The connections.

Everything in me stills.

Knox keeps talking, too fast now. "I didn't know it would go there. I just followed the accounts. I didn't know it would hit your family. I didn't know it would hit you. So I reached out to Mercer."

"And how exactly does a glorified data pirate with trust issues get the damn FBI on speed dial?" I ask, my voice laced with venom.

Knox grimaces, and it's the first time I've ever seen guilt on his face. "I've had a deal," he mutters.

I blink. "You what?"

Mercer speaks for him, calm and clinical. "Knox has been an off-record asset for two years. Cyber-intelligence. Quiet contracts. He flagged the Volkovs during a shell routing sweep that was already under active surveillance. When he followed the money to Langford Holdings, we stepped in."

Of course. Of course Knox is working with the feds. Of course no one tells me anything until I'm already in the damn blast radius.

I turn back to the screen. "So what do you want from me? A wire? A recording? Blood?"

Mercer doesn't blink. "Nothing. Yet."

Knox opens his mouth like he wants to say something else, but I don't let him.

I straighten, smooth my coat. Then I say it. "This doesn't change anything. I'm still going to the engagement party. I'm still walking into that room with my fiancé."

Knox freezes, then looks up sharply.

"...*Fiancé?*" His voice hits the room like a gunshot. "You're *engaged* to one of them?"

I meet his eyes, unflinching. "You didn't think I was doing this for a research project, did you?"

"You said you wanted anything I could find on them," he says, voice rising. "You didn't say you were one of them!"

The reality of what he said slaps me in the face and I go numb. Because I will never be like them.

"No," I say coldly. "Because if I had, you would've backed off. And I needed you to dig."

He looks like he wants to argue—maybe punch a wall, maybe scream—but Mercer speaks again, voice level.

"She signed the paperwork over a month ago. It was filed through Langford's private legal office. Quiet, internal, heavily redacted. The announcement hasn't gone public yet, but yes, this is real."

I look at them both.

My traitorous hacker.

My government babysitter.

And I realize, in this moment, that I'm the only one in the room who has nothing left to lose. "I knew what I was getting into," I say. "I just didn't realize how many of you were already playing the game behind my back."

Mercer tilts his head, studying me like a puzzle he can't quite solve. "You're in deep," he says. "You're not walking out untouched." He steps closer, reaching into his pocket, and hands me a different burner phone. "We'll be in touch." His voice is calm. Like he's handing me a favor. But it's not a favor. It's a leash.

"And if I don't answer?"

His smile doesn't reach his eyes. "You don't want to find out, Ms. Langford."

I snatch the phone from his hand and tuck it into my coat. I don't say another word. Not yet. Because the next one? Will change everything.

-

It's been a few hours since I met with Knox and I'm still seething. The FBI? Really? He brings the FBI into this. As if this situation is complicated enough, let's throw in another curveball.

I'm pacing my room right now. Thank goodness Thalia's downstairs because I'm pretty sure she would hold me hostage until I told her everything that's happened within the past forty-eight hours.

By the time I make it downstairs, the common room is a mess of autumn vibes. There's a Spotify playlist drifting through the Bluetooth speakers. Someone lit the apple cinnamon candle we're technically not allowed to use in shared spaces. The windows are cracked just enough to let in the November light, and the room smells like cider.

The exec board is spread out across the couches and mismatched chairs, laptops open, nails clicking, iced matchas sweating into cupholders. They're all in comfy sweatshirts and half in control—hair tied up, glossed lips, gold earrings that say *we're chill but also wildly competent.*

I slide into the armchair closest to Kennedy.

"Okay," Poppy announces, flipping to a new page in her rose-gold binder, "we need to finalize details for the sisterhood brunch next weekend. Theme, colors, flowers, menu. I'm thinking something cozy and classic—like chic cottage core meets Pinterest board come to life."

"Does that mean more burlap or less?" Marist mutters from the corner, pulling her oversized hoodie over her knees like a blanket.

"Less," Poppy says, scandalized. "We're not hosting a hoe-down. I'm talking woven basket accents. Neutral tones. Linen napkins, not mason jars."

"We had mason jars last year," Sloane says, barely looking up from her phone. "You can still find glitter in the cracks of the fireplace."

"I had glitter in my bed for *two weeks*," Kennedy adds. "And I didn't even *attend* the brunch."

"That's because you were hungover from the SAE after-formal," I say, sweetly.

Sloane grins. "Allegedly."

"I say we lean into fall without doing too much plaid," I offer, slipping into the rhythm easily, naturally. "Think warm-toned florals, tapered candles, spiced cider that doesn't taste like potpourri. Understated luxury, not basic November energy."

Poppy snaps her fingers. "Exactly. Emilia gets it. Elevated cozy. Like ... if Vogue did Thanksgiving."

"Can we still serve mimosas?" Marist asks.

"We can call it an 'apple cider prosecco bar' and pretend it's festive," Sloane says.

"Or pretend it's not 11 a.m. on a Sunday and we're all trying to recover from questionable life choices," I add.

Laughter ripples across the room, and it's warm, genuine. And just like that, I'm in it again. Not as the girl who walked out of a meeting with the FBI a few hours ago. Not the girl who's engaged to the Russian mafia. Or who's been sold a lie her whole life. No. Right now, I'm the chapter president. The one who knows the budget, the calendar, and exactly how to order $150 worth of flowers that look like they cost twice that.

"You guys realize," Poppy says, eyes lighting up, "we could do a floral arch for photos. Like one of those Pinterest installations with pampas grass and dried oranges and little hanging lanterns—"

"That sounds like it costs actual rent money," Thalia murmurs, typing away.

"Actually," I interject, tapping my pen against my planner, "we could DIY it with copper piping and fishing wire. Spray paint the base, anchor it with cinder blocks, then cover the frame with eucalyptus and faux florals. Add battery lanterns and boom—budget-friendly centerpiece."

Thalia smirks. "And this is why she's our president."

Sloane sighs dramatically. "I want to be Emilia Langford when I grow up."

"You'd have to start waking up before noon," I say, dry as bone.

Sloane shrugs. "Never mind."

Another wave of laughter. The good kind. The kind that bubbles over and sticks around. I lean back, crossing one leg over the other, letting the smile settle on my face like a crown.

This is mine. This house. These girls. This moment.

And no one here knows I'm preparing for a war behind the scenes.

They don't know that I've already picked out the dress I'll wear to my own engagement party—the one I didn't choose, the one no one asked me if I wanted. They don't know the weight of that contract sitting in my family's vault or the gun Mercer might have tucked into his blazer when he warned me that I was now officially on every watchlist that mattered.

All they see is me—polished, organized, smiling.

Still running the room.

Still running everything.

And I'm going to keep it that way.

-

This week has been brutal—like the universe decided to stack every worst-case scenario on top of each other and dared me to crawl out from underneath it with my sanity still intact. I've barely slept, can't eat without feeling like I'm swallowing glass, and every time I close my eyes, I'm back in that room, back in that chair, back in that moment where the world tilted just enough to make everything that came before it feel like a lie. I thought if I kept moving—if I threw myself into coursework and obligations and group texts about Halloween hangovers—I could box it all up, file it away in some back corner of my brain like an archive I never planned to revisit. But the human brain is cruel. It loops the worst moments, plays them louder than the rest, refuses to let you forget even when your body begs for numbness.

Honestly, I almost didn't go to class today. I stared at the ceiling for an hour, weighing the consequences of just ... not showing up. A hooky day. A self-prescribed screw-it kind of morning. But then Max texted me, simple and casual, like the world hadn't cracked beneath our feet this weekend:

Max: *Want to meet up for coffee at the same place as before? I could use the distraction from this paper.*

At first, I stared at the message, thumb hovering, brain fogged with the kind of exhaustion that makes you question why you say yes to anyone anymore. But Max—he's … different. There's something about him I can't quite name. Something warm and easy and familiar in a way that shouldn't be possible. So I text back:

Sure. 20 minutes?

Thalia's already gone by the time I drag myself out of bed, her half-drunk smoothie still on the dresser and her laptop open on a paused lecture video. I shuffle into the bathroom and stare at myself under the fluorescent lights that make my skin look paper-thin. I don't bother with the usual routine—no concealer, no mascara, no curling iron. Just a splash of cold water, a tie of hair into the messiest of buns, and a silent middle finger to the imaginary voice of my mother, who would no doubt gasp at the sight of me in leggings and an oversized hoodie, declaring something painfully on-brand like, *You represent the Langford family, Emilia.* The irony punches me straight in the gut. Joke's on her—I'm not actually a Langford.

By the time I push open the front door of the house, the air hits me like a sigh I didn't know I needed. It's overcast, moody in the way fall tends to be—gray sky, gold leaves, a bite to the breeze that sneaks under your clothes and lingers on your skin like memory. I keep my head down, earbuds in but not playing anything, and try to pretend I'm just another college girl headed for caffeine and not a girl whose identity was shattered by one envelope and a room full of people who smiled as they detonated it.

I catch movement from the side of the house—Keller and Ruiz, of course, lingering like shadows with earpieces and too much tension in their shoulders. I flick a glance toward them. Keller sees it. I give a small shake of my head, a silent *not today,* and he rolls his eyes so hard I can feel it from across the lawn. He doesn't argue, though. He knows how this goes. Knows I'll make it ten steps before he or Ruiz picks up my trail again from the other side of the street. They don't guard me. They haunt me.

The café isn't far—ten minutes tops—and when I step inside, the smell of roasted beans and cinnamon pastries wraps around me like a sweater. It's warm here. Dim. Intimate. The kind of place where time moves slower and everyone speaks a few decibels quieter. I scan the back corner, and there he is.

Max.

Seated at the table we chose last time, hair messier than usual, hoodie sleeves pushed to his elbows, and—damn it— gray joggers that should be illegal on a man with thighs like that. He stands when he sees me, a mega-watt smile and boy- next-door charm, and for a second, just a second, I almost forget why I'm holding my breath.

I smile back, walk over, and slide into the chair across from him. My heart doesn't stop pounding. But I pretend it does.

Because this is just coffee.

It's just Max.

And I'm a very good liar.

Max slides my drink across the table before I've even asked, like he memorized my order weeks ago. I eye the drink, then wrap my fingers around the mug, letting the heat bleed into my skin.

"You look…" He pauses, eyes scanning my face, taking in the bare skin, the hoodie, the general screw-it-all aesthetic I'm giving off like perfume. "Cozy."

I huff a dry laugh. "Translation: I look like I've been hit by a semi."

He shrugs, a half-smile tugging at his mouth. "A very cute semi."

I roll my eyes and take a sip to hide the way my lips twitch. "That's the line you're going with today? Not exactly Pulitzer-winning."

"I'm pacing myself," he says, leaning back in his seat. "Don't want to peak too early."

It's easy with him. Too easy. That's the problem. He doesn't push, doesn't pry. He doesn't look at me like I'm fragile glass or radioactive material. He looks at me like I'm human. Like I'm still allowed to be a little screwed up and still worth something. And maybe that's why I said yes. Maybe that's why I'm here. Because pretending nothing's wrong, even for ten minutes, feels like the closest thing to sanity I've had all week.

I toy with the sleeve of my hoodie, watching the way his fingers move as he opens his laptop. "Still working on that paper?"

"Trying," he says. "But I've got the attention span of a gnat today."

"What's it on again?"

"Russian foreign policy and post-Soviet influence. Light reading." He smirks over the rim of his coffee.

"Sexy," I deadpan.

He grins. "If only my TA agreed."

We lapse into a moment of silence, not uncomfortable, but not weightless either. There's something hanging in the air, unspoken, unnamed. I feel it. I think he does too. But neither of us reaches for it.

Then he says, "I've gotta hit the bathroom. Don't let anyone steal my laptop, yeah?"

"Only if they offer me a better grade," I quip, watching him slide out of the booth with a lazy stretch that does nothing to help me focus on my drink.

He leaves his phone on the table.

I don't notice it at first. I'm mid-sip, eyes on the window. But then the screen lights up—just briefly—and my name is the second thing I see.

The first is Nikolai's.

A message. Not long. No preview. Just his name and the time stamp. A fresh notification. From him.

Something cold curls low in my stomach, and my pulse skips, not in fear, not even in suspicion, just ... in that quiet way your body knows something your mind hasn't caught up to yet.

I glance toward the hallway. No sign of Max.

I shouldn't look.

But my fingers are already moving, slow and cautious as I pull the phone toward me. It's not locked. The thread is still open.

I don't read every message. I don't need to. There are hundreds of them. Messages between Max and Nikolai—some terse, some long, some timestamped around moments I remember too clearly. There's no decoding to be done. It's all there, threaded through updates, conversations about me.

About who I've spoken to.

Where I've gone.

What I've said.

And I just sit there, staring, the shop noise dissolving around me like water down a drain. I feel ... hollow. Like I've been scraped out and left with nothing but skin. My coffee goes cold. The knot in my throat tightens. I put the phone down gently, as if setting it too hard might confirm what I've just seen.

I don't move when Max returns. He doesn't see the phone at first, doesn't register the shift in the air. But then he sees my face. My hands.

His steps slow.

"Emilia?" he says carefully, eyes flicking to the screen and then back to me.

I say nothing, but I watch it happen—the moment he realizes what I saw, the way his face goes slack for half a second before it smooths over again.

I lean forward, voice low and flat. "How long?"

He doesn't ask what I mean. Just looks at me, guilt etched into every part of his expression. "Since the beginning."

I nod slowly, letting the words settle over me.

"Was I a class assignment?" I sneer. I'm over politeness.

He winces. "No."

"Then what? Just surveillance? Keeping tabs on the American girl?"

"It wasn't like that." He runs a hand through his hair, letting out a shaky breath before he looks at me again.

I laugh, but there's no humor in it. "You knew who I was. You knew exactly who I was, and you still pretended to be my friend."

"I didn't lie about who I was."

"No?" I raise an eyebrow. "Because I didn't see 'Volkov' anywhere on your profile."

He exhales, slow and quiet, like he's still weighing whether to reach across the table and try to bridge the wreckage between us, like he thinks one small gesture might soften the edges of what he's done, but he doesn't, and that tells me everything.

"I didn't want to hurt you," he says, voice rough with something too close to regret.

But I don't think Volkovs have regrets. I don't flinch. Don't look away. "I'm not hurt."

And I mean it. Not because I'm cold, not because I don't feel anything, but because hurt implies a wound from someone who mattered, and Max never got that far. Not really. What I feel now is something different, something heavier, something colder. This isn't heartbreak. It's betrayal. Calculation. The bone-deep chill of realizing I was never looking at a friend—I was looking at a mirror with a false reflection, one I mistook for something safe.

This isn't about Max. Not really. This is Nikolai's doing—his network, his power play, his name stitched into every corner of my life like a thread I never saw coming until it cinched tight.

The silence stretches, taut and suffocating, and I know I can't sit here one second longer without doing something reckless, so I reach for my bag with slow precision, stand without a word, and lean forward across the table, just enough to catch his eyes one last time.

"I didn't care about your last name," I say, voice low, steady, dangerous in the way quiet things often are. "But if you ever try to talk to me again, look in my direction, or so much as breathe near my name, I'll put you on a government watchlist so fast your own family won't be able to find you."

Something flickers across his face. Not fear. Not shame. Just this quiet, familiar resignation, like he expected this, like he knew from the start this would be the end of whatever we were pretending to be. He doesn't apologize. Doesn't beg. I don't expect him to.

I don't say goodbye. I don't curse him out or flip him off or demand closure.

I just walk out, my spine straight, my chest hollow, my pulse thundering behind my ribs like it's trying to remind me I'm still here, still standing, still learning.

And as the door swings shut behind me, I feel the bitter sting of clarity settle in like smoke through my lungs.

I should've known.

I should've seen this coming.
But I didn't.
And now?
Now, I'll never forget it.

-

Max

I hate surprises.

They're unexpected. Like a knock at your door in the middle of the night—no warning. Which is exactly why I should've stayed away from Emilia Langford. From the start. Like Nikolai told me to. No, like he ordered me to.

I wasn't even supposed to be here. I had a job lined up in London with the Russian Embassy. Clean. Distant. Respectable. But then Niko called, cashed in a favor he knew I owed. I said no at first. Thought I could stand my ground. But he's my cousin, and I know what he's up against. So I caved. Like an idiot.

Two months later, I know everything there is to know about her. Emilia Langford. The golden girl of American politics. Perfect on paper, lethal in silence. What no one realizes—not even the people closest to her—is that she's not the image they've sold to the press. Beneath that polished sheen, there's someone dangerous. Calculated. She doesn't just play the game—she studies the board, rearranges the pieces, and waits until no one's watching before making her move.

The scandal Irina uncovered—about her parentage, her bloodline—that's the match. And when it drops, the whole powder keg is going up. But the thing that stands out to me the most? She was born for this world. Not the staged politics of Capitol Hill. No. She's a Bratva heir in everything but name. A Petrov. And that blood doesn't run cold—it burns.

225

The Arrangement

I used to think I left that life behind for good. I said all the right things—told them I wanted a proper education, a safer future. But the truth? I wanted out. Away from my mother and her poisoned ambition. Away from my uncle—my late father's twin brother— and the bottle he uses to forget he failed his own brother. Away from the bodies and the debts and the rules etched in blood. But the thing about running from fire? It always finds a way to follow you.

That's why I agreed to help Niko. Because he doesn't just want to escape, he wants to burn it all down. The Bratva. Our family's corner of it, at least. And Emilia? She's the variable. The spark. The storm none of us accounted for.

That's why I've been watching her. Not because I didn't trust her, but because I finally understood why Nikolai was so obsessed. She's magnetic. A lethal wildfire. And if we're not careful, she's going to turn this entire legacy into ash.

My phone is warm in my hand when I finally speak. "She knows."

There's silence on the other end, but I can feel Nikolai's anger simmering through the line. Cold. Measured. Dangerous.

"Fix this, Max."

I swallow the sigh clawing up my throat. "I'll try."

"You better do more than try. Don't screw this up any worse than you already have."

The call ends with a hollow click. No goodbye. No grace.

I don't move. Just stare at the empty seat she left behind. The coffee's still there. Still warm. And I sit there, like a ghost, wishing I'd never agreed to come here in the first place.

Chapter 11

Emilia

I've been avoiding public spaces ever since the Max revelation.

Max.

Even thinking his name feels like biting down on tinfoil: sharp, metallic, wrong. I'm almost certain that's not even his real name, and honestly, that wouldn't surprise me. Just another lie in a growing collection. It's been two days since I last saw him, and I've done everything possible to erase his presence from my life. His number is blocked. In Kerr's class, I've taken to sitting beside Wells Ballard, a decision that has unfortunately inflated his already overblown ego. He thinks I'm interested. I'm not. But if it's a choice between the class creep and the guy who pretended to be my friend while reporting back to a Volkov? I'll take the lesser evil. Even if it comes with cologne headaches and unsolicited winks.

On the contrary, I did something I never imagined possible: I skipped the sisterhood brunch. A true faux pas. Never in Chi Omega history has a President failed to attend an event … unless she was sick, dead, or committed to something more pressing.

The Arrangement

When I told Clara, she looked utterly appalled, as if I just informed her Sephora has stopped carrying Laura Mercier products. In true presidential fashion, I reassured that, as VP, she was more than capable of handling a brunch on her own.

And now it's Saturday ... the day of the brunch ... and I'm standing in the middle of a boutique. My mother—ever the orchestrator of public image—has arranged for a "mother-daughter bonding day" under the guise of finding the perfect engagement dress. Her words. Not mine. I still can't look her in the eyes without seeing the years of lies reflected back at me. The things she hid. The truths she buried. Our texts this week have been brief, transactional at best. I reply only when necessary. Like today. Today is for her. Only her.

The boutique she chose feels like a love letter to Elle Woods. So much pink. Blush, coral, fuchsia ... every hue imaginable, smeared across every wall, pillow, and wretched dressing room curtain. The sales associate is practically vibrating with energy, nodding along to my mother's every word like she's taking orders from a queen. Her eyes gleam with commission hunger, and I already feel a migraine building behind my eyes from the sheer amount of brown-nosing in the room.

Everything is pristine in that unsettling, too-perfect way—marble floors polished to a mirror-like sheen, gold-framed mirrors reflecting my disinterest back at me from every angle, racks upon racks of silk and velvet arranged like curated museum pieces.

And me?

I hate it here.

Most women would be thrilled to shop for their engagement party dress. But most women are free to choose who they marry. Not me. Today isn't about love; it's about the dress I'll wear when they present me to the world like a perfectly bred racehorse. Not a wedding dress, thankfully.

That nightmare's still months away. No, this dress is for the engagement party—the announcement, the debut. The moment where Emilia Langford smiles in a thousand photos and everyone claps politely and pretends they don't see the cage closing around her.

The cream satin whispers as I pull it up over my hips, slipping into place like a second skin. It's a masterpiece—of course it is. Strapless, the neckline just daring enough to suggest rebellion without slipping into scandal. The bodice molds to my curves like it was cut from a mold of my body, boned and structured to hold me up even when everything else crumbles. The skirt falls in a smooth, weighted line to the floor, the hem skimming the tops of my heels. No embroidery. No frills. Just the quiet, devastating elegance of old money and older expectations.

I step out onto the platform.

My mother watches from the sidelines like a general inspecting her troops. Her arms are folded neatly over the front of her cream cashmere coat, her manicured fingers tapping once against her sleeve as she circles slowly, taking in every inch of me.

"That one," she says, after a long moment.

The attendant—all bright teeth and frantic approval—claps her hands together. "Exquisite choice. The cream brings out the warmth in your complexion. So polished, so poised. It will photograph beautifully."

I force my mouth into a smile that doesn't reach my eyes. "Exactly what I wanted. To photograph beautifully."

Thalia, sprawled in a velvet chair with her legs crossed at the ankle and a champagne flute dangling lazily from two fingers, snorts so quietly only I can hear it. She catches my eye in the mirror and raises her glass in a tiny, mocking salute.

I almost laugh. Almost.

Instead, I turn back toward the mirror and study my reflection.

The dress is perfect. There's no question about that. But I look like a Langford. I look like I was born for this. And it makes me want to claw my own skin off.

My mother moves behind me, adjusting the fall of the skirt, smoothing a phantom wrinkle with a hand that's gentle only on the surface. "You'll be breathtaking, darling. Everything they expect."

Everything they expect.

Not everything I am.

I meet my own gaze in the mirror, and for a moment, I don't see a girl stepping into her future.

I see a girl trapped in a cage. A golden cage.

-

The dining room looks like something straight off Pinterest: long wooden tables pulled together end to end, burlap runners scattered with little gold pumpkins and mismatched candles flickering in mason jars. There's way too much food crammed onto every surface—turkey that's already picked over, mountains of mashed potatoes swimming in butter, pies that have been preemptively "taste-tested" by at least three girls, and a frankly absurd amount of wine for a sorority dinner.

The air smells like cinnamon, thyme, and a low hum of excitement that Thanksgiving is next week.

I hover near the window for a second, a mug of apple cider warming my hands, just soaking it in—the noise, the clutter, the laughter that feels a little too big for the room but somehow fits anyway.

Ava's perched on the back of one of the couches, arguing with Tinsley over whether or not sleeping with your roommate's ex officially violates girl code.

"It doesn't count if it's been over six months," Ava insists, waving her fork dramatically. "Statute of limitations, my friends."

"Since when do we have statutes?" Tinsley huffs, stealing a bite of stuffing off her plate. "You made that up."

"It's an unwritten rule," Sloane chimes in from across the room, where she's halfway through her second glass of wine. "Like ... driving laws. Everyone pretends they're suggestions until someone crashes."

"That's not reassuring," Marist says, wide-eyed.

I smirk behind my mug. "Neither is dating anyone who calls you 'bro' during sex, but here we are."

The table erupts. Ava nearly spits out her drink. Tinsley howls. Even Thalia, who's been quietly scrolling through her phone in the corner, snorts into her cider.

"You're kidding, who?" Ava gasps, fanning herself.

I shrug innocently. "Ask Clara."

Clara, who has the grace to turn cherry red from across the table, groans and buries her face in her hands. "I told you that in confidence!"

"You told me that after two tequila shots and a game of truth or dare. I don't make the rules," I say, sweetly.

"You're evil," she mutters, throwing a dinner roll at my head, which I easily dodge.

"That's why you love me," I toss back. She doesn't, but boy, does it feel good to get even with her.

The laughter crackles and stretches, filling up every corner of the room. It's stupid and messy and loud, the kind of joy that feels slightly drunk and slightly invincible, even when none of us really are.

Across the table, Sloane leans in, dropping her voice to a stage whisper. "Okay, but has anyone heard about Lila and the Phi Delt president?"

Immediate uproar.

"No."

"Yes."

"Shut up."

"Tell me everything."

Sloane smirks like a cat who found the canary. "Apparently, he broke up with his girlfriend last week. Cried about it for like three days. Then hooked up with Lila in the courtyard after their Halloween party. Still wearing his costume."

"What was he dressed as?" Ava demands.

"A priest," Sloane says.

Dead silence for a beat.

Then Clara screams-laughs so hard she almost falls out of her chair.

"You're telling me he had a fake rosary in one hand and Lila's ass in the other?" Thalia says dryly, finally looking up from her phone.

"Allegedly," Sloane says, doing that innocent blink that fools no one.

Someone knocks over a glass. Tinsley screams. I smile until my cheeks hurt.

Because it's easy here. Because it's messy and stupid and real, and for a moment, it lets me forget that a ticking clock is winding down somewhere far too close to my future.

I'm halfway through a conversation about Spotify Wrapped predictions when my phone buzzes in my back pocket, and a chill runs straight up my spine.

Not the main line.

The burner phone Mercer gave me.

I excuse myself with a smile and step into the relatively private side of the hallway. The old wood floors creak under my feet as I pull out the phone and read the message.

Mercer: *Movement on Project Daggerfall. Be ready.*

My heart stutters once, twice, then falls back into an even, deadly rhythm.

I slip the phone back into my pocket and plaster a smile back onto my face before stepping into the kitchen to help slice the pie. Because tonight is Friendsgiving. And tonight, I still get to pretend I'm normal.

-

Later, curled into the corner of my bed with the lamp casting a soft, honey-colored pool of light across my blankets, I call Grace. I feel bad that we haven't spoken in a while, outside of our weekly texts. After all, she's still my sister.

The FaceTime rings twice before Grace answers, her face filling the screen in chaotic Gen Z glory. She's lying sideways across her bed, hoodie sleeves stretched over her hands, claw clip half-falling out of her hair, and an iced coffee balanced dangerously on the edge of her nightstand.

"Wow," she says, one brow raised. "She lives."

"Barely," I mutter, adjusting the phone against my pillow.

Grace squints at me. "No offense, but you look like you just got hit by a truck full of AP tests and emotional trauma."

I sigh. "It's been a week."

"Clearly," she says, popping her gum. "I texted you, like, four times. At one point, I thought you were being held hostage by your fiancé. Blink twice if he's in the room."

"He's not," I deadpan.

"Suspicious response, but okay."

I let out a laugh that doesn't quite reach my chest. "Sorry I went dark. Things have just … been a lot."

She adjusts the camera and flops onto her back, hair fanning across a ridiculous Hello Kitty pillow. "Well, I missed you. Even if you're mid–mental breakdown right now. Want me to distract you with stories of high school drama and existential dread?"

"Please."

She launches into a play-by-play of her week: how Anna tried to steal her French quiz, how she might be lowkey feuding with her chem teacher, how a random video of her lip-syncing in the cafeteria blew up on TikTok. "I'm literally famous in my own comment section," she says, like it's both a curse and a badge of honor. "But also, I hate everyone. So..."

I smile, just watching her. She's a little older every time I see her. Her jaw's sharper now. She's wearing mascara. Her braces are finally gone. And her hazel eyes—warm, golden in the corners, lined in glittery eyeliner—don't match mine at all.

Not like they used to when we were kids, and I convinced myself we just took after different grandparents.

She doesn't know. She can't. She's all freckles and sarcasm and loud music and cracked phone screens ... and still untouched by the kind of truth that ruins people.

"So," she says, brushing hair from her face. "Are you gonna tell me if the mystery fiancé is still a thing or if you've faked your own death and run off with a barista yet?"

I blink. "What?"

"Don't 'what' me," she says. "You told me you were engaged and then ghosted. Like? I need updates. Am I going to be a bridesmaid or what?"

So Mother never told her. How odd.

I exhale. "Yeah. It's still happening."

She makes a face. "Okay, well, is he hot at least? Like ... you want to jump his bones hot?"

I hesitate.

She gasps. "Wait. Is this a no-chemistry-arranged-marriage situation or a you're-secretly-into-him-but-emotionally-repressed situation?"

"I'm not getting into this with you."

"That means it's the second one."

"You're exhausting."

"You love me."

"I do," I say, and I mean it more than she knows.

She rests her chin on her arm, expression softening just slightly. "You okay though? Like ... actually?"

I want to lie. I really, really do. But she's watching me too closely.

"I don't know," I say quietly.

She nods. Doesn't push. Just chews her gum and says, "Well, if you need someone to fake food poisoning and get you out of whatever rich-people brunch Mom has planned, I'm your girl."

I laugh for real this time. "Good to know."

"Call me again soon, okay? Like, don't disappear. I'll send an embarrassing slideshow to your future in-laws."

"Threats now?"

"Always." She ends the call with a peace sign and a dramatic eyeroll.

And when the screen goes dark, I'm left alone again ... my own reflection staring back at me.

Green eyes. Not hazel.

Not hers.

And no matter how many times I call her sister, that truth never goes away.

Chapter 12

Emilia

Bancroft's campus basks in brittle November sunlight, the sky a washed-out blue, the grass sharp with frost that hasn't yet melted from the shadowed corners of the quad. It should feel ordinary, safe even, the way it always has—students hurrying across the pathways with backpacks slung low, coffee cups clutched like lifelines, laughter floating in the cold air—but there's an unease threading through everything today, a static charge prickling just under my skin, and it doesn't take long to find the source.

He's there before I even make it to the lecture hall, posted up like he's just another student killing time between classes. One foot propped against the edge of the stone planter, arms crossed, a black notebook tucked beneath one arm like he's trying to blend in.

But he doesn't.

He never did.

Max, or should I say Maksim Volkov, sticks out the way snakes do in gardens. Yeah, I did my research on the guy.

He's too still. Too careful. Like the world's already moved around him and he's three steps ahead, waiting for the rest of us to catch up.

His eyes lift as I approach, that unreadable, practiced expression on his face, and I can't tell if he's nervous or if he just wants me to *think* he is.

I don't slow down.

"Emilia," he says as I pass, falling into step beside me like it's nothing.

"Max." I say it flat, unbothered, but my grip tightens on my coffee cup until the lid creaks.

"I wasn't sure if you'd show."

"Why wouldn't I?" I glance at him just once. "This is Comparative Politics, not a funeral."

He actually flinches at that. Not much, but I catch it.

"That bad, huh?"

"You tell me," I say. "You've been here since the start of the semester, right? Taking notes on everyone, keeping tabs, reporting in. You probably have a full dossier on my sleep habits by now."

He stays quiet for a beat. "That's not what I was doing."

"Sure," I say, giving him a sardonic smile. "Just shadowing me for the sake of it."

We approach the steps of the lecture hall, and I feel the shift ... students clustering around the doors, voices bouncing off stone and glass, none of them realizing what's happening just beneath the surface of this scene. I slow, enough to peel off to the side, out of the crowd.

He follows.

"Look," he starts, voice lower now, "I didn't expect it to go like this."

"No?" I turn to him, lifting a brow. "You didn't expect to get caught? Or you didn't expect to actually like the girl you were spying on?"

That gets him. Barely. But enough.

"I didn't come here to hurt you."

"Well, you're batting a thousand."

He sighs, dragging a hand through his hair, the movement frustratingly familiar. I hate that I notice. Hate that a piece of me still wants to trust him … not because he deserves it, but because *I* wanted to believe he could've been real.

"You're mad," he says quietly.

"No," I say, voice clipped. "I'm humiliated. There's a difference."

He nods, eyes on the concrete. "I never wanted to be the guy who—"

"Spied?" I cut in. "Lied? Played friend in the mornings and asset by night? No? Didn't want to be that guy? You are that guy, Max. Doesn't matter how you say it."

There's a moment. A beat between us so tight I could slice through it with a look. And then I see it … the flicker of guilt. Not superficial. Real.

"I stopped reporting on you weeks ago."

That makes me pause. I stare at him. "What?"

"I didn't tell him anything after midterms," he says. "Nikolai. I didn't see the point. You weren't a target anymore."

"And what was I before that?"

He doesn't answer.

I step back, just enough to breathe. Just enough to not be in his shadow. "Do you know what it's like," I say, quietly now, "to let your guard down for *one second*, and find out someone was *watching* the whole time?"

He says nothing.

"Yeah," I whisper. "Didn't think so."

The doors open behind us, and the rush of students break the moment. I move past him without another glance.

But just before I disappear inside, I hear him.

"I didn't stop because I was told to," he says, almost too quiet to catch. "I stopped because I didn't want to look at you like that anymore."

I freeze. But only for a moment. Then I keep walking. Because that confession isn't for me. It's for the guilt he'll carry back to his cousin. And I'm done making space for anyone else's shame but mine.

-

Knox finally gets back to me, a short message with no fluff, no warning, no buffer to soften the blow: *Email sent. DNA confirmation's attached.* That's it. No context. No 'Are you ready for this?' No 'You might want to sit down'. Just the kind of cold, clinical delivery that tells me everything I need to know about what's waiting for me on the other side of that screen. I've been sitting here for what feels like forever, staring at my laptop like it might open itself, like maybe if I wait long enough, the file will disappear, or the truth will change, or time will rewind. But it doesn't. It just sits there: quiet, patient, damning. My hands won't stop shaking. My leg bounces beneath the desk. The cursor hovers over the zip file and I tell myself, one more breath, one more second, but all that does is stretch the dread tighter until it starts to strangle.

So I do it. I click. Before I can talk myself out of it, before my nerves can catch up to my impulse, before the weight in my chest can glue me to the chair entirely. I double-click the zip, and then the PDF, and watch the screen go white for half a beat as it loads. I expect a name I've heard before, something familiar, something political: a senator's son maybe, a donor, some faceless man with a Georgetown education and a file full of glossy photos at Republican fundraisers. Someone who looks like me, someone who fits the script. That's what I think I'm going to see. What I *want* to see. What I've spent my entire life being told I should see.

But then the file opens.

And the name staring back at me is nothing like what I prepared myself for.

Ivan Petrov.

Two words. No face. No photo. Just that name, centered on the page like it's been waiting there for years. Like it's been lurking behind everything I didn't want to see. At first, the letters don't register. They're just shapes: foreign, sharp, wrong. And then they click into place, and I realize I have no idea who this man is. He isn't American. He isn't someone I recognize in the D.C. circuit. He isn't even traceable. He's a stranger. A ghost. A name that doesn't belong in my life and yet, somehow, does.

A sound tears out of me, guttural and broken, too loud in the silence of my room, and for a moment, I don't even realize it came from me. I jolt, eyes flicking toward the door like someone else must've heard it, like someone must be here, must be standing over me to witness the moment my entire world falls out from under me. But there's no one. Just the hum of my laptop and the echo of my own scream hanging in the air like smoke. I slam the computer shut on instinct, pushing away from the desk like I've just touched a live wire, heart pounding in my ears, throat closing up so fast it feels like I might suffocate on the weight of this one single truth.

But after a minute—or maybe five—I go back.

I have to.

Because maybe I imagined it. Maybe I read it wrong. Maybe my mind is playing tricks. So I open the laptop again, hands still shaking, and the file reappears with cruel clarity. The name is still there. Ivan Petrov. And below it, in sharp, emotionless font:

*Biological Father: Confirmed. Test Date: August 2004.
Mother: Veronica Langford. Child: Emilia Rose Langford.
Result: Positive.*

There's no other detail. No face to pair with the name. Just the fact of him. Just the brutal finality of blood.

I open a new tab and type it in, Ivan Petrov.

Nothing comes up.

No social media. No press releases. No arrest records or corporate listings. Not even a poorly edited Wikipedia page. A couple of scraps: foreign business filings, a ship manifest from a decade ago, a customs record buried behind broken links, but none of it tells me who he is. Just enough to confirm he's real, and just enough to make it clear someone's worked very hard to make sure I'll never know more than the name.

And that's what sends the chill down my spine ... not that he's a stranger, but that he's been erased.

Because erasure means power. It means danger. It means that this man isn't just someone my mother met on a European vacation twenty-one years ago. It means this wasn't an accident. It means someone made a choice—a choice to bury him, to bury me, to rewrite a bloodline and hope the lie held long enough that I'd never ask the question.

But now I have the answer. And I don't know what to do with it.

Because I'm not who I thought I was.

I'm not a Langford.

I never was.

And now I'm staring at the truth like it's a reflection I don't recognize ... like the girl in the mirror is someone entirely new. Someone forged out of secrets. Someone born from silence.

And whoever Ivan Petrov is, one thing is suddenly very, very clear:

I wasn't supposed to find him.

But I have.

And nothing about my life will ever be the same.

-

The next morning dawns brittle and gray, the sky a slab of dull steel overhead, the air cold enough to sting the inside of my nose when I step outside. I bundle deeper into my coat, a heavy navy wool thing my mother picked out last Christmas, and head towards the edge of campus where Mercer said to meet him.

Noon sharp.

The world feels strangely empty as I walk, like everyone else has been cleared out for this moment, like the universe is giving us space to conduct whatever treason we're about to discuss.

The diner Mercer picked looks like it was built in the 50s and never got renovated. Dim lights. Greasy smell. Fogged windows. Booths so worn the stuffing peeks through the seams.

He's already here when I walk in, sitting in the back corner like a scene out of a bad spy movie, the hood of his jacket pulled low, a cup of untouched coffee steaming in front of him. He doesn't wave, doesn't smile. Just watches me cross the room like he's marking a target.

I slide into the booth opposite him, shrugging off my coat but keeping it close, an old instinct I'm not in the mood to unlearn.

"You're late," he says, voice low and unimpressed.

"You're lucky I showed up at all," I reply, matching his disinterest beat for beat.

He doesn't bother with a comeback. Instead, he leans forward, the heavy, acrid scent of stale leather and stronger coffee clinging to him like a second skin. "You're going to listen," he says, tone flat and absolute. "And you're not going to like it."

I lift a brow, feigning boredom, but my hands stay curled loose and ready under the table.

"You're not a bystander anymore, Langford. You're inside the Volkov web now. Close enough that you can see things no one else can."

I say nothing.

He slides a tiny mic across the table between us, the black plastic scuffed and cheap. I don't reach for it yet.

"This," he says, tapping it with one blunt finger, "is how you're going to stay alive."

"You're asking me to spy," I say quietly, no inflection. Great, another person I'm spying for.

He huffs a humorless sound that might almost be a laugh if there were anything human left in it. "No, sweetheart. I'm telling you. There's no more asking."

The words hang heavy in the air, thick and metallic.

I don't flinch.

He smiles slightly, but it's not friendly. Just acknowledging the obvious. "You don't get to play Switzerland here. You're either useful or you're a liability. And I don't protect liabilities."

I tip my head slightly, considering. "And if I tell you to shove it?" I ask, my voice dripping with false sweetness.

Mercer leans closer, his voice dropping low enough that I have to strain to catch it. "Then you and your sister," he says, almost gently, "become a very inconvenient set of loose ends."

The bottom drops out of my stomach, but my face doesn't move, not even a flicker.

He smiles wider, slow and sure. "We've got eyes on her," he says, like he's commenting on the weather. "Soccer practice. Parties. School." He shrugs, slow, deliberate. "Accidents happen."

My nails dig into the worn vinyl of the booth, but I don't let the rage show anywhere else.

Instead, I reach out, pick up the mic with two fingers, and slip it into my coat pocket like I'm pocketing a receipt.

"Information only," Mercer says. "Movement. Meetings. Names."

I rise slowly, sliding my coat on, the movement smooth and unhurried even though my blood is a drumline in my ears.

"And if you try to double-cross us," he adds, tilting his head just slightly, "you'll wish the Volkovs had gotten to you first."

I don't give him the satisfaction of a reply. I just turn and walk out into the freezing November air, the mic heavy against my ribs, the weight of his threat sinking into my bones with every step.

The cold sinks deeper into my skin as I walk back across Bancroft's campus, the heavy gray sky pressing lower with each step. The quad has emptied out, students scurrying toward warmth, but I take the long way back, my boots scraping over the uneven stone paths, the burner phone in my coat pocket feeling heavier than the weight of the whole sky. Every breath comes sharp and shallow, every noise—laughter from the library steps, a bike rattling by—grating against my ears, too bright, too alive, too far from the silent war that just got declared in that crappy diner booth across town. Mercer's words hammer in my skull with every step. Grace. They threatened Grace. Maybe not in so many words, maybe not with a gun to her head, not yet, but it doesn't matter. The message was clear enough. Do what we say, or your sister's the first casualty.

By the time I push through the heavy oak door of Chi Omega, the noise inside hits me like a tidal wave. Laughter spilling from the living room, music thudding from upstairs, the kitchen clattering with the sounds of someone burning another attempt at homemade mac and cheese. It's normal. So damn normal I could scream. I slip past the ruckus without speaking, my coat clutched tightly around me, my boots thudding up the staircase louder than necessary, every step vibrating in my bones. I reach my room, kick the door closed behind me harder than I mean to, and toss my bag onto the floor, the sound sharp in the stillness.

For a second, I just stand there.

The mic burns a hole through my pocket, but I don't touch it. I can't. I move instead, pacing the small space, my hands flexing at my sides, nails biting into my palms. The pressure builds so fast it's almost laughable—days, weeks, months of playing the perfect daughter, the perfect student, the perfect damn chess piece—all of it choking me from the inside out until I can't breathe around it anymore.

I grab the first thing within reach—a stupid, overpriced pillow Thalia made me buy during recruitment week—and hurl it across the room with a ragged, animal sound tearing from my throat. It slams into the far wall, knocking down a framed photo from our pledge class, the glass shattering on the hardwood floor with a clean, satisfying crack. I don't stop. I can't. I drag my hands through my hair, pulling at the roots until my scalp burns, the rage bubbling higher, sharper, uglier.

"Crap," I hiss under my breath, pacing faster, kicking the broken frame out of my way. "Crap, crap, crap."

It isn't fair. None of it is fair. They get to make all the rules, and I'm the one who has to bleed for it.

I slam my fist into the closet door, the cheap wood rattling against the hinges, the jolt of pain radiating up my arm in a white-hot spike that barely registers over the fury roaring through my veins. I'm supposed to be smarter than this. I'm supposed to be better at hiding it. But right now, all I want to do is break everything I can get my hands on until the world makes some kind of sense again.

The door creaks open.

I don't look up at first, breathing hard, my shoulders heaving with the effort of holding myself together by threads that feel ready to snap.

"Em?" Thalia's voice slices through the noise, low and cautious, like she already knows what she's walking into.

I drag my gaze up and meet hers. She stands just inside the door, taking it all in with one sharp sweep—the shattered glass on the floor, the dented closet door, the pillow sprawled like a fallen soldier across the far wall, the mess of me standing in the middle of it all, shaking with rage and something dangerously close to grief.

She doesn't ask what happened. She doesn't need to. She moves instead, crossing the room with steady steps, grabbing the trash can by my desk, crouching down to gather the shards of glass with her bare hands, not flinching even when a sliver bites into her thumb and beads of blood bloom along her skin. She works quietly, methodically, cleaning up the mess without asking permission, without saying a word about how bad it looks, about how bad I look.

"You don't have to—" I start, my voice cracking on the edges of the words.

She cuts me off with a glance, sharp and warm and infuriatingly understanding, the kind of look that says shut up, I'm not going anywhere.

By the time she sweeps the last of the broken frame into the trash, my hands are trembling so hard I can barely keep them fisted in my lap. Thalia nudges the bin out of the way with her boot and straightens, brushing her palms clean against her jeans.

She doesn't say anything at first.

She just looks at me ... really looks at me ... and then she opens her arms in a simple, silent offer.

For a second, I can't move.

Then, without thinking, without overanalyzing the thousand ways it could break me worse, I stumble forward, and collapse into her hug.

It's not graceful. It's not elegant. It's ugly and desperate and absolutely everything I didn't know I needed until she's there, warm and solid and real around me, anchoring me when the whole world feels like it's sliding out from under my feet. I clutch at the back of her sweatshirt, digging my fingers in hard enough to hurt, and squeeze my eyes shut against the burn rising up from somewhere deep in my chest.

Thalia says nothing. She doesn't promise me it'll be okay, doesn't lie to fill the silence, doesn't pretend she can fix this. She just holds on, like she's willing to carry some of it, even if she doesn't know what it is yet.

And for the first time in a long, long time, I let her.

I let myself need someone.

Just for a minute.

Just long enough to remember that I'm still here.

Still breathing.

Still standing.

Maybe not for long.

But long enough to fight.

Chapter 13

Emilia

The thing they don't tell you about disasters is that the world doesn't stop spinning when yours does. You still have to go to class. You still have to answer emails. You still have to sit in a lecture hall surrounded by over-caffeinated, overdressed twenty-somethings pretending they know what they're doing with their lives while your own future burns quietly at the edges.

Tuesday morning smells like burnt coffee and cold rain, the quad slick with mist, the kind that seeps into your bones before you even realize it's there. I tug the sleeves of my sweater down over my hands and shoulder my way into Global Institutions—room 302, third floor, the one where the heaters clank so loud it feels like you're learning next to a dying war machine.

Charlotte Kleins already has her laptop open on the third row, tapping away like she's curing cancer instead of rewording her Model UN submission for the fifth dang time. She glances up as I pass and gives me a tight, polished smile that doesn't reach her eyes.

I don't bother returning it. Fake diplomacy is her game. I'm too tired to play today.

The Arrangement

The professor drones about transnational governance structures, and I stare at the clock above his head, watching the second hand drag itself in slow, agonizing circles. My notes are a disaster ... half-finished thoughts, arrows connecting ideas I'll never bother to clean up ... but I keep scribbling anyway, the motion of it keeping me tethered to the present when my mind keeps trying to spiral off into a thousand different futures I can't control.

The engagement party is in five days.

Five days until I'm dressed up like a trophy and paraded in front of half the city's elite, a perfect Langford heir; the latest in a long, unbroken line of chess pieces carved and polished for public consumption.

Five days until I smile for the cameras, sip champagne I won't taste, and stand next to a man whose empire bleeds in languages I haven't even begun to understand yet.

Five days until everything that's been hiding under my skin detonates, one way or another.

I tap my pen against my notebook, trying to bleed off the tension coiling tight between my shoulders. The lecture drags on, the buzz of my phone vibrating once, twice, in my pocket.

Not the burner.

Not Mercer.

My regular phone.

I fish it out under the desk, shielding the screen with my notebook.

Mother: *Reminder: Final dress fitting Thursday, 5:30 PM. Do NOT be late.*

A second text pings immediately after.

Mother: *The Langfords do not make a poor showing.*

I let out a bitter scoff, the sound sharp in the back of my throat. Of course she knows I'm not a Langford, she's known all along. She's the one who kept me in the dark, fed me a name that was never mine, built an entire life around a lie and never once looked back. I should hate her. I should delete the thread, block her number, pretend she doesn't exist. But there's a part of me—raw, aching, infuriatingly human—that still wants to know why. Why lie? Why hide it? Why let me live my whole life chasing a truth she never intended me to find?

The urge to launch my phone across the room is almost unbearable. If it accidentally clipped Charlotte on the way down, well, bonus. But I'm in class, trapped under harsh fluorescent lights, surrounded by the soft-clicking chaos of laptop keys and students highlighting bullet points like the world outside isn't quietly disintegrating. Like everything isn't shifting beneath my feet while someone in the back row whispers about finals, completely unaware that mine already started … and I'm failing.

So instead, I slide the phone back into my pocket.

I press my thumbnail into the side of my finger until it hurts.

And I keep my eyes locked on the front of the room, pretending to absorb the lecture, pretending like I'm not unraveling word by word, breath by breath.

Because if there's one thing I learned from her—one lesson she drilled into me better than any name or bloodline ever could—it's this:

Even when the truth guts you, you keep your shoulders back and your chin high.

And you smile like it doesn't burn.

-

By the time class ends, my head's pounding with a low, miserable throb that no amount of caffeine is going to touch. I shove my laptop into my bag, my hands stiff and clumsy, and elbow through the crowd of students pouring down the hallway, my body moving on autopilot while my mind chews itself to pieces.

My phone buzzes just as I hit the stairs outside.

Thalia: *Mae's. Fifteen minutes. You're buying.*

I stare at the screen for a second, the cold biting into my fingers, and think about blowing her off, crawling back into bed, hiding under my covers until it's time to pretend I'm normal again.

Instead, I type back.

Me: *Fine. But I'm not tipping if the sandwich is soggy.*

Thalia sends back a middle finger emoji, followed by a GIF of someone throwing a sandwich across the room like a grenade, and somehow it makes me laugh, a quick reprieve from the past few weeks.

-

Mae's is a hole-in-the-wall cafe sandwiched between a used bookstore and a vape shop, a place that smells like burned toast, cheap black coffee, and whatever soup of the day they're trying to hock for five bucks a bowl. The floors are sticky, the tables wobble if you lean on them wrong, and the windows sweat year-round no matter what season it is. It's the kind of place that's too stubborn to die, even if it probably failed every health inspection they ever had.

Which is exactly why I love it.

Normal places are too clean, too polished, too ready to swallow you whole.

Mae's just lets you exist.

I shove the door open with my hip, the little brass bell above it jangling sharply, and find Thalia already crammed into a booth in the back, her coat shoved into the corner, her boots up on the opposite bench like she's claiming the whole thing for herself. A chipped mug of coffee steams in front of her, the kind that tastes like regret and bad decisions, and she raises it in salute when she sees me.

"You look like you got hit by a bus," she says cheerfully.

"You're a ray of sunshine," I mutter, sliding into the seat across from her, my bag thudding onto the floor.

The waitress wanders over, a notepad tucked into the back pocket of her jeans, and Thalia rattles off our order without asking—two grilled cheese specials, two tomato soups, and a refill of whatever black sludge they're passing off as coffee today.

"You're bossy when you're hungry," I grumble, slumping back into the booth.

"I'm bossy all the time," Thalia says, smirking. "Being hungry just sharpens it."

She kicks me lightly under the table and I almost smile—almost—before the reality of the next five days crushes down hard enough to steal the air out of my lungs.

Final dress fitting Thursday.

Langford family "Thanksgiving party" Saturday—the one nobody knows is actually an engagement announcement in disguise.

Five days.

Five days left of this version of my life.

Thalia sips her coffee, watching me over the rim of her mug with that look she gets when she knows I'm lying before I even open my mouth.

"You ready?" she asks casually, but her eyes are sharp.

I drag my nails down the side of my cup, the ceramic squeaking faintly under the pressure. "Ready's not the word I'd use," I mutter.

"Terrified?" she offers helpfully.

"Not terrified," I say, and it's almost true. "Just ... bracing for impact."

Thalia snorts and leans back, stretching her arms over the back of the booth. "Classic Langford response. Smile pretty, brace for impact, pretend you're not bleeding out the whole time."

I flinch. Not because she's right, because she is. But because she doesn't know that I'm technically not a Langford.

If Thalia notices my discomfort, she keeps it to herself.

The food arrives—two sad little grilled cheese sandwiches oozing neon-orange cheese, two bowls of watery tomato soup that smell like home and heartburn—and we eat in silence for a while, the kind of silence you only get with someone who knows you too well to fill it with crap.

Halfway through her sandwich, Thalia wipes her hands on a napkin and says, "You know, if you did want to run, we could make it work."

I freeze, my spoon halfway to my mouth, the words hitting harder than they have any right to. "You think it's that simple?" I ask, my voice rough around the edges.

"I think nothing about your life is simple," she says. "But simple's not the same as impossible."

I set my fork down carefully, my appetite disappearing like smoke. "You don't know the half of it," I whisper, mostly to myself.

Thalia leans in, her voice low, her eyes steady. "Then tell me."

I meet her gaze across the table, feeling the words—the truth—lodge in my throat like broken glass. I can't. Not yet. Maybe not ever.

Because if I drag Thalia into this, if I hand her the matches and the map to the powder keg under my feet, she won't walk away. She'll strike the match herself and smile while she does it.

And I'm not ready to lose her, either.

I push my soup away and lean back, folding my arms across my chest. "I'm fine," I lie, the words hollow and weightless.

Thalia doesn't push. She just sits there, steady and infuriatingly patient, like she's waiting for the rest of me to catch up.

I don't know if I ever will.

-

Outside Mae's, the cold clings to my skin, even through the wool of my coat, and the wind has started to whip down the sidewalk in long, clean gusts that tug at my hair and sting my eyes. Thalia's still talking, walking half a step ahead of me, flipping through something on her phone and muttering about the Winter formal in January. I catch fragments: Zeta wants fairy lights again, we're under-budget on decor, someone keeps changing the theme on the shared doc. I nod when I need to. She doesn't notice that my mind's already a block ahead, pacing through the next seventy-two hours like I'm tracing escape routes.

She breaks off down the side path toward her seminar, still talking. I keep walking.

The house is warm when I push the door open, a little too warm, actually—the kind of artificial heat that clings to your clothes and makes the air feel thick. Someone left a holiday-scented candle burning in the front hall again. Vanilla and cinnamon, too strong, too sweet. It makes me want to gag.

I walk through the front room without slowing down. Someone waves at me from the couch ... maybe Sloane ...

but I'm already on the stairs. I'm halfway to my room when I hear Clara's voice behind me, fast and breathless.

"Em, wait, do you have a sec?"

I pause long enough to make it look polite. "A minute. What's up?"

She catches up, clutching her tablet, cheeks flushed like she sprinted in from the backyard. Her hair is still damp from a shower, and she smells faintly like eucalyptus and too much dry shampoo. She blinks at me once, then lowers her voice.

"Okay, I just wanted to confirm—Zeta's saying the January formal is capped at seventy. That still work for us?"

"That's fine," I say. "We'll trim the list."

"Cool. And can you check the menu link when you get a sec? Marist's already being annoying about dairy-free options."

I nod once, and she hesitates, just for a second, her eyes flicking over my shoulder toward the open crack of my bedroom door.

"You have a dress up for something?" she asks, too casually.

I glance back, where the cream satin still hangs against the closet door. I should've taken it down. Should've hidden it. But I didn't, and now she's seen it, and Clara doesn't miss details.

"It's just for Saturday," I say, evenly. "You know … my family's annual party."

"Oh," she says. "I figured you'd wear something black. That looks … different."

I don't blink. "It is."

Clara stands there a second longer, like she wants to keep poking but doesn't know what she's poking at. She smiles, sort of. "Anyway. I'll email the RSVP doc."

I nod. "Thanks."

She takes the stairs two at a time, disappearing back toward the second floor before I can exhale properly.

I push open the door wider and step inside, shutting it behind me with a soft click. The room is quiet now. No noise. Just the creak of old wood and the faint, slow hum of the radiator rattling somewhere under the floor.

The dress still hangs where I left it. I cross the room, grab it by the hanger and shove it into my closet. Then, I sit on the edge of the bed, pull my phone from my pocket, and open the screen.

There's one unread message.

> **Unknown**: *Don't make plans for Friday. We need to talk. You'll be picked up at 7 pm.*

I stare at the screen for a moment, my reflection faint in the black glass once the message fades.

I don't even have to guess who this is … I already know. He doesn't ask me if that's okay. Just assumes I'm available. What a douche.

I place the phone face-down on the nightstand and lie back on the bed, eyes on the ceiling, arms at my sides, body still. I don't move. And somewhere in between, I fall asleep, clothes and all.

-

The first pin catches just beneath my ribcage, and I suck in a breath so sharply it feels like I've stepped into ice water. The seamstress doesn't notice. She continues marking the dress with pins, oblivious to the pain her rough hands are causing. If anyone else sees, they don't comment.

To my left, my mother sits stiffly, a Vogue magazine perched on her lap like a prop. On my right, Thalia is draped over an armchair, ankle crossed over her knee, her fingers flying across her phone. She's been more withdrawn lately, and I wonder if it has something to do with Sebastian. She never mentioned him after that Halloween party—the one where she came back wearing his shirt. That's the thing about us: we don't ask questions. If she needs me, she knows I'm here. The same goes for her.

I close my eyes for just a moment and take a deep breath, but the silence is quickly shattered by my mother's voice—sharp and cold, like the snap of a whip.

"The waist is fine, but the neckline needs to come down an inch. She looks constrained." Her tone is critical, as if critiquing a sculpture in a gallery, not her own daughter.

Thalia finally looks up from her phone. "Yeah, because that's the main problem here," she says dryly. I have to bite back a laugh and shoot her a small grin in the mirror. She winks.

Veronica ignores her. She always does. I'm not sure she even likes Thalia, but she tolerates her for the sake of appearances. Thalia's family is well-connected. Her father, Lorenzo Reyes, is a Supreme Court justice, and her mother, Lydia, is a high-powered defense attorney.

The seamstress—a thin woman with gray-streaked hair and trembling fingers that somehow never miss—hums quietly in agreement and adjusts the fabric with surgical precision. Her chalk glides along the bodice edge, but the next pin scrapes across my skin again. I hiss softly.

The door opens with a muted thud, and every head turns except mine. I stay focused on the pin hovering near my side.

Irina Volkov steps into view. She's dressed in black, tailored to perfection. Her silk blouse catches the light effortlessly. Her hair is twisted into a chignon so sleek it could slice glass, and diamond studs gleam at her ears—understated, yet impossible to ignore. Her heels barely make a sound.

She doesn't speak at first, just surveys the dress. "It suits you." That's all. No elaboration. And honestly, that might be the highest compliment I'll get from her.

I don't know Irina. Not really. I only met her a few weeks ago, and even then, I didn't recognize her for what she was. Or maybe I refused to. But she's Max's mother. The resemblance is subtle but there: the same blue eyes, the same curve of the mouth. And even though Max's betrayal still stings, I know in my bones he's nothing like her.

I say nothing. My mother offers a clipped nod. "She wears the dress well."

Irina gives a faint smile, a mere tilt of her mouth. "Nikolai will be pleased."

The seamstress doesn't flinch. Thalia glances up again. The silence stretches, thick and expectant.

I don't react. I simply turn on the pedestal as instructed, letting the hem of the dress sweep in a slow, deliberate circle. The weight is perfect. Balanced. When I face forward again, I catch Irina's gaze in the mirror and let the quiet do the talking.

"I hope Nikolai appreciates the effort," I say lightly, detached. Because truthfully, I couldn't care less if he likes the dress. I didn't get a say in this arrangement. He doesn't get one in the dress.

Irina's smile doesn't grow, but it sharpens. "Nikolai doesn't appreciate anything until it's taken from him."

Behind me, my mother goes still. Thalia leans forward slightly. Everyone waits for my reaction. I give them nothing. Just my reflection in the mirror—centered, poised, silent.

The seamstress places the final pin and steps back. "We're done."

I nod. I don't turn to the others. I don't wait for approval. The mirrors already tell me what I need to know. The dress is perfect. The color is muted but unforgettable. The fit is sculpted, clean. It was made for photographs. It was made to make a statement. It was made for someone who is done pretending she didn't choose this.

Maybe that's the real trick.

Because beneath the satin and posture and polish, the girl in the mirror doesn't look like she's being dressed for a celebration.

She looks like she's preparing for a war she never asked to fight.

Chapter 14

Emilia

Nikolai doesn't lie. He never has to. The car is there at exactly 6:58: black, gleaming, and deliberately imposing, idling just close enough to the steps of Chi O to make it clear that this isn't a ride. It's a reminder.

My fingers smooth the fabric stretched across my thighs, the tights already clinging too tightly to skin flushed from the heat of getting ready. My boots pinch with every step—too tall, too new, too everything—and yet I chose them. Chose the height. The ache. They'll be unbearable in an hour, maybe less, but that's a problem for the girl who gets to go home. I'm not sure she exists anymore.

The driver, Boris, steps out with all the enthusiasm of a statue. No greeting. No smile. Just clinical silence wrapped in a six-figure salary and a security clearance that could probably make me disappear without a trace. I nod my thanks because it's the only language I have left that doesn't cost me something.

The door closes behind me with a whisper, and then we're off, Chi O shrinking into the background like a fading echo, one more part of a life that no longer belongs to me. Just another warm place I'll never fully return to.

The drive drags, not in time but in weight, the kind of quiet that thickens with every turn of the tires. The city melts into wealthy residential sprawl which gives way to woods so private they seem almost deliberate. There are no porch lights here. No neighbors peeking from behind curtains. Just tall trees and darker intentions. By the time we hit the gates, there's no need for names or clearances. They open as if the estate itself had been waiting for me.

And maybe it had.

The house rises like a secret too beautiful to be spoken aloud. Not opulent. Not ostentatious. Just ... correct. Everything about it screams precision. Discipline. Wealth so old it forgot how to brag. Clean lines, glass and stone, gold-hued path lighting that doesn't blind, it guides. This isn't a fortress like the Volkov estate with its looming shadows and guards at every door. This is something quieter. Smarter. A place that doesn't beg to be feared but earns it.

Boris opens the door again, silent as ever, and I step out, my boots sinking slightly into gravel as the cold air brushes against my skin. I inhale slowly, grounding myself. Shoulders straight. Jaw locked. Heart pounding with the kind of rhythm that comes from high-stakes games and no exits.

The front door swings open. I expect a servant. A butler. An assistant with a clipboard and a bloodless smile. But it's him.

And he's barefoot. And I'm thrown off.

Nikolai stands in the entryway like a man who owns more than property ... like he owns gravity. The black shirt is unbuttoned at the chest, his sleeves rolled carelessly to the elbows, and his dark jeans sit low on his hips like comfort was a calculated decision. His hair is a little tousled, like he's spent the afternoon running his fingers through it, frustrated or amused or both. I'm not sure which is worse.

This is not the version of him I was prepared for. I had braced for armor: tailored suits and weaponized elegance. Not this. Not bare feet and too-easy charm and a grin that threatens to unmake me.

"Early," he says, voice smooth like wine poured into a too-full glass. "I thought you'd make me wait. Or not come at all."

"I figured if I made you wait, you'd send Boris to knock until I answered."

That grin sharpens. "Not knock," he says, and there's a pause just long enough to feel deliberate. "Drag you out of the house."

I don't smile. I don't even flinch. I walk past him, chin high, because I refuse to let this be his win.

The house is warm in the kind of way money can't buy. It smells like garlic and rosemary and something deeper: smoke, maybe, or old wood. A meal. A memory. A promise I don't trust.

"Planning on giving me a tour?" I ask, pretending his proximity doesn't make my skin feel too tight.

He shrugs. "Do you want one?"

My eyes flick up. "Isn't that what good hosts do?"

That panty melting grin again, like he knows exactly how much he's getting under my skin. "I'm starving," he says instead, and turns.

And I follow.

Not because I want to. Because there's nowhere else to go.

The hall is long, the light golden and low, the floors a dark, expensive wood that doesn't squeak even under his weight. The house is clean, yes, but not sterile. There's personality here, lurking between the details: muted paintings, leather-bound books worn soft with use, a jacket slung over a low chair like it had been shrugged off carelessly and never corrected. A coffee cup chipped at the rim. Framed vinyls in narrow hallways. A house designed not to impress but to contain. A man's house. His. I want to ask him how long he's lived here, but I'm afraid of the answer I'll receive.

That unsettles me more than any opulence ever could.

But what really stops me is the dining room. Not the table—it's elegant but simple. No centerpiece. No candles.

It's the two men already seated that kill the breath in my throat.

Max.

Sebastian.

Both with half-empty glasses, both watching me with expressions that toe the line between amusement and assessment. And I do what I've always been taught not to do. I turn to leave.

Nikolai's hand touches my shoulder, gentle but grounding. "Please," he says softly. "Don't."

I pause. I don't look at his hand. I don't look at the table. I look at him. Really look. And for the first time since this arrangement began, I see something that looks like sincerity.

I don't say yes. But I don't leave.

I take the seat across from Max. I feel his gaze like heat under my skin, and I have to force myself not to react. Not to glance at him. Not to throw a glass or ask him why he ever thought betrayal was a language I'd understand.

Sebastian leans forward, elbows on the table, and offers me a smile that doesn't quite reach his eyes. "Good to see you again, Emilia."

"Wish I could say the same," I reply sweetly.

Nikolai reappears, plates in hand like he doesn't notice the tension threading through the air. The food smells too good to hate. Seared steak, garlic potatoes, warm rolls folded into a napkin. It's domestic. Intimate. So real it feels like fiction.

He pours the wine himself. "Cabernet," he murmurs, placing the glass in front of me. "I figured you'd prefer something with backbone."

"And if I didn't?"

"Then I'd know you were lying."

The meal begins, quiet and deceptively ordinary. Except nothing here is ordinary. Not the food. Not the men. Not the way they're watching me … not like a woman, but like a weapon they haven't decided how to use yet.

Max is the first to break. "You look well."

My fork pauses. "That's funny. You look like you've been carrying guilt like a parasite."

Nikolai clears his throat, like this wasn't the script. "I invited you here for clarity."

I sip the wine. Let it settle. "Then ask the right question."

His gaze holds mine like it's a challenge. "Why did you sign the contract?"

And there it is.

The truth sits at the base of my throat like a curse. I could say it was for Grace, for my sister's future, for safety. And that would be partly true. But there's more. So much more. There's the hunger to tear this world apart from the inside. There's the exhaustion of watching men like my father win. And yes, there's a part of me, small and desperate, that still wants the boy who wrote me letters under a Russian winter moon.

But I don't say any of that.

"Protection," I say, and it sounds like a sin.

Nikolai nods slowly, his expression unreadable. "You'll have that."

Silence curls between us, thick and slow.

"And the rest?" I ask. "The posing? The affection? Do I smile on cue or kiss you like I mean it?"

He leans forward, elbows braced. "A kiss would help."

"I'll try not to vomit."

But we both know I won't. We both know I've spent too many nights imagining the taste of that particular lie.

He studies me like I'm a secret he's trying to remember. "I want them to believe you're mine."

I tilt my head. "And are you mine, Nikolai?"

The pause stretches so long it becomes a second heartbeat in the room. "I think," he says finally, "you already know the answer." And that's the most dangerous thing he's said all night.

I hastily excuse myself to go to the bathroom. The hallway is long, with abstract wall art that seems out of place. I find the bathroom and shut the door behind me. The mirror reflects a woman who on the outside, seems put together, but on the inside, she's humming with anticipation. I pretend to wash my hands because the bathroom was just an excuse to get away. When I open the door again, I expect a deserted hallway, but instead, Max is standing outside, back leaning against the opposite wall.

I stop short, my eyes darting around for an exit, but I don't see a way out. I'm trapped. I'm annoyed. And the last person I want to talk to is Max.

-

Max

I told Nikolai I was going to talk to her. To clear the air. I didn't like how we left things, and the longer the silence stretched between us, the more it felt like something was fracturing permanently.

So when she excused herself to go to the bathroom, I took it as my opening. The perfect chance to talk, without eyes or ears or anyone turning it into a scene.

But now it's been a few minutes, and I'm starting to get nervous. There's a small window in there—not big enough for most people, but she's scrappy. Wouldn't be the first time she ran when things got too real. Not that she's trapped. She's free to walk out the front door if she wants. But something about the delay sets me on edge.

Then the lock clicks.

The door opens.

And there she is.

My chest tightens, because up close, she looks good. *Too* good. Her makeup's subtle, barely there, but enough to draw the eye. Not that she needs it. I've seen her without it—half asleep, mascara smudged, hair a mess—and she was still the most beautiful person in the room. But right now? She's striking. Confident. Sharp-edged in a way that hurts to look at.

I shove the thoughts down. This isn't the time.

I'm here to fix what I broke.

I see it ... the flicker in her eyes, that split second where she contemplates walking right past me without a word. Maybe even running. But she doesn't. Instead, she crosses her arms, leans against the doorframe like she owns the hallway, and narrows her eyes.

"What do you want, Max?"

She's annoyed. She's cold. And she has every right to be. I deserve worse.

I inhale slowly, try to steady myself, but the words come rushing out anyway, tumbling over each other like they've been waiting too long to be said. "I know I don't deserve your time. I just ... please, just hear me out."

She raises a brow, tapping her foot like she's waiting for me to implode.

Then she gives a little wave of her hand. "Go on."

So I do.

"I'm a selfish idiot," I admit, bluntly. "I should've told you my last name from the beginning. I shouldn't have hidden it."

Her reaction is immediate. She rolls her eyes, sharp and unbothered, and for a moment I'm distracted because—holy crap—her eyes really are that green. That kind of green you only notice when it's too late to forget it.

"You think *that's* why I'm mad?" she snaps. "Because you didn't tell me your last name?"

I blink. "Yes?" It comes out like a question, and I instantly regret it.

Because now I don't know.

I assumed it was the Volkov name. The weight that comes with it. That's why I hid it. I didn't want her to see me as *them*.

She throws her hands up like she can't believe how dense I am. "Just stop, Max. You're completely missing it. I don't care about your last name. I don't give a crap about your family. We all come from messed up people." She takes a step forward, frustration spilling from every inch of her. "I'm mad because you lied about why we became friends in the first place."

The words hit harder than I expect.

Right. That.

I scratch the back of my neck because, yeah. She's not wrong.

She finally shuts the bathroom door behind her with a soft click, like she's cutting off the past along with it. Her expression softens just slightly, but the disappointment in her eyes is still there.

"If you still don't get why that matters," she says, shaking her head, "then I don't think you ever will."

I open my mouth, desperate to stop her. "Em—"

But she raises a hand before I can finish. "Don't." Her voice drops lower. Not cruel. Just final. "We can't be friends, Max. And it's not because of your last name. Think about that." She turns and walks down the hallway, each step pulling her farther from something I didn't realize I needed until I'd already lost it.

And me?

I just stand there. Stuck. Watching the space she left behind and wondering how in the world I screwed this up so badly that the one girl I'd risk everything for won't even let me be her friend.

-

Emilia

I'm still fuming by the time I make it back to the dining room, the kind of hot, focused anger that doesn't sit in your chest—it simmers in your bloodstream, makes every step feel too loud and every breath feel earned. Sebastian and Nikolai are talking in hushed whispers, their heads tilted in just enough to be conspiring, but not enough to be obvious about it. I stop just beyond the doorway, cloaked in shadow, tucked into the edge of the hall where I can see them, but they can't see me, and for a second, I just watch. Because I need the space, and because I need the time.

From here, I can see Niko swirling his wine around in the glass with that particular kind of boredom that only men like him have perfected … the kind that doesn't mean disinterest but control. Calculated detachment. That ability to let the world burn around him while he finishes his drink. Sebastian, though, looks pissed, and not in the way that invites confrontation … more like someone replaced the milk in his Cheerios with water, and he's still being forced to eat them with a silver spoon and a fake smile.

I don't know Sebastian well enough to trust him. Or hate him. He exists in that dangerous in-between: neutral on the surface, unreadable beneath. After I had Knox run background on everyone close to Nikolai, Sebastian was the only one who came back spotless. No records. No scandals. No smudges. Which is suspicious as hell. People in this world don't come clean. They're scrubbed, polished, or erased.

All I've managed to dig up is that he's from old money on the outskirts of London. Shipped off to boarding school at a young age. Like me. An only child. Somehow ended up best friends with the heir to a Bratva faction. The math doesn't add up, and I've played this game long enough to know when someone is holding cards they're not showing.

He's a wildcard. The kind of man who doesn't show all his cards because he doesn't need to. If life was a game of Uno, he'd be the one slapping down a draw four just to watch the room burn, grinning while everyone else scrambled to recover.

I can't hear what they're saying, and maybe that's for the best because I'm not sure I'd like it if I could. I'm about to step into the room and cut whatever conversation they're having short when I feel a hand press lightly against the small of my back, fingers just barely brushing against the fabric of my sweater, and the annoyance rises so fast I'm already biting back a groan before I turn.

"Spying's not a great look on you, Emilia."

Max. Of course.

I roll my eyes without even turning to face him, already over the sound of his voice. "That's rich coming from you," I mutter, shaking his hand off before it lingers. "Same could be said for you, Maksim."

I don't have to look over my shoulder to know he winces. I hear it in the way his breath catches, the way the space between us shifts, the sudden quiet that says he wasn't expecting me to weaponize his full name but should've known better.

Both of them look up when I enter. Sebastian looks irritated, like I've interrupted a conversation he didn't want to pause. Niko just watches me, eyes steady, unreadable, like he's measuring the damage and already deciding how to use it.

For a second, I think he's going to ask if I'm okay. He doesn't. He never does. Because for all the red flags he drags behind him like royal robes, Niko's only green flag is this: he knows when I'm not okay, and he doesn't pretend otherwise.

I walk briskly to my seat, grab my purse with a single fluid motion, and turn back to him.

"Thank you for dinner," I say, calm and clipped. "It was … lovely." I pause on the word. Let it drag, sweet and acidic, like a poisoned cherry. Then I give Sebastian a nod. Barely. Max doesn't even get that.

I turn on my heel and head for the door, focus narrowed to the exit and nothing else, until I hear the footsteps behind me … deliberate, fast, heavy.

A hand closes around my arm, and before I can pull away, I'm spun around so fast it makes my stomach flip, and I'm suddenly face-to-face with Nikolai, his eyes dark and sharp and way too close. He's looking at me like he wants to say something but can't, like the words are lodged behind his teeth, too dangerous to let out and too bitter to swallow. He opens his mouth, shuts it again, jaw clenched so tight I swear I can hear the crack of tension radiating off him. He drags a hand across the back of his neck like it'll somehow clear the storm in his head, and for one stupid second, I think he might actually say something kind.

He doesn't.

He leans down, mouth so close to my ear I can feel the heat of it against my skin, and his voice is low, firm, unshakable. "Don't screw tomorrow up, Langford." Then he pulls back, steps around me, and opens the door from behind like I'm nothing more than a guest overstaying her welcome.

And I stand there, frozen—not because of fear, not even because of anger—but because of how easily he can knock the air out of my lungs with five words and a stare.

I don't give him the reaction he's waiting for.

I don't even look at him.

I just flip him off as I walk out the door, climb into the back of the car without a word, and let Boris close the door behind me with a soft, final click.

As the car pulls out of the circular drive, the lights of the estate shrinking in the distance, I check my phone.

Three messages.

One from my mother, reminding me to make sure everything is ready for tomorrow.

One from Thalia: *Did you survive dinner or do I need to kill someone?*

And one from the burner phone.

Unknown: *We're watching you tomorrow, Emilia. If you screw this up, it'll be your own funeral. Think of Grace. Of Thalia. Of anyone you've ever cared for.*

I let the screen go dark and rest my head against the window, eyes closing before the panic can creep in. Because maybe … if I'm lucky … when I wake up, it'll all just be a dream.

But I already know it won't be.

It never is.

-

If you'd told me six months ago that I'd be engaged right now, I would've laughed in your face. Heck, I probably would've looked at you like you were hallucinating. Because that? That would've been impossible. My relationship with Preston imploded half a year ago, and I haven't had a boyfriend since. I made it a point … no more getting serious with strangers. Especially not marriage. Especially not this.

And yet, here we are.

Today's the day. Not the wedding, praise for that. That spectacle comes later. Today is the announcement. The official, PR-orchestrated unveiling of our engagement. Publicly. To the world.

I groan, low and guttural, and fling the sheets off like they're to blame. My phone screams from the nightstand, its bright white numbers searing judgment into my eyes.

9:00 a.m.

Wow. I actually slept. Not well—it felt like wandering through someone else's dream with no way out—but still, more than I expected. The kind of sleep that tricks your body into thinking it's fine while your mind keeps pacing in circles.

I drag myself to the mirror—the tall one in the corner by the window—and stop cold.

The girl staring back doesn't look like someone preparing for one of the most strategically choreographed engagement announcements in modern history. She looks like she barely made it through the night. Hair tangled. Mascara still clinging under one eye like a bruise. Eyes too green and too tired. Skin pale from stress and not enough sunlight.

Still me but hanging on by a thread. There's a tightness in my chest I can't shake. Not panic. Not grief. Just that slow, dawning ache of knowing today was never really about me. It was about legacy. Optics. Control. By tonight, half the country club crowd will be buzzing that I'm engaged to a man whose hands are probably still stained with the blood of every covert deal my "father" ever signed off on.

And I should care. I should rage. But after the last few months? I'm just … exhausted. So exhausted.

It's one thing to be forced into marrying someone you don't love. It's another to discover that the man you've called "Dad" your entire life, the man you've sacrificed yourself to please isn't even your biological father. No, that honor goes to a Russian criminal with a name that makes FBI agents twitch.

And let's not forget the Bureau has me under 24/7 surveillance. A single misstep and they'll bury me in legal misery with a metaphorical gun to my head. So no, my father's black-ops history isn't at the top of my worry list. Not in a city where corruption is practically currency.

I twist my hair into a messy knot and splash cold water on my face like that's going to fix anything. It doesn't. I still look like the girl who almost let Nikolai Volkov kiss her last night. The girl who stood in his house—a house that felt like danger and safety all at once—and pretended none of it meant anything.

I'm dead tired. Bone-deep, soul-cracking tired.

I grab my phone and scroll through group chats without a care, just to feel something … anything. The messages are flying about the Winter formal: finalizing set-ups, confirming lighting cues, coordinating playlists. Clara is asking if the violinist confirmed. Someone's panicking over seating cards.

It all feels fake. Like we're acting out a script none of us auditioned for.

Then, a knock.

Two sharp taps.

And Thalia's voice, muffled but unmistakably impatient. "Emilia Langford, if you don't open this door in the next ten seconds, I will throw away this coffee, and you know you need the caffeine to survive today."

I close my eyes, inhale, and brace myself. There's no escaping her. She's my best friend. My co-conspirator. My buffer against the madness. My mirror.

And this morning? She's about to be a pain in my ass.

I crack open the door just wide enough to see her standing there, already dressed in a silk robe, coffee in one hand, phone in the other, under-eye masks perfectly in place.

She takes one look at me and doesn't bother to sugarcoat it. "Oh, babe," she sighs, pushing her way in. "You look like generational trauma ran you over with a bus."

I groan and collapse back onto the bed. "That's because it did."

And it really, really did.

-

The room feels suffocating. Too many people. Too many eyes. And all of them on me.

My mother stands off to the side, practically glowing in her element, her gaze sweeping over me like she's inspecting a product she's about to ship off. From the cream satin glued to my skin—strapless, impossible to breathe in—to the makeup that's been caked on and sprayed stiff enough to survive a hurricane. She lingers on every inch of me like she's waiting to find a flaw.

I catch a glimpse of myself in the mirror. Pearl drop earrings. Blush pink nails. I look exactly like the person they want me to be.

And I hate how easy it is to play the part.

The makeup artist, Harper, I think, adds the last bit of gloss to my lips, then steps back like she's unveiling a masterpiece. She glances to my mother for approval, because apparently, she's the final authority on my face.

My mother gives a curt nod, and Harper lights up like she just landed a Vogue cover.

I give her a weak smile. It's not her fault. She's just doing her job. But man, I would give anything to feel even an ounce of her excitement.

The room buzzes around me, all too loud and all too fake. Assistants rush in and out like they're running a drill. Through the window, I can already see cars pulling up.

Of course my parents went all out; the Langford Annual Party isn't just tradition, it's spectacle. Or, if we're being honest, a campaign stunt dressed up in hors d'oeuvres and string quartets. A donor thank-you. A PR power move. Another chance for Trent Langford to showcase the empire he's been assembling piece by calculated piece. But what none of the guests know, not yet, is that tonight isn't just about champagne and carefully staged photo ops. Tonight is the setup. The warm-up. The soft launch for the real headline they're saving for later.

My engagement.

So help me.

Thalia's perched in the window seat like she's watching a slow car crash. Her blush chiffon gown spills over her legs. Hair pinned up. Champagne glass balanced on her knee. She's scrolling, pretending to be bored, but when our eyes meet in the mirror, she gives me a soft, knowing smile.

I shove out of the chair, ignoring my mother's hiss of disapproval, and make my way over to Thalia like gravity's pulling me there. I drop onto the couch next to her and lean my head against her shoulder. Somewhere behind us, the stylist makes a strangled noise like I've just committed a capital offense against my hair.

"You're way too quiet," Thalia murmurs, not looking up. "It's creeping me out."

I keep my eyes on the chaos in front of me. "Do you ever feel like you're watching yourself from the outside?"

She tilts her head slightly, smirking. "Yeah. Usually when I'm doing something hot and catastrophically bad for me."

I let out the ghost of a laugh. "So, always."

"Exactly."

Before she can say more, the door creaks open and a pair of deliberate, slow heels click across the marble.

Grace walks in like she owns the place. Hair pulled back in a high ponytail, soft curls bouncing, not too formal, not too casual. Her periwinkle dress hugs her at the waist and flows just enough to make it look effortless.

She shuts the door behind her and raises an eyebrow. "You look ... different."

I blink. "Thanks?"

"No, seriously. You look ... regal. Like a statue someone would be scared to touch."

Thalia smirks. "Finally. Someone gets it."

Grace saunters over and perches on the armrest of the couch like it was made for her. "I just spent an hour having my scalp boiled by a curling wand. If I don't get a good photo out of tonight, someone's getting sued."

I study her. Really study her.

The caramel highlights in her hair—natural, lightened by the sun and hours on the soccer field. The way her jaw clenches when she's thinking, just like her dad. Or rather, her *real* dad. Not mine.

But it's her eyes that hit hardest.

Hazel. That exact, muted gold-brown. Our father's eyes. Eyes I've never had.

Mine are green. Darker. Sharper. My features are narrower. More angular. And suddenly I can see it, everything I missed before. The subtle differences I chalked up to coincidence or genetics skipping a generation. But no. It's more than that. Her softness is inherited. Mine is borrowed. I am a stranger inside my own bloodline.

Because Grace is the true Langford heir. My mother's pride and joy. And I am the reminder of the man she never talks about. The Russian. The real father. The secret mistake that was hidden.

The realization settles like lead in my stomach.

A knock at the door breaks the moment.

"Miss Langford?" a voice says, muffled but urgent. "It's time."

My mother turns from her assistant and sweeps toward the exit like a bride entering her own funeral. As she passes Grace, she gently touches her arm, an unthinking gesture, intimate and habitual.

Grace stands, smooths her dress. She hesitates at the door. Glances back at me like she wants to say something. But there's nothing left to say. Instead, she raises her hand and flips our mother off behind her back before stepping out into the hallway.

It almost makes me laugh. Thalia, next to me, is already grinning.

She finishes her champagne, sets the glass down, and stands.

"Well," she says, brushing off invisible lint, "you ready to go lie to a room full of politicians and millionaires?"

I exhale, square my shoulders. The dress pulls taut across my chest, but I don't flinch.

"Let's make it convincing."

-

The marble stair treads glide beneath my feet, cool and indifferent, as I descend at Thalia's side with the kind of composure that's no longer learned—it's bone-deep. We don't speak. We don't need to. We descend in rhythm, our gowns brushing the edges of our legs like whispers, our faces polished into effortless calm, as if we were born into nights like this, into chandeliers and candlelight and wine glasses shaped like promises.

The ballroom swells below us, golden and gleaming, bodies clustered like expensive perfume clouds—donors, press, family, snakes in silk. To them, this is just another Langford party. Just another November excuse for a thousand-dollar guest list and a too-long toast from the Vice President himself.

No one looks up.

Except him.

My breath stutters ... uninvited, unwelcome ... the second I find him near the far end of the room, flanked by Max and Sebastian. Nikolai Volkov stands in black, full black, with the kind of precision that turns tailoring into weaponry. The suit hugs his frame like it's been hand-stitched to match the exact tension in his spine. His shirt is unbuttoned just enough to hint at something beneath, skin and heat and danger, and his posture is maddeningly relaxed—one hand in his pocket, the other wrapped lazily around a glass of dark liquor, like this entire night is happening for his amusement.

When he sees me, he doesn't smile. Doesn't look surprised. Doesn't straighten. He just watches—all dark eyes and unholy stillness—and then that slow, deliberate, entirely too sinful smile ghosts across his lips like he's tasted something I haven't even offered yet.

And just like that, my body betrays me.

There's a flush ... low and sharp and hot ... curling up my chest, a pulse behind my knees, a prickle down the back of my neck that makes me want to scream at myself. My spine stays straight, my expression cool, but inside? I'm heat and instinct and the slow-burning realization that I want to taste that mouth, just once, just to know what power like his tastes like when it's pressed against mine.

What I wouldn't give to kiss those lips. Just once. Just to ruin myself a little.

Thalia leans in, her voice soft and dry. "You're staring."

"He started it," I mutter, lips barely moving.

"That man looks like temptation in a custom suit," she replies, sipping from her champagne. "And I say this with love—you're not immune."

"I don't have to be," I hiss, "I just have to survive." But even as I say it, I feel the shift in the room.

Because it's not just Nikolai.

They're all here.

The Volkovs.

I spot Alexei first—tall, silver-templed, flanked by two men in dark suits, his eyes scanning the crowd with the kind of cold efficiency that feels off-putting. He stands with his back impossibly straight, his mouth drawn in a line I wouldn't dare cross, and even from across the ballroom, I feel the iron of him. Next to him is Irina dressed in a dark red gown which skims the floor as she sips from a crystal flute, gaze sharp enough to cut glass. She sees me. Her head tilts slightly. She doesn't smile. I didn't expect her to.

To the left of her stands Dimitri. His eyes locked on me like he's calculating the distance to something I haven't noticed yet. Behind them, more men. More shadows.

Thalia notices too. Her voice is lower now, edged with something unreadable. "Did you know they'd be here?"

"No. But it doesn't surprise me."

"Lovely."

By the time my heels land on the marble at the bottom of the stairs, I've slipped fully into the version of myself they all know—the one with the easy smile and the measured laughter, the one who belongs here like the crown molding and the champagne. I let my chin tilt at just the right angle. Let my shoulders glide back. My mouth curls around a soft smile so well-practiced it could be trademarked.

It doesn't take long for them to find me.

"Holy crap, look at you," Poppy breathes before she's even halfway across the floor, her pink tulle dress bouncing around her knees like she walked out of a Valentine's ad. "You look like a Bond girl who also owns the bank."

"She looks like she'd murder someone on the Riviera and get away with it," Sloane says, looping her arm through mine like we're at prom, her clutch swinging from two fingers like a weapon. "In heels. Without smudging her lipstick."

Clara circles next, drink already in hand, eyeing me like she's doing a cost-per-wear analysis. "Okay, but is that custom? Because that's not off the rack. That bodice? That's illegal in six countries."

I smile, just slightly. "I plead the fifth."

Sloane spins me in a half-circle. "I'm sorry, this is what you've been hiding in your room? You could've warned the rest of us. I would've brought backup lashes."

"You would've brought a defibrillator," Clara mutters, sipping again. "The neckline alone could stop traffic."

"I mean, I knew you'd look good," Poppy says, stepping closer, eyes scanning the gown from hem to collarbone, "but this? This is main character energy. You don't just walk in dressed like that for nothing."

My stomach tightens. I smile wider. "I just liked the cut," I say lightly, lifting my champagne glass to my lips before they can press further.

"Oh please," Clara scoffs. "No one wears cream satin unless they're about to announce an engagement or burn down a country club."

"Preferably both," Sloane adds, laughing.

I hum, noncommittal, and scan the crowd like I'm only half-listening. They keep going—because of course they do—overlapping voices, compliments, questions. Who did my makeup. Who tailored the dress. Whether I saw that Georgia from Delta Gamma hooked up with Drew Callahan and was apparently bragging about it like it wasn't a community service project.

Poppy leans in again, lowering her voice to a conspiratorial whisper. "Okay, but seriously, is that Nikolai over there?"

I don't answer. I don't flinch. I don't even blink. Just lift my glass again.

"That's him, right?" she presses. "Tall, scary-hot, looks like he has a gun collection and secret childhood trauma?"

"He looks like a sex contract waiting to happen," Sloane says, a little too loudly.

"He looks like a PR nightmare," Clara mutters, but she's eyeing him with interest as well.

"I'm sorry," Poppy says, "but why is he here? And why is he looking at you like—"

"He's not," I cut in, smoothly. "He's probably just bored."

Clara narrows her eyes. "So you do know him."

I smile again, soft, elegant, impenetrable. "He's a family … acquaintance."

Thalia, miraculously still at my side, snorts into her drink.

Sloane's already distracted again. "Okay, but like … what's his story? Mafia vibes or just bad boy investor chic?"

"Does it matter?" Clara says. "He looks like he'd ruin your credit score and your life."

"That's the dream," Poppy sighs.

They laugh. I smile again. My mouth is starting to hurt from it, but the whole time, I can feel him.

Nikolai hasn't moved. Still watching. Still waiting. Still anchored at the far side of the room like the storm I haven't admitted is coming.

My Chi O sisters are beautiful. Loud. Real in the way that only people untouched by consequence can be. They see me, but only the parts I allow—the dress, the hair, the easy charm I wear like perfume. They don't see the leash. They don't see the Volkovs. They don't know the earth is already shifting under their feet.

Not yet.

Nikolai hasn't stopped watching me. Not once. Even surrounded by the Volkovs—Alexei rigid and regal, Irina poised like she's curating the entire damn room, Max perfectly silent beside him—Nikolai stands at the center of it like gravity. He's not smiling anymore. He's not doing anything. He's just *there*. Anchored. Burning. Like the match hasn't been struck yet, but it's close, and he's already warm with the anticipation.

The voices start to lower before the music fades.

It's gradual, the way the room begins to hush, the way heads start to turn. The kind of silence that builds not because someone told them to stop speaking, but because the air shifts and the tone drops and suddenly people just know something's about to happen.

And then my father's voice, perfectly amplified, smooth as aged bourbon, rolls across the room from the far end of the grand piano. "I want to thank you all for being here tonight. It's always a privilege to host so many friends, colleagues, and members of our extended family under one roof." He waits, lets the applause rise and fade like a well-trained tide.

I brace myself.

"Each year, this night marks the beginning of the holiday season—a tradition we've carried on for over two decades…"

I don't hear the rest. Not clearly. Because that's when it happens. A hand—cool, poised, with urgency—finds my arm just below the elbow.

Mother.

She doesn't pull. Doesn't tighten her grip. Just presses her fingers there, light and firm like a whisper from a blade. She's beside me in her champagne silk gown, pearls at her throat, expression lifted into something that reads as maternal warmth from five feet away and glacial control from two.

"Now," she says under her breath. "Smile and walk."

I turn. Slowly. Meet her eyes.

"I'm talking to them," I say. I don't know why. Maybe because I need to remind her I'm not just a pawn in this moment. That I can see what's coming.

"They'll survive," she murmurs. "You'll thank me later."

"I doubt it."

She doesn't flinch. "That's not required."

She's already moving before I can say anything else. Her hand never leaves my arm, and the smile on her face never breaks. Not when she guides me gently but absolutely through the crowd.

Not when Sloane's voice calls out behind me, "Wait, where are you going? Did we say something—?"

Not when Clara watches me with narrowed eyes and Poppy's mouth opens to ask another question I'll never hear.

We pass the Volkovs, and for a moment, I swear the entire room tilts.

Irina's gaze meets mine, steady and glittering, like she's watching a scene she's already read in a script. Alexei doesn't look at me, but I feel the chill that radiates off him like marble. Malkov gives me nothing but a flicker of something unreadable, and Max … Max tracks every step like he's logging angles for later.

But Nikolai? He doesn't move. Doesn't speak.

His eyes follow me as I walk past, slow, deliberate, like he's watching the moment I'm handed over. Like he knows I've just crossed the point of no return. And for a second, I think he might say something.

But he doesn't.

He just lifts his glass slightly, the ghost of that smirk returning to his mouth—the one that isn't meant to mock. The one that says *there's no going back*

And then we stop.

Just behind the grand arch near the raised platform, tucked slightly from view. Not hidden, not revealed. A place to watch. A place to wait.

My mother releases my arm.

I hear my father's voice again, louder now, rehearsed and warm. "…but this year, it's different. This year, we're proud to share something close to our hearts…"

Her eyes flick to mine.

She doesn't say, *Are you ready?*

She doesn't say, *You'll be fine.*

She just smooths the line of her sleeve and says, in the softest, most polished tone I've ever heard, "Fix your posture."

And then the room goes still.

I don't move. I don't blink. I don't let my hands tremble where they rest at my sides, even though my heart is beating so hard it feels like it might crack through my ribs and spill everything I've been trying so fucking hard to hold together. My mother doesn't look at me again. She doesn't need to. She knows I'll do what I'm supposed to. She raised me to. Raised me to smile through silence. To nod through betrayal. To make it look easy when it's anything but.

Across the room, the crowd has shifted. Their attention fully turned toward the front of the room now, toward my father, still standing at the mic like he was born there, his voice the only thing anyone hears.

"...and so," he says, with that practiced warmth that makes even the lies sound like gospel, "it brings me great pride tonight to introduce someone very special to our family. A man whose reputation and accomplishments speak for themselves, but whose future, I believe, will speak even louder."

I feel it before I see it.

The subtle movement. The pause in the room. The way the air sharpens.

My mother leans in.

"This is it," she says, smiling with her mouth, dead behind the eyes. "Now walk."

I step forward.

Not because I want to. But because it's already happening.

There's a low murmur, a ripple through the guests, as I cross the floor towards my 'father'. I hear my name once, soft, questioning—maybe Poppy's voice, maybe Clara's—but I don't turn. I can't. My heels click like a countdown, the dress sweeping in elegant defiance behind me.

My father continues without missing a beat.

"Please join me in welcoming not just an ally, not just a partner, but a future member of the Langford family—"

The pause is precise.

"—Nikolai Volkov."

It detonates like a silent explosion. No screams. Just gasps. Just the collective *tilt* of the room, the quiet thud of realization hitting a hundred people at once, the shifting weight of expectations being rewritten in real time.

And then I feel him. He's there. Beside me.

I don't know when he moved. I didn't hear his footsteps. Didn't see him cross the room. One moment he wasn't there, and now he is.

He stands just to my left, close enough that I feel the warmth radiating from him, his arm brushing mine for half a second before he pulls away again. He smells like spice and leather and the kind of scent that makes my thighs clench. Which makes me hate him even more for the effect he has on me. I can't look at him, not yet, not with the crowd watching. But I know. I can feel the smirk. Feel the satisfaction.

He's standing like he's been beside me all along.

My father extends an arm toward us, welcoming the applause now stirring through the room—slow, uneven, unsure.

"To celebrate the engagement of my daughter, Emilia Rose Langford," he says, pride thick in his voice, "and Nikolai Adrian Volkov."

There it is.

Final. Unyielding. Public.

My full name. His full name. A weaponized truth. A political contract. A legacy binding itself to something older, darker, more dangerous than anyone in this room has the spine to understand.

I smile. I have to.

The applause swells. The cameras rise. The flashes begin.

I turn to him slowly, like choreography, and he meets me with that calm, wicked expression that tells me he's not just surviving this—he's winning.

"Congratulations, darling," he murmurs, so low only I can hear. "You're mine now."

Then he slides the engagement ring onto my left hand. I glance down to see a fairly substantial-sized diamond surrounded by tiny emeralds and I want to hate it, but I can't. Because it's the exact ring I offhandedly mentioned in one of my letters to him all those years ago. He remembered. My gaze whips up to him, a small o forming on my lips. He sends me a wink, and I lift my champagne glass to his, eyes glittering with the kind of fire they'll all mistake for joy.

"Don't get comfortable," I murmur back. "I bite."

He clinks his glass gently against mine. "Good."

The applause fades, but the sound doesn't leave. It echoes. Inside my ribs. Behind my eyes. My ears are ringing, and for a moment, I can't tell if it's from the lights or the blood rushing hot and fast through my veins. I stand tall. I smile. I tilt my head just slightly, just enough to look picture-perfect beside him. And I don't move.

Nikolai's hand brushes mine again, deliberate this time, his fingers curling just enough to suggest that if I took it, the whole room would explode. I don't. Not yet. But I can feel the question in the air around us, feel it rising on champagne bubbles and disbelief.

Behind the smile, I want to scream.

He leans closer, his voice warm and soft and dripping in things I don't have the energy to parse. "You're shaking," he says.

"I'll steady," I answer. "Don't flatter yourself."

"Wouldn't dream of it," he murmurs.

The crowd is moving now, stirring like a crazed beehive. Conversations restarting in low tones, lips against wine glasses, a hundred half-finished sentences and widened eyes disguised as polite curiosity.

My mother reappears before I can blink, already nodding to someone near the front—probably the photographer from The Times. Her smile is sharp. Her steps smoother than they should be. She whispers something to my 'father'. His hand drops from the mic. The performance, for them, is already done.

But not for me.

The moment we step off the platform, the swarm closes in.

Poppy reaches us first. Her eyes are wide, her mouth hanging open in a silent *what the hell* as she stares between me and Nikolai like we just walked off the cover of a scandal. Sloane is right behind her, grabbing my wrist and holding it up before I can protest.

"When were you going to tell us?" she hisses.

"Congratulations," Clara says coolly, her voice the same tone she uses when she knows there's gossip too fresh to touch. "Guess we know who picked the dress."

I manage a laugh, airy, rehearsed, empty. "It all happened very fast."

Poppy blinks. "You're engaged. To him."

I glance at Nikolai. He's watching them like he's being presented with prey he doesn't plan to eat—yet.

"To me," he says, extending his hand toward Sloane like this is just another fundraiser, just another name to add to the donor wall. "Nikolai Volkov. A pleasure."

Sloane shakes it like she's not sure if she should call security or ask for a selfie.

Clara doesn't move. She just sips her drink and stares at me like she's doing calculus behind her eyes.

"You move on pretty … fast," she says, her eyes dropping to my hand.

Nikolai's head turns just slightly.

I smile wider. "When you know, you know."

"Holy crap," Sloane says, and then promptly throws back the rest of her drink.

A hand taps my shoulder. My father's aide. I barely register what he says before I'm being guided toward another cluster of guests—all suits and names I've heard whispered behind closed doors. Nikolai follows, of course. Never more than a step behind. Never once hesitating.

I nod. I laugh. I thank them for their congratulations. I lie so beautifully it should be criminal.

Max lingers near the Volkov family—except here, no one calls him Max. Here, he's Maksim, standing straighter, speaking in Russian with Alexei, the easy charm from campus replaced with something colder, sharper. It takes me a second to reconcile it—the same boy who cracked jokes on campus now folded back into the machine that made him. Eyes scanning. Posture alert. Like he's waiting for someone to screw up.

Irina drifts closer, offering a brief nod and a smile so tight it could slice skin. She says something in Russian I don't catch, but Nikolai answers without looking her way. The exchange is short. Sharp. Intentional. Family business. Volkov business.

Alexei stays rooted to his spot, his glass of amber liquor untouched now, fingers resting against the rim as he speaks low and even in a voice that doesn't invite interruption. His gaze doesn't touch me, but I feel it anyway, like a wire looped gently around my throat.

One woman leans in close, pressing her hand over mine like we're old friends.

"You must be thrilled," she says, smile just a little too fixed. "Such a strong match. Such ... powerful families."

"Thrilled," I echo. "It's been a whirlwind."

Nikolai's voice brushes my ear again, that signature low rasp that never sounds rushed, never sounds unsure. "You're lying better than I expected."

I look up at him, the edge of my smile never dropping. "You'd know. You've had a lot more practice."

He chuckles softly, a private, dark sound that sits too low in my chest.

When the photographer calls for a formal shot, we move in sync. He places a hand at my waist—warm, steady, too confident—and pulls me into the frame like we've done this a thousand times. I lean in just enough to sell it. Our shoulders touch. His jaw brushes the top of my head. The camera clicks.

"Smile," he whispers, just for me.

"I am," I breathe. "Don't mistake it for affection."

Click.

We break apart.

Applause again somewhere behind us. The sound of a toast being proposed. Someone already drunk is saying something about power couples and dynasties reborn.

I catch Thalia's eye from across the room. She lifts her flute, expression unreadable, mouth pressed into the thinnest of lines. She knows. She knows this is no fairy tale.

And I know this is only the beginning.

To be continued...

Coming Soon!

The Unraveling

Bancroft University Chronicles Book 2

The Unraveling is the final book in this dark romance duet.

The hardest part of senior year was supposed to be surviving the Chi Omega house.

Not questioning every truth she was raised to believe.

Emilia Langford is tearing through the lies: the ones her family told, the ones she told herself, and the ones that shaped her into someone easy to control.

Now everything is shifting. Power. Loyalty. Blood. And at the center of it all is the man who won't let her go.

She doesn't know if Nikolai is protecting her or positioning her for something worse. But either way, she's done pretending not to see what's coming.

She was raised to obey.

She's learning how to destroy.

Some truths burn everything down on the way out.

"He thinks he has me fooled. He has no idea what's coming..."

About the Author

S.D. Lettie has been writing since she was young, beginning with notebooks of fanfiction before turning to darker, immersive stories that blur the line between fiction and reality.

What started as an obsession with creating alternate worlds grew into a lifelong passion for crafting characters who feel real enough to frustrate, tempt, and break your heart.

A devoted reader of dark romance, Lettie creates stories that capture the grit, allure, and moral complexity that make the genre so addictive.

Her goal is to craft tales that feel as dangerous as they are relatable, pulling readers so deeply into her heroines' journeys that they experience every moment alongside them.

Music often sparks her writing, whether it's rock, pop, or hip hop, with songs inspiring the emotions and scenes that later unfold on the page.

Most of her words come alive late at night or in the quiet of early morning, always with a Dr. Pepper nearby. When not writing, she can be found at the soccer fields cheering on her kids or catching MLS matches on Saturday nights.